TELL ME ABOUT IT

FRANCES MENSAH WILLIAMS

First published in Great Britain in 2025 by Boldwood Books Ltd as *Sorry, Not Sorry*. This edition published 2026.

Cover Design by Alice Moore Design

Cover Images: iStock and Shutterstock

A CIP catalogue record for this book is available from the British Library.

Paperback ISBN 978-1-80600-684-7

Large Print ISBN 978-1-80600-683-0

Hardback ISBN 978-1-80600-682-3

Trade Paperback ISBN 978-1-80635-350-7

Ebook ISBN 978-1-80600-685-4

Kindle ISBN 978-1-80600-686-1

Audio CD ISBN 978-1-80600-677-9

MP3 CD ISBN 978-1-80600-678-6

Digital audio download ISBN 978-1-80600-679-3

This book is printed on certified sustainable paper. Boldwood Books is dedicated to putting sustainability at the heart of our business. For more information please visit https://www.boldwoodbooks.com/about-us/sustainability/

Boldwood Books Ltd, 23 Bowerdean Street, London, SW6 3TN

www.boldwoodbooks.com

Sometimes, sisterhood can be all the therapy you need.
To my sister-friends, with love.

We can't escape the past. We can only make peace with it.

PROLOGUE

THREE YEARS EARLIER...

Delilah tramped through the thick grass in the cemetery, her cheeks wet with tears. The sticky heat and scorching midday sun added to her misery as she struggled to keep a grip on the wilting bouquet in one hand and the voluminous skirt of her wedding dress in the other. She blinked hard, clearing her blurred vision just in time to clumsily sidestep a clump of vicious-looking stinging nettles, wincing as the straps of the ivory bridal shoes dug into her feet. She raised the layers of tulle clear of the stalks of yellow dandelions scattered across the field and tripped when the unfamiliar heels caught in a tangle of weeds, only just managing to keep her balance.

Gulping down the tearing sobs ripping at her chest, forcing her breath to emerge in ragged, shallow bursts, she limped over to the relative safety of a gravel path running outside the cemetery chapel. Sweat ran down her back, and her arm ached from the weight of the heavy skirt, but still she ploughed on, head down and eyes trained to the ground, her long, freshly plaited braids falling into her face. When she passed the chapel, she skirted a path round a roped-off section of old, neglected graves marked by headstones sunken crookedly into the ground, their worn inscriptions obscured by dried moss and winding ivy.

Hang in there, Del! She knew it was only her imagination, but her mother's voice sounded so reassuringly clear that it was hard to believe she hadn't heard it in, what... fifteen years and... eight months?

Almost there.

She staggered towards a clump of trees on the far side of the cemetery, hobbling past a weathered stone statue of a cherub with a missing arm, before finally stumbling to a halt in front of a grave sheltered by a towering oak tree.

Calm down, Del. You're okay now. I'm here. Her mother's soothing voice seemed to do the trick. Delilah clasped the drooping bouquet to her chest and released her grip on the dress, slumping to the ground and letting the voluminous skirt puff up into a soft cloud around her. Her gaze fell onto a brass vase holding a display of white roses, their long stems partially obscuring the white marble headstone. She and her sister had made it a tradition to bring Mum flowers so she could celebrate the big events in their lives and, judging from the perfect floral arrangement, the super-efficient Salome had got there first. *Well, you were too quick this time, Sal.*

Delilah ripped away the crumpled cellophane and laid her bouquet next to the roses, starting to cry again when the flowers flopped listlessly onto the marble. They wouldn't survive in the punishing heat, but she hadn't noticed she was still holding the freshly delivered bouquet until after she'd raced out of her sister's house. Breaking up with her fiancé in a blind panic a day before their wedding and bolting from her sister's house without stopping to change out of her wedding outfit hadn't been the plan when she'd woken up this morning. The *plan* was that she and Noah would bring her bouquet here tomorrow, after—

Delilah's heart clenched with a pain so intense she couldn't finish the thought.

Never mind the flowers, Del. What's going on? This time, her mother's voice sounded grim rather than soothing.

'Hi Mum.' Delilah's voice emerged as little more than a whisper, and she cleared her throat. Her eyes were puffy, and her head hurt from crying, but when she tried to take a breath, it felt like someone had reached into her chest and tied her lungs into a painful knot. *Get on with it, Del. Confession time.*

'I know I've let you down, Mum, but I can't go through with it. I just *can't*! You'd be furious with me if you were here. Sal probably thinks I've lost the plot—'

She broke off in despair, remembering how she'd abruptly ended her call with Noah before pushing past an open-mouthed Salome without a word.

As the enormity of her actions hit her afresh, hot tears flooded Delilah's eyes. 'Mum, this time I've really fuc— I mean, messed up.' She caught herself just in time. Swearing was a no-no as far as Mum was concerned.

Delilah swiped her wet cheeks with the back of her hand and sniffed hard, plucking at the grass with trembling fingers while silently berating herself. Maybe if Salome hadn't insisted on a final try-on of the dress before the big day tomorrow, she wouldn't have panicked and called the whole thing off. Maybe if Noah hadn't picked that exact moment to ring her... *maybe* if Noah hadn't said—

Delilah raked her fingers through her hair, clutching the braids tightly as if that would stop the unruly thoughts tumbling around her mind.

'He's perfect, Mum. You'd have loved him,' she said in a low voice, feeling a fresh tear trickle down her cheek.

Her words hung in the stillness of the deserted cemetery, a murmur in a silence broken only by the sound of birds chirping in the branches overhead.

But if he's perfect, Del, why did you run? Relieved that her mother now sounded concerned rather than angry, Delilah closed her eyes and sighed.

'Because he said... because he – he scared me.'

1

It was safe to say the counselling session wasn't going well.

Janine Henderson appeared every inch ready for battle. Glaring at her husband, she tapped out a rapid tattoo on the polished parquet flooring with the metal-tipped heel of her new stilettos. Brian was seated across from her, his gaze firmly fixed on the scuffed toes of his boots, and looking less like a gladiator than a visibly upset middle-aged man.

With half an hour of the session still to go, Delilah was floundering. Any hope that she could shift the couple in her office from outright hostility to some form of mutual understanding was rapidly draining away. The few minutes for reflection she had suggested while she mentally flipped through her communication skills toolkit had made no discernible difference. Janine's expression hadn't budged, and Brian was clearly fuming.

Delilah flicked her gaze from husband to wife with mounting frustration. The Hendersons' fragile relationship was unravelling faster than she could have predicted, and while Brian would easily have won an award for exasperating husband of the year, Delilah simply couldn't afford to have another client walk out on her. She had slogged her way through a gruelling two-year course to make it as a trainee relationship counsellor, and since starting the all-important final year of practical training and supervised practice with a roster of clients, two of her couples had requested a change of counsellor while another three had quietly quit the programme. Having stubbornly refused to admit to Polly, her supervisor, that she was struggling with the Hendersons, Delilah had exhausted every tool in her counselling repertoire and was bitterly regretting not asking for help.

The sound of Janine's heel tapping was growing increasingly more irritating, and Delilah fought the urge to snap at her. It wasn't the woman's fault that her relationship was wedged on the rocks. After twenty-two years with a man whose marital expectations were better suited to the 1950s than the 2020s, Janine had finally reached the end of her tether, and it was hard not to feel a sneaking sympathy for her. If Delilah had been forced to live with Brian's long list of requirements – not least expecting his dinner to be on the table at six-thirty sharp with no exceptions – she would be doing a lot worse than boring a hole in the flooring.

Your personal opinions have no place in relationship counselling, Del. Polly's frequent admonition popped into Delilah's head, and she refocused her attention on the couple. After her recent run of bad luck with clients, it was time to calm the troubled waters.

'Now, Brian, refusing to compromise doesn't sound like a very helpful way of thinking,' Delilah said gently. 'What other way do you think you could show Janine you understand her perspective?'

'But I – I *don't* understand, do I?' Brian broke his silence, sounding so outraged that his words emerged in staccato bursts. 'We've been doing alright for more than twenty bloomin' years. Now she's gone and got all these ideas from God knows where. Does she just expect me to roll over and accept it? How's that fair?'

'*How's that fair?*' had already come up several times in the session, and Delilah tried not to roll her eyes.

'Look, Brian, I understand things have changed in the relationship, which you're not yet comfortable with, and that's perfectly understandable. But, at the end of the day, you are both here because you want to make your marriage work – for *both* of you. Okay, let's move on.' She softened her voice, trying not to sound impatient. 'I want you to try a different exercise. Think about three things you love most about Janine. Go on – dig deep.'

The muscles in Brian's jaw moved, but no words emerged. The heel tapping paused, but as the silence lengthened, Janine's cheeks reddened with anger. She narrowed her eyes and flipped back her newly highlighted blonde waves – her latest act of defiance against Brian's stated preference for her previously straight brown hair.

'Yeah, Brian, *think*! Remember what we learned last week about how you need to "use your words"?' Janine's voice dripped with sarcasm as she crooked her fingers into air quotes.

The previous week's session, which had focused on communicating in a loving tone, had clearly gone over Janine's head, and Brian's ruddy features paled at his wife's taunting. Trying to control the damage, Delilah hastily intervened.

'Brian, I know it can be challenging to delve into your emotions, but Janine is trying to express to you that after many years of marriage, she feels like you no longer see her. So, if you can tell her how much you appreciate her and give specific examples of why you love her, it will strengthen the foundation of understanding between the two of you. I believe what Janine is trying to communicate here is that when you sound... er...' *Careful, no opinions!* '...inflexible in your requests, it makes her feel—'

'It pisses me off is what it does!' Janine cut in with an impatient wave of her manicured hand. 'For twenty-two bloody years I've had to cancel everything just so you can have your dinner on the table at half-six. Anyone would think you'd drop dead if you didn't eat bang on the half hour! Well, like Delilah says, it's high time you realised I've got my own needs. Which means if I want to go to my Salsa class on Tuesdays at six, I bloody well *will*!'

Brian's mouth worked silently while his complexion went from pallid to puce, and Delilah bit her lip in dismay. Janine clearly didn't do nuance and was wielding Delilah's carefully crafted words encouraging the couple to establish mutually respectful boundaries like a sledgehammer and making an already tricky situation worse. Taking advantage of Brian's temporary inability to use his words, Delilah jumped in.

'Janine, that's not what I said! Look, Brian, I think what's important here is that you acknowledge Janine's needs and let her know you're sorry for what could be seen as... well, being a bit domineering.'

'Only thing I'm bloody sorry about is wasting my *bloody* time coming 'ere!' Brian's fleshy chin quivered with fury as he finally found his voice. 'Come on, gel, we're going!' he bellowed.

Janine's eyes bulged in shock as Brian jumped up and pulled her out of her chair. Before she could protest, he bundled her out of the office and slammed the door behind him.

2

Delilah stood frozen in the middle of her office staring in shock at the closed door. The silence in the room following Brian's furious departure and forceful door slam was so electric she could feel the hair rising on her arms. Moments later, the door opened a few inches, and a head poked through the gap.

'Del? Are you alright?'

Delilah's expression seemed answer enough because the door opened wider, and a brown-skinned woman wearing black jeans and a purple jumper with a matching headwrap slipped into the room and quietly closed the door behind her.

'What the hell happened? I was next door typing up my session notes and it sounded like World War Three had broken out in here.'

Delilah drew in a shaky breath and shook her head in bewilderment. 'It was the Hendersons trying to score points off each other again. She kept pushing his buttons, but this time he completely lost it... I can't believe what he just did, Armenique.'

'I heard him through the wall! It's just as well I didn't have any clients with me, because—' She broke off and pursed her lips. 'You okay, hon?' she asked softly.

'No, no I'm not! I have tried everything with those two but it's like talking to a brick wall. *He's* a domestic tyrant and she's got the communication skills of a raging bull.'

'So, not exactly your dream pairing, then?' Armenique said with a rueful smile, leaning her back against the door. 'Well, it makes sense. They wouldn't be here for couples counselling if they were love's young dream now, would they? He sounded furious, though. Have you talked to Polly about them or brought this up in supervision?'

'Not exactly,' Delilah muttered. She ducked her head and her braids swung forward, hiding her face. She had grown close to Armenique since they'd started their training together, but Delilah had never admitted her terror of sounding incompetent in a group setting or shared how uneasy it felt for her to admit to difficulties within an open forum.

'Del, it's no secret that you loathe supervision,' Armenique said pointedly, 'but the whole point of it is to share challenges we're having with clients – and let's face it, you've had more than your share of bad luck with some of yours lately. If you haven't given Polly a heads-up on this couple and she finds out what's just happened—'

She broke off at the sound of a peremptory knock, quickly stepping aside as the door opened and a slightly built woman wearing a poppy-patterned knit dress came into the room.

'Hi Polly,' said Delilah with a weak smile, not altogether surprised to see her manager. Everyone on the floor had probably heard Brian's stormy exit.

Armenique pulled a face, mouthing a silent 'good luck' to Delilah, before slipping out of the room and closing the door behind her.

Polly stood inside the room with her arms folded, her usual cheery smile nowhere in evidence. 'So, what happened this time?' she asked bluntly.

Delilah inhaled sharply, stung by the implication behind Polly's words. It wasn't as if clients slammed their way out of her office every day.

'It wasn't my fault, Polly! You know how tricky the Hendersons have been to work with.'

'Do I?'

'Well... okay,' Delilah hedged. 'I suppose I could have been a bit more specific about their situation.'

'You think?'

Delilah shrugged off the sarcasm. 'I didn't want to make a big deal about it to you because I thought I could handle the situation, but honestly, those two are a proper nightmare! I don't blame Janine because it's obvious *he's* impossible, but she knows which buttons to press to wind him up. I was trying to keep things calm, but she kept taunting him, and in the end it set him right off. It was awful, Polly – he literally *dragged* her out of here!'

'Take me through what happened, please. Step by step.'

It took a lot to ruffle Polly's feathers, and seeing her supervisor looking so grim set Delilah's alarm bells ringing. Relationship counselling was her dream job, but some recent client sessions had ended with couples engaging in shouting matches or walking out mid-session, and she was growing increasingly anxious that despite all her hard work, the dream could be slipping through her fingers. Polly had been patient and encouraging, but this was the third incident with a disgruntled client in as many weeks, and even Polly's tolerance had its limits.

'Well?'

Unnerved by the uncompromising tone, Delilah squashed her rising panic and quietly related the events of the session, while Polly sank into an armchair and listened without interruption.

'So, if I'm understanding you correctly, you described Mr Henderson as domineering?' Polly asked evenly.

Delilah's nerves were beginning to jangle, and she sat down in Brian's recently vacated chair. 'I wasn't making a personal judgement. I was trying to get him to understand how she sees him.'

'I get that, but from your own description, Mrs Henderson sounds like a woman who can speak for herself. You do know your job is to facilitate their communication and not put words in their mouths, don't you?'

Delilah opened her mouth and then shut it again. *Listen, consider, acknowledge, speak.* Isn't that what she told her clients to do during difficult conversations? She drew in a calming breath and suppressed the urge to defend herself. With only eight months of practical training left to earn her diploma and qualify as a counsellor, she had to make it to the finish line. Polly clearly hadn't fully grasped what had happened during the session or appreciated that there was only so much Delilah could have done with two people bent on pushing their own agendas and refusing to communicate like adults. She tried again.

'Polly, I hear you and I can understand why you might think it was down to me, but the truth is Brian – Mr Henderson – has resisted counselling from the get-go. He only agreed to come with her because Janine threatened to leave him if he didn't. I know he says he loves his wife, but he acts like it's either his way or the highway.'

'How do you know that?'

Baffled, Delilah stared at her supervisor. 'Because that's what Janine says and—' She broke off as Polly shook her head, looking exasperated.

'It might be *Janine's* truth, Del, but that doesn't mean it's the absolute truth. You know from your training that you have to listen to everything, but also question everything. Our clients' emotions can cloud their judgement, which makes them unreliable narrators. If you only take one person's perspective on a situation, then all you know is what they choose to tell you – which is never the whole truth!'

'I agree,' Delilah argued. 'But it doesn't help the situation when the man clams up any time he's challenged.'

When Polly remained silent, Delilah ignored the voice in her head telling her to stop digging and instead kept going. 'I've tried very hard to get Brian to open up and communicate, but today Janine kept goading him, and it all suddenly got super intense.'

'Dealing with couples in dispute *will* get intense, but it's your job to manage the situation and create a safe space for your clients to work through their emotions,' Polly said brusquely. 'You can only help them fix what's broken and build a stronger relationship if they understand what's led them to where they are now. Of course, you can challenge their reasoning, but your role is to make it easier for them to have honest and constructive communication, which means *not* taking sides.'

'I was trying to get him to acknowledge how his behaviour impacts her,' Delilah said doggedly, wounded by the unfair criticism. 'Brian acts like a caveman throw-back, and I know Janine can be a bit full-on but quite frankly, she deserves better.'

Polly's expression shifted, and her light blue eyes narrowed into a probing gaze. 'What's going on here, Delilah?'

'What do you mean? I've told you what happened. I suggested a standard exercise to help Brian understand Janine's perspective. I followed all the steps.'

'Yes, but what's *really* going on here? Why were you so insistent that he should see himself the way you appear to have painted him?'

Delilah squirmed under Polly's laser stare. Suddenly lost for words, she could feel her pulse quickening again and her eyelid beginning to twitch – a sure sign that she was feeling under stress. She turned away and smoothed her hair back with fingers that had unaccountably started to tremble.

'I – I don't think... It – it's...' She stopped stammering and closed her eyes for a moment, shaking her head as if it would throw her scattered thoughts into a coherent sentence.

'It sounds to me like there's a strong element of projection taking place here, Del, and, if I'm honest, it's not the first time.'

Polly's blunt words were like a kick to Delilah's chest and her lungs tightened painfully. She had worked so *hard* on this course! Was her job really at risk because she was trying to help a headstrong couple and save a woman from her domineering husband?

'I know it seems like I've been messing up lately, Polly, but I'm doing my best.' Delilah could hear the tremor in her voice, and she sucked in a breath, trying to steady her jumping nerves. 'This job's really important to me. I'll do anything! I'll apologise to Brian and Janine and—'

'No,' Polly interjected. 'I'll speak to Mr and Mrs Henderson and explain you overstepped, and that what happened today was an unfortunate misunderstanding. But, Delilah, I need you to think carefully about what's been happening with your clients over the past few weeks and decide if this line of work is really for you.'

3

It was dark, and the autumn wind was biting. Delilah burrowed her chin into the thick woolly scarf wrapped around her neck and picked up her pace. She could almost taste the strong, steaming cup of tea she intended to brew as soon as she reached her sister's house.

While keeping a wary eye on the pavement that was slick with wet leaves from the overhanging trees, she failed to notice the woman approaching from the other end of the street until she reached Salome's front gate. Several inches taller than Delilah's petite five feet two inches, the woman appeared to be in her sixties and was elegantly dressed in a tailored camel-coloured coat, a matching fur-trimmed hat and knee-length black boots. Caught unawares, Delilah could only stare at her in silence, painfully aware of her own scuffed leather jacket and striped football scarf.

'Hi, Mrs West,' Delilah said eventually, the steam from her warm breath curling up into the chilly evening air.

The woman returned the tentative greeting with a hostile glare, drawing in her breath sharply and flaring her nostrils as if outraged at being spoken to. Without saying a word, Mrs West opened the gate to the adjoining front garden and closed it firmly behind her, marching up the path and into the house next door without looking back.

* * *

Delilah pushed her way into Salome's house, almost knocking over the man holding the door open.

'Whoa! Slow down, Del!' He peered into the darkness for a few moments and then shut the door before turning to Delilah, who was unwinding her scarf and trying to catch her breath after running up the garden path.

'What's wrong? Were you being chased by a fox?' There was a hint of humour beneath the concern.

Shaken by the encounter with Mrs West, Delilah kicked off her trainers and scowled at him. 'Less of the sarcasm if you don't mind – there really *was* a fox following me last week! No, I just ran into that witch next door. I said hello – because at least some of us have manners – and she looked at me like I was something she'd stepped in, and then totally ignored me. *Again*. You'd think I'd be used to it by now, but – anyway, where's Sal?'

'Hello to you, too. It's lovely to see you, and, yes, I'm fine.'

'Sorry, Farhan,' Delilah mumbled sheepishly. Her brother-in-law was the most chilled man on the planet, but that was still no excuse for rudeness. Farhan smiled and nodded in the direction of the stairs.

'She's upstairs changing Arin if you want to give her a hand?'

'Er, no thanks.' Delilah grimaced, shrugging off her jacket. 'You know dealing with dirty nappies is not my thing. What I *do* want, though, is a huge mug of tea.' She hooked her jacket onto the coat rack and stamped her feet to get some warmth back into her frozen toes. 'It's seriously nippy out there and I'm parched.'

Farhan shrugged. 'Well, you know where the kitchen is. I'm in the study if anyone needs me. I've got to finish a report and send it out to my team before I can call it a day.'

'You're not still working, are you? It's Friday night!'

Farhan had been working from home for almost three years and seemed to spend twice as much time on call as when he had gone into the office. But Salome was happy to sacrifice her treasured dining room for her husband to use as an office in exchange for having him on hand to help with their two young children.

'No choice, I'm afraid,' he said. 'We've just started a new project, and I've got to get a bunch of information to the folks in Mumbai before they start work on Monday morning. I'll see you in a bit.'

Farhan disappeared into his office off the hall and Delilah stood at the bottom of the staircase and shouted, 'Sal! I'm here!'

'I'll be down in a minute!' came the reply.

Rubbing her chilled hands together, Delilah pulled up her thick socks and made her way to the kitchen. As soon as she turned on the light, she relaxed into the comforting warmth of her favourite room in the house. It was spacious with high ceilings and spotlessly clean appliances, and the crayoned drawings Blu-tacked onto the walls were an indication that Salome's obsession for neatness was superseded only by her obsession with her children. Delilah padded over the slate-tiled floor to the sink to fill the kettle and while she waited for the water to boil, she went to sit at the large pine dining table.

Her mind returned to the disturbing conversation she'd had with Polly earlier that afternoon with the persistence of a tongue probing a sore tooth. The implied threat to her job had unnerved her enough to rush straight over to her sister's for reassurance, and as if the fear of losing her job wasn't enough, the universe had thrown her into the path of Mrs West. The woman clearly still hated her, despite Delilah's efforts to make things right with her after—

The click of the kettle roused her from her brooding, and she went to the cupboard, standing on tiptoe to retrieve her favourite mug and the large box of PG Tips Salome bought in especially for her.

She had just taken her first sip of hot tea when the door bounced open, and a little girl wearing a pair of Paddington Bear pyjamas and holding a teddy bear skipped into the kitchen.

'Auntie Del! Auntie Del!' she screeched, her silky dark curls bouncing around a chubby, pink-cheeked face as she rushed to Delilah.

'Ma-*ya*!' Delilah quickly put down her mug, splashing tea onto the spotless counter in the process, and opened her arms to scoop up the child, hugging her tightly and inhaling her sweet, just-bathed scent until the child wriggled away.

'Now tell me the truth, Maya-moo! Have you grown taller since I saw you four days ago?' Delilah crouched down until she was at eye level with the child and scrutinised her with a mock-serious expression.

'No, Auntie Del! I'm still small,' Maya replied, her giggle revealing a missing front tooth. Then her smile disappeared, and she waved her teddy bear in Delilah's face. 'Look – Arin chewed off Bertie's ear. Mummy stopped him from swallowing it and she's going to sew it back on when it's dry again.'

'Oh no, poor Bertie! That was naughty of Arin. Did you tell him we don't eat bears, and we certainly don't eat Bertie?'

Maya's expression darkened. 'I've told him he will be in *big* trouble if he does it again!'

Her niece's temper was such that Delilah didn't fancy Arin's chances if he crossed his sister. But before she could comment, a dark-skinned woman in jeans and a knitted top walked into the kitchen carrying a toddler with the same chubby cheeks and silky curls as Maya.

'Hi Sal.' Delilah's face lit up at the sight of her sister.

'Hi hon, how's it going?' Salome greeted her with a weary smile. 'Let me put the little man in his chair and give you a proper hug.'

In contrast to Delilah's curvy build, Salome was tall and lean, although she had the same high cheekbones and thickly lashed brown eyes. She slipped the baby into the highchair at the table and strapped him in with practised ease before opening her arms to Delilah and crushing her into a hug.

'Me too! Me too!' Maya squealed, running over to grab them both by the legs.

'*Salome!* You are literally smothering me!' Delilah protested, her voice muffled by the thick wool of her sister's jumper.

Laughing, Salome released her and walked over to the cupboard, taking out a box of herbal tea. As she reached for the kettle, her eyes lasered onto the tea Delilah had spilt on the counter.

'Honestly, Del, you are so messy!' She tutted, immediately tearing off a strip of kitchen paper to wipe up the liquid.

Delilah rolled her eyes with exasperation. 'And you are such a neat freak. Sal, it's literally a *drop* of tea!'

Salome tossed the used tissue in the bin and reached for the kettle, giving it a gentle shake. 'Is there enough water for another cup?'

'Yes, and it just boiled a minute ago.' Delilah walked over to the highchair and kissed the baby's cheek, ruffling his soft curls gently.

'Hi, Arin,' she cooed sweetly.

Unmoved, Arin pursed his lips and stared back through huge unblinking brown eyes before sticking his thumb in his mouth.

'Come on, sweetie, give your favourite auntie a smile. I've had a ton of stress today. I've already been given the fishy-eyed treatment from the Wicked Witch of the West, so please be nice to me.'

Salome had been pouring hot water onto a teabag, and she stopped and looked at Delilah with raised eyebrows. 'You ran into her *again*?'

'Imagine! Second time in two weeks. I think the gods are punishing me.'

'That's so weird. I live next door, and I hardly see anything of her. Did she speak to you?'

'What do you think?' Delilah said derisively. 'Nope. Just glared at me, as usual, and walked off.'

Salome steered a path around Maya, who was sitting cross-legged on the kitchen floor behind Arin's highchair, playing with Bertie, and set her mug on the table. Pulling out a chair, she sat down while Delilah retrieved her cup of tea from the kitchen counter and came to sit across the table from her sister.

'Honestly, Sal, she's so *rude*!' Delilah said moodily.

'Who's so rude?'

Farhan walked into the kitchen and strolled over to the fridge. Taking out a small bottle of water, he twisted off the cap and took a long sip before repeating his question with eyes bright with curiosity.

'Your next-door neighbour,' Delilah muttered. 'I don't know what the hell... *Oops!*' She caught herself and glanced guiltily towards Maya, who could be relied upon to repeat anything she heard. 'I don't know what I need to do for her to stop treating me like I'm some kind of serial killer.'

Farhan scoffed, and Salome shot him a warning look. 'Never mind about Mrs West, Del. You sounded really upset when you called earlier. What's going on? Is there a problem at work?'

Farhan was mid-swallow and promptly choked on his water, earning a glare from Delilah.

'*What* is so funny?' she demanded.

'You.' Farhan gestured towards her with the bottle. 'I should have been smart enough to put a bet on how long it would take you to jack in this job. Although, to be fair, you've lasted a lot longer this time round.'

Delilah gripped her mug and fumed in silence. She knew Farhan was only teasing, but in her current frame of mind, his words were as welcome as ice-cold water on a sensitive tooth.

'Take no notice, hon. He's just trying to wind you up,' Salome intervened.

'Sweetheart, can you take the kids into the living room for a bit so Del and I can chat? Without interruption,' she added pointedly.

Farhan grinned. 'Come on, Del, lighten up. We've always had a laugh about your career – or should I say careers?'

'Farhan...' Salome warned.

Farhan ignored his wife's attempt to silence him. 'Let's see, you're now on, what, your fifth career change?'

'Fourth,' Delilah replied through gritted teeth. 'You know full well I was only waitressing until I worked out what I wanted to do.'

'Hmmm... two years is a bit of a stretch for a temp job, but whatever. Okay, then there was that stint in the call centre, then the traffic warden job, and after that – remind me, what came next?'

'I was a guide at the Cultural Archive Centre. Have you finished or is there any other part of my life you'd like to dissect while you're at it?'

'Hey, I'm not judging you. It's all good, Del. We know you don't do commitment, but we love you anyway.'

Delilah's grip tightened on the mug and her knuckles turned white from the strain of not hurling the contents at her brother-in-law. She had happily joked about her serial career moves in the past, but things were different now. She loved her job, and just the idea of being fired made her feel physically sick.

'Okay, you two, that's enough!' Salome frowned and glanced meaningfully in Maya's direction. 'Young ears are listening.'

As if sensing he might have upset her, Farhan flashed Delilah an apologetic smile before going to release Arin from the highchair. 'Come on, my son. I think the ladies want some alone time. Maya, grab a couple of the juice boxes from the cupboard and let's leave Mummy and Auntie Del to chat.'

As soon as the door shut behind her husband and children, Salome reached across the table to touch her sister's hand.

'What's wrong, Del? You know you can tell me anything. *Is* there a problem at work?'

With Farhan having just painted her as an unserious job-hopper, there was no way she could admit to Salome she was at risk of being fired. Instead, she swallowed the words she really wanted to say and the reassurance she desperately needed and forced a smile. 'No, no... it's nothing. Work's been incredibly busy, and I haven't been sleeping well. I suppose... it just feels like a lot, sometimes.'

Salome nodded sympathetically. 'I get it, hon. But Del, you *would* tell me if there was something wrong, wouldn't you? You know I'm always here for you.'

'I know, Mama,' Delilah said, pulling her hand away, ready to change the subject. 'Which reminds me, I haven't been to the cemetery for a couple of weeks. Have you?'

'No, I meant to go yesterday but Farhan was called into the office for an urgent meeting and there was no way I was taking the kids on my own. I'm still cringing after the last time when Maya pulled the flowers out from the grave next to Mum's. Besides, the weather's been crappy over the past few days, and the ground gets so muddy this time of year—' She broke off and examined her sister. 'Del, are you *sure* you're okay? If you're feeling... well, you know, anxious or upset, you don't have to deal with it alone and—'

Delilah cut her off with a dismissive wave of her hand. 'I'm a counsellor, Sal. *If* I need help – and I don't – then, trust me, I know where to get it.'

'We all need help sometimes,' Salome said quietly. 'If I didn't have my sessions with Alison every fortnight, I don't know how I'd cope. It wouldn't hurt if you at least tried—'

Delilah groaned loudly and dropped her head onto the table. When she raised it again, she looked her sister straight in the eyes. 'Please, Sal. Can we talk about something else?'

Salome opened her mouth and then shut it without a word. For a few moments she sipped her tea, and the silence was broken only by the low hum of the fridge and the muted sound of Maya's shrieks coming through the kitchen door from the living room.

Salome finished her tea and dropped the mug onto the table with a thump. 'Okay, fine, let's talk about something else. You said you bumped into Mrs West on the way here again. What happened?'

It wasn't the change of topic Delilah had been hoping for, but anything was better than Sal trying to coax her back into therapy.

'I don't know what the woman wants from me,' Delilah said with a resigned sigh. Her mind went back to the brief encounter outside and, remembering the look of scorn laced with contempt on the older woman's face, Delilah pounded her fist on the table in frustration.

'I've apologised to her God knows how many times and she *still* won't give me the time of day! I know she's nice to Maya and acknowledges you and Farhan, but she's always evil to me. I honestly don't know how you can stand to live next door to her – she's unbearable!'

Salome pushed her chair back from the table and reached over to pick up Delilah's empty mug. Standing up, she studied her sister pensively. 'Look, I know the two of you have your issues, but she's really not that bad.'

'Hang on, whose side are you on here?' Delilah looked up in disbelief.

'You know I always have your back, hon,' Salome said calmly. 'But to be fair to the woman, you *did* leave her son at the altar.'

4

FOUR YEARS EARLIER…

Delilah stared at the blue recycling bin, wondering how to get it open without dropping the armful of packing boxes she had just crushed.

'Hey, do you need a hand with that?'

The voice came from behind her, and she turned, craning her neck to see around the precariously balanced pile of cardboard. It took one look at the man with chocolate-brown skin and full, sensuous lips standing on the pavement for Delilah's mouth to fall open and her heart to wobble.

He walked up the garden path towards her without waiting for an answer – which was just as well since she suddenly found herself struggling to find the most basic of words. A moment later, he was standing close enough for her to see the dark flecks in his light brown eyes and a faint stubble along his sculpted jawline. His sudden proximity set her heart racing, and the faint lemon scent of his cologne wafted into the small space between them. She could feel her face burning and couldn't prevent the tiny gasp that escaped her when he leaned in closer to flip open the dustbin lid.

'Um, thanks,' she mumbled, mortified by her body's response to the attractive stranger. She quickly crammed the torn cartons into the wheelie bin, dropping a few pieces of cardboard in her haste.

He dropped down to pick up the bits just as she crouched to retrieve them, and their eyes locked. Mesmerised, she couldn't look away, and for a moment neither of them moved. Then Delilah blinked and stood up abruptly, trying to catch the breath hovering somewhere around her chest. He slowly straightened and without the cardboard barrier between them, she had a clear view of a lean, muscular body in jeans and a T-shirt.

'Hello again. I'm Noah. Noah West.' He towered over her petite frame, forcing her to look up at him.

'Delilah... um, Braithwaite.' She swallowed hard and squeezed out the words, her voice sounding breathless and wispy.

'So, you must be the new neighbour. My parents live next door.'

'Oh, right! But not to me. To – to my sister. Salome,' she stammered. 'She and her family are the ones that live here.' Her neck and cheeks burned with embarrassment as she heard herself babbling like a starstruck teenager.

'Are you close?'

'Excuse me?' She looked at him, perplexed, and he smiled impishly and cocked an eyebrow.

'Close. You know – like, do you visit her often?'

'Oh right! Yes – very!' she added fervently. Then, unaccountably, her nerves vanished, and she felt a smile tugging at the corners of her lips. 'What about you? Are you close?'

'I don't even know her!' His disarming grin revealed white teeth that sparkled against the dark brown of his skin.

'I meant as in close to your parents!' Delilah said with a giggle.

'I know. Sorry, couldn't resist that. Yeah, I usually come by on Sundays to see my oldies.' He glanced at his watch. 'I'm sorry, I'd really love to chat some more but I'm running late. Maybe I'll bump into you again? Soon?'

She exhaled, feeling her chest relax and her breath flow freely again. 'Sure.'

She tossed the bits of cardboard she was still clutching into the bin and closed the lid before turning to watch him stride down the road, not caring if he turned around and caught her.

* * *

'Isn't that right, Delilah?'

The sudden silence in the room catapulted Delilah back into the present to find two sets of eyes staring at her. She flushed, embarrassed at the irony of not paying attention while leading a session on mindful communication. It was a struggle concentrating on the real-life people in the room after a restless night of fitful dreams about a man she had forced herself to forget, but she was already skating on thin ice, and annoying more clients was not an option. She smothered a yawn and smiled brightly at the woman who had posed the question.

'Well, I suppose that depends, Sammie,' she said cautiously, trying to remember what they'd been talking about before her mind had wandered off.

Sammie, a freckled redhead in her thirties, had clearly been expecting more productive feedback, and she frowned and tucked her hair behind her ears, turning to the ruggedly built man sprawled in the armchair opposite. His muscular legs were outstretched, and he looked visibly bored.

'I don't understand why you're being so moody, Ross,' she said plaintively. 'We agreed in the last session that we'd do the questionnaire and share our results today, didn't we, Delilah? Look' – Sammie waved a purple notebook in the air – 'I wrote all mine down off the computer.'

She glanced at Delilah, who gave her an encouraging nod, and then continued. 'My results show that my dominant love language is words of affirmation.' She paused and looked across at Ross, who responded with a careless shrug. 'That means it's really important for me to hear you say nice things about me. It really wouldn't hurt you to pay me a compliment every now and then or tell me how you feel about us.' Her voice wavered, and Delilah gave Sammie an enthusiastic thumbs up.

'That's brilliant, Sammie. You've expressed yourself very clearly. Ross' – she ignored his audible sigh and continued – 'now, I appreciate this might feel a bit uncomfortable, but like we've discussed, if you understand how Sammie prefers to receive love, it will help you communicate so much better. It's your turn. What was your primary love language?'

Suddenly animated, Ross leaned forward and rubbed his hands vigorously, his beefy biceps straining the sleeves of his sports jacket.

'Physical touch, 70 per cent,' he said with a smirk, waggling his eyebrows suggestively.

No surprise there, Delilah thought, trying not to scoff out loud. From the first counselling session, Ross had made it clear that right at the top of his long list of grievances was what he'd bluntly described as 'not getting enough of the old S-E-X'. His refusal to acknowledge any responsibility for his relationship crisis had led Delilah to set the couple the love languages exercise, which she hoped would help Ross better articulate his needs and – with any luck – provoke him to reflect on how to meet Sammie's.

'Is *that* all you care about?' Sammie asked reproachfully.

'Well, what's better than sex, eh?' Ross said, chuckling. When Sammie refused to look at him, his smile turned into a frown. 'For God's sake, lighten up, will you? I was only joking!'

'Yeah, well I don't think it's funny!' Sammie's eyes moistened. 'When you go on about sex all the time... it makes me feel devalued. It's like that's all I'm good for.'

Ross clutched his head and groaned dramatically. 'Jesus, you're too bloody sensitive, d'you know that? Delilah said we had to be honest about our scores.'

Delilah cleared her throat, and they looked at her expectantly. 'Okay, so Ross, your scores indicate that feeling close to Sammie is important to you. Whether it's holding hands, hugging each other...' She tailed off in exasperation at his incredulous expression. 'Ross, physical touch doesn't just mean sex! It's about all the ways Sammie can show you how she loves you. It can be through touching or caressing or just cuddling. There's scientific evidence that cuddling releases oxytocin, which helps us bond with each other.'

'It's all a bit soppy, this. No offence, but I thought you'd be helping me sort out my missus not wanting to – well, you know...' He shrugged again and crossed his legs to rest his ankle on his knee.

'You and Sammie both made a commitment, as part of this counselling therapy, to be willing to open up and try new approaches to deepen your connection with each other,' Delilah said patiently. 'You know, I once went out with someone who was... well, a bit emotionally closed off, I suppose you could say. But when I started to get more tactile with him, doing things like holding his hand and stroking his arm and – and giving him lots of hugs, it made all the difference.'

When Ross muttered something unintelligible, Delilah persisted. 'Ross, would you be willing to offer Sammie some compliments and share how you feel about her a bit more? I'm sure Sammie, for her part, would be willing to spend time cuddling up with you on the sofa. Maybe when you're watching telly – Sammie, you said earlier you'd love to watch TV with Ross more often, right?'

'You won't catch me wasting my time on the reality rubbish she watches,' he scoffed.

'That's not fair!' Sammie protested. 'Football bores the life out of me, but I still watch it with you. And didn't I sit through that boxing match last night watching those blokes knock chunks off each other? I was practically falling into your lap to get you to notice me, and you wouldn't even hold my hand.'

'Christ, it's not like watching a heavyweight title fight is what gets me in the mood for a cuddle, is it? Anyway, I was up for it later until you started with your usual "I've got a headache",' he mocked in a whiny tone and then shook his head, as if bored of the conversation.

Sammie's lip wobbled. 'I *did* have a headache after watching that fight – not that *you* cared!' she added tearfully.

Delilah could feel a headache of her own brewing, and she massaged her right temple surreptitiously. Her eyes felt dry and gritty from the lack of sleep and a pulsating pain was starting to radiate across her head. Three cups of strong coffee hadn't made up for a night of disturbed dreams about... She willed her thoughts away from dangerous ground and pressed on.

'Okay, let's keep going. Sammie, what was your next highest score?'

For a moment Sammie looked set to continue the argument, but then she flipped the page of her notebook and sucked the end of her pen while she scanned her notes. 'I got 35 per cent for acts of service.'

'Good. Now, Ross, what does "acts of service" mean to you?' Delilah asked.

Ross rubbed his jaw furiously and uncrossed his legs, shifting his bulk in the chair and looking as comfortable as a caged tiger. 'I don't know. Like giving her a hand with things around the house... stuff like that?'

'Well, yes, that's part of it. It's being aware how important it is for Sammie to see you doing things that are helpful to her. Maybe cooking dinner occasionally, which I'm sure she'd appreciate after a hard day's work, or offering to run some errands. Or, you know, doing the shopping?'

Ross glanced at Sammie's sceptical expression and his eyes darted round the room as if searching for escape. Ross wasn't the only one in need of rescue, Delilah thought morosely. The throbbing behind her eyes was growing more intense and her head felt like it was caught in a vice. But while it was tempting to apologise and end the session early, she owed it to Sammie to help her turn her troubled relationship around.

'Ross, is this an area you think you can improve on to help Sammie feel loved?' Delilah asked, trying not to sound as weary as she felt.

'I do the washing up, don't I?' he muttered.

'We've got a bloody dishwasher!' Sammie shot back. Her tears had vanished, and her green eyes flashed with annoyance below her deep auburn fringe. 'Honestly, Ross, if you spent a fraction of the time you put in at the gym picking up after yourself at home and doing your share of the housework, I might actually want to have sex with you!'

Ross scowled, his face darkening with anger, and Delilah sighed. She really didn't need this today.

5

Delilah leaned back against the cushioned headrest of her office chair and closed her eyes. The painkillers she had taken the moment Sammie and Ross's session was over had kicked in and she felt the tension between her temples begin to ease. At the sound of a gentle knock, she opened one eye and glanced warily at the closed door. The last thing she needed was Polly showing up and accusing her of napping on the job.

'Who is it?' she called cautiously.

'It's me,' came a muffled reply. 'It's pretty quiet in there. Just checking you're still alive.'

'Come in.' Delilah sat up and smoothed back her braids. Her head was heavy, and her brain still felt like someone had swapped it for cotton wool, but Armenique was safe.

Armenique came in and sat down facing Delilah's desk, leaning forward to peer closely at her. 'What's wrong? Did I wake you up or something?'

'No, resting my eyes. I have a pounding headache and just took some paracetamol a few minutes ago.'

'You do look pretty knackered,' Armenique observed.

'Cheers,' Delilah mumbled sarcastically. She yawned widely and covered her mouth. 'Sorry. I didn't get much sleep last night.'

'Woohoo! Someone's finally having some fun!' Armenique broke into an infectious belly laugh, throwing her head back with such gusto she nearly lost her blue headwrap.

Delilah pulled a face and then smiled reluctantly. 'Haha, very funny. I've told you I'm not dating.'

'Ah yes, Miss I'm-taking-a-sabbatical-from-men.' Armenique grinned and wiped under her eyes. 'So, if it's not bedroom action keeping you up, what's the problem?'

'Who knows. Too much thinking, I suppose,' Delilah said, swivelling her chair to avoid Armenique's questioning gaze. 'Never mind about me, what I don't get is why every single one of my clients wants to cause drama. I'm trying to keep on Polly's good side, but it's *so* flipping stressful trying to control some of these people! Take my couple that just left. She's trying to hold their relationship together while all he cares about is getting his leg over! I swear it's like pulling teeth getting Ross to show her a bit of consideration.'

'Sounds like an arrogant tosser,' Armenique said sagely. 'But don't quote me. I'll deny ever using such judgemental language.'

'I thought I'd be used to him by now, but he was acting like *such* an arse today.' Delilah closed her eyes and let out a deep sigh. 'I don't know why poor Sammie puts up with it.'

'Maybe because she loves him?'

Delilah's eyes flew open, and she turned her chair back to face Armenique, her headache momentarily forgotten. 'How can you possibly think love excuses abuse?'

Armenique raised an eyebrow at Delilah's sharp tone. 'Hang on a minute, no one's talking about abuse here. The bloke sounds selfish and insensitive, but that hardly makes him an abuser!'

'But that's how it starts, isn't it?' Delilah's voice rose. 'You give an inch, and then another, and the next thing you know, you've got a man taking advantage and calling all the shots.'

Armenique tilted her head to the side. 'Are we still talking about Ross?'

'Him – and guys just like him. I've gone out with enough of them to recognise the pattern.' Delilah struggled to keep the bitterness out of her voice.

Armenique studied Delilah thoughtfully. 'We've been mates since we started this course, but this is the first time I've heard you talk about your exes this way. I always assumed you were the happy-go-lucky, love-'em-and-leave-'em type.'

'I'm fine until a guy starts to get possessive or controlling,' Delilah replied shortly.

'So maybe that's why clients like Ross trigger you.' Armenique hesitated. 'Come to think of it, it always seems to be your male clients you have a problem with.'

Delilah tried to row the conversation back from the direction it was taking. 'I was talking about me. It's got nothing to do with my clients. We've both done the training and trust me, I know how to keep my personal views out of counselling sessions.'

'Well yes, in theory,' Armenique said slowly. 'But we're not miracle workers, Del, we're human and it's easy to let our own experiences get in the way of being objective. *This* is why you need to come to supervision, and it's something you should explore with your therapist.'

Although the peer group sessions were mandatory, Delilah found them stressful, and when no one had pulled her up after she'd ducked one or two, she continued to find excuses not to attend. She dropped her head back against the headrest and closed her eyes, but Armenique didn't let it go.

'You've got away with missing most of the supervision sessions, and yet you're obviously struggling with your clients. This work can really weigh on us and we all need support. You need to take this seriously,' she said.

When Delilah made no reply, Armenique sighed heavily. 'Del, I'm your friend and I love you, but I've got to be honest, babe. If you don't sort this out, it's going to cost you.'

6

Delilah stood outside Polly's office, willing herself to knock on the door.

'Calm down! There's nothing to panic about,' she muttered aloud, as if hearing the words would remove the sick feeling that had lodged itself in the pit of her stomach since opening Polly's email. Polly usually asked for a catchup by sticking her head around the door of Delilah's office, so the formally worded email requesting a meeting at ten that morning had read like the business equivalent of 'we need to talk'.

Delilah cleared her throat and inhaled deeply to steady her racing pulse. When that didn't work, she shuffled her feet on the carpet and wiped her suddenly damp palms down the side of the smart grey skirt she kept for work. *Come on, Del. Get a grip!* Things were finally settling down and there had been no dramas with her clients for over two weeks – if she didn't count the incident of the dog whose preference for sleeping in his 'mummy's' bed had led his owners to seek counselling. As the couple were leaving at the end of a heated session, the much-loved pooch had broken free of his leash and scampered around the building for twenty minutes before being recaptured. But there was no way Polly could hold Delilah responsible for her clients' dog's behaviour, so why this meeting? *For crying out loud, knock on the bloody door, Delilah!* She squared her shoulders and raised her hand – just as the door opened.

'I thought I heard a noise out here,' Polly said, puzzled. 'Why on earth didn't you knock?' Without waiting for a reply, she stood back and ushered Delilah inside.

Delilah had always loved Polly's office, a light and airy corner room with huge windows on two walls and a bright rainbow rug in the centre of the parquet flooring. Half the room was dominated by a huge bookcase stacked with books, with the rest of the space taken up by a squashy grey sofa with soft pastel throw cushions and three armchairs. Polly's desk, small and unobtrusive, was tucked into a small alcove next to a tall potted palm.

The office's charm was the last thing on Delilah's mind as she made an anxious beeline for the sofa, sitting up with her hands resting on her knees. Polly took a seat at the other end and shifted round to face her.

'I'm sorry for the short notice but I'm glad you were able to make the time.' Polly paused for a moment. 'How are things going, Delilah?'

'Absolutely fine,' Delilah replied with a confident smile totally at odds with her upright posture and the nervous fluttering in her belly.

Polly gazed at her thoughtfully until Delilah, unnerved by the silence, dropped her calm façade and blurted out, 'What's this all about? Is there something wrong?'

She could hear the tremor in her voice, and Polly must have heard it too because her expression softened.

'It's nothing to worry about, Del, but I do want us to talk about your progress and see how best I can help you through your training. I know how much this job means to you, but it wouldn't be fair of me to pretend that things are going swimmingly when we both know that's not the case.'

Delilah squashed the instinctive impulse to leap to her own defence, and let Polly continue.

'I've been reviewing your notes from your client sessions, and I have some concerns about the way you're facilitating your couples' conversations.'

'Like what?' Delilah demanded, her voice rising defensively.

Polly raised an eyebrow, and Delilah bit her lip and said quietly, 'Sorry. I meant to ask, what kind of concerns?'

Reaching behind her, Polly picked up a manila folder from the side table and opened it, flipping through a sheaf of papers as she spoke. 'I've printed off some of your notes which I thought we could discuss. Let's start with the session you had a couple of weeks ago with Sammie Wilson and her fiancé, Ross Diamond.'

Delilah relaxed slightly; she had bent over backwards to support that couple. 'The session went fine,' she said firmly. 'We talked through their communication feedback reports and how to use their learning from the love languages exercise. Sammie has been working hard to get Ross to improve his communication style, although between you and me, I don't see Ross as someone who's committed to doing the work. He seems keen on her, though, and at least he's turned up to the sessions.'

Polly slipped on her glasses and scanned a page. 'Reading through your notes, you seem to put more focus on Ross's behaviour than on Sammie's. Keep in mind they're seeking our help as a couple, and if our clients think we're being partial or judgemental, they can feel under attack and shut down, which makes us ineffective. I'm curious about why you're not challenging Sammie's perspective more?'

Delilah shifted uneasily on the sofa and stared at the rainbow rug, trying to marshal a defence. Other than remembering she had been exhausted and suffering from a pounding headache that day, her recollections from the session were hazy.

'It says on Ross's feedback form that you referenced a past relationship of yours during the session?' Polly continued.

Delilah's head jerked upright. '*What?* No, I didn't!'

'So you didn't say something along the lines of...' Polly flipped over a sheet and read out loud, '"I went out with someone emotionally closed off, but I would do things like hold his hand and stroke his arm and hug him, and it made a big difference"?'

Mortified, Delilah remained silent.

'Delilah, surely I don't have to remind you that we don't bring our personal stories into counselling. At the very least, you risk hijacking the session and making it about you, never mind keeping clear boundaries and the ethics of the situation.'

Moving on before Delilah could speak, Polly plucked a sheet from the file and waved it. 'I went through your report on the session with Rob and Malcolm Turner-Jones. You're helping them work through their relationship after Malcolm's affair, right?'

Delilah nodded, keeping tight-lipped until she knew where Polly was going with this.

'Obviously I wasn't in the room during the session, but your notes focus a lot on Rob's feelings and I'm not seeing much here regarding Malcolm and what drove him into the affair. Is this an area you're helping him explore?'

'Of course I am, Polly,' Delilah said with a resigned sigh, wondering if her supervisor planned to pick holes in every one of her client interactions. 'Malcolm is very sorry about what he did and he's desperate for Rob to forgive him. We've done some exercises to help Malcolm reflect on what he thought was missing in the relationship, but he's keen for us to support Rob through his feelings of rejection and that's why we focused on Rob in that session.'

'But has Malcolm been able to articulate *why* he felt the need to look elsewhere?' Polly probed gently. 'If he's not clear on his motivation, how will he recognise when he might be in danger of it happening again?'

Delilah groaned silently, feeling distinctly under attack, but Polly didn't appear to have finished. 'Okay, so let's talk about that session you had earlier this week with the Hendersons. Now, I'm going to be candid, after what happened in your previous session, I had thought about reassigning them to another counsellor, but I wanted to give you the opportunity to reset your relationship with them. I appreciate they aren't the easiest of couples, but I'm still concerned about how you are facilitating their sessions and maintaining boundaries.'

Delilah's eyebrows shot up. 'The *easiest* of couples? Come on, Polly – Brian is a nightmare, and Janine has been a saint to put up with his rules and regulations all these years. If *I* lived with him, he would have driven me completely up the wall by now!'

Polly's voice switched from gentle to crisp as peanut brittle. 'That's the point, Delilah. Deciding who is right or wrong is not a useful approach to helping a couple. Their relationship isn't about you, which you should know by now.'

'I'm not saying it is! I just want Janine to feel confident about setting boundaries for herself. She obviously feels suffocated by Brian and he didn't want to acknowledge that in the session, so—'

'—so you thought you'd do it for him?'

Hearing the incredulity in Polly's voice, Delilah hesitated. 'Not – not exactly. Anyway, it's not just Brian – Janine can be a bit all over the place with her words at times, so occasionally I try to summarise her thoughts—'

'—which you should have let her do herself. You can't do Janine's work for her; yours is to give them the space and support to work through their situation without judgement.'

Polly referred back to Delilah's notes. 'Looking at your notes from this and earlier sessions, you've made several references to the husband's insistence on his wife making him dinner. Have you explored whether acts of service might be his primary love language and if his wife could be encouraged to see it that way or perhaps find a way they might align – or were you just focused on judging him?'

'Polly, you weren't there! Despite everything the woman says, it's so obvious she's compromising her truth. She's not getting through to him and all I did was try and help her articulate what Brian didn't seem to be hearing.'

Polly's face turned a deep pink, and she sucked in her cheeks and took a breath, looking as close to furious as Delilah could remember. After an anxious few moments, Polly relaxed her face and faced Delilah squarely.

'These are the sort of challenges you should be raising with me and bringing to your supervision group. Talking of which, how are your supervision sessions going? Before you answer, you should know I've checked the attendance logs and from what I can make out, you seem to have skipped almost as many as you've attended.'

Polly closed the folder and placed it back on the table before folding her hands in her lap. 'Del, I'm going to be honest with you.' She spaced her words out carefully. 'I know how motivated you are, and I know you desperately want to help people, but our work is to support couples to resolve the challenges in their relationships without projecting our opinions and biases. I understand it's frustrating to see someone's pain and feel for them, and we've spoken in training about how we can often feel helpless in the face of our clients' difficulties. However, while you might think you're being useful, diving in helps no one. If you get it right, your client learns nothing, and if you get it wrong, then you've lost their trust. You went through all this at the beginning of your training, and yet you still seem unable to separate your emotions from your clients' situations and remain within your professional boundaries. A key part of your training when you started this programme was the mandatory therapy sessions. I don't know how I've missed this until now, but you are at least five hours behind your minimum required personal counselling. What's going on?'

Caught off-guard by the change of topic, Delilah stared at her mutely. Polly was unlikely to see it her way, but Verity, the humourless therapist Delilah had been assigned to for personal counselling, had been completely wrong for her. Her persistent probing had put Delilah's back up and driven her into a resentful silence. Furthermore, Verity's tactic of asking questions and then sitting patiently through their allotted hour, as if hoping the weight of the silence would provoke Delilah into responding, had failed miserably. After three virtually silent sessions, Delilah had quietly opted out of attending any more. She had assumed, since Verity hadn't ratted her out at the time, that the therapist was equally relieved to be spared the hassle.

Polly heaved a deep sigh. 'Okay, I think I'm seeing a pattern here. Delilah, you have enormous potential as a counsellor, but our first responsibility is to our clients. That means being aware of our own issues and dealing with them – or at least being willing to work on them. Counsellors also need support, which is why we insist they undergo therapy to increase their self-awareness and help them recognise their own vulnerabilities and biases.'

Where is all this going? Delilah shook her head, trying to make sense of Polly's words swirling around her brain. Crossing her legs, she hugged her knee to her chest, finding a sliver of comfort in the reassuring solidity of her body when her mind seemed unable to focus.

Polly observed her and then said softly, 'You aren't a mother hen taking ownership of people's issues, Del. If you go down that path, you will crumble under the weight of other people's problems. It's critical in our work to have empathy, and I know that makes it tempting to take on our clients' burdens, but it's not the best way to help them. We absolutely must set boundaries if we're to have any hope of managing our emotions.'

Polly paused and Delilah's stomach immediately started to churn. *Oh my God, this is it!* Her supervisor clearly thought she was hopeless and now she was going to be fired from the only job she had ever loved. She swallowed hard and tried to find her words. 'I admit I haven't been great at keeping up with the group sessions and I should have told you ages ago that the therapist and I didn't click. But I promise that going forward, I'll do anything to make up for it. I'll – I'll go to every single supervision session... I really care about my clients, Polly. I *know* I can make a difference, so please – *please* give me the chance.'

'Delilah, you're a lovely team member and always ready to go the extra mile, but you've got to admit you can't carry on like this.'

'I know...' Delilah tailed off dejectedly.

'You have the highest number of clients leaving the programme out of all the trainee counsellors on the course, and at the end of the day, our organisation has targets to meet. You must understand that I can't afford to let this continue.'

And here it comes. All the hours of studying and cramming for the exams, all the time she'd put into helping her clients – *none* of it counted. As far as Polly was concerned, Delilah had failed to take the programme and her training seriously, and now she was out. Lost in a fog of self-recrimination, it took her a moment to realise Polly was still speaking.

'Before you completely derail all the work you've put into the course, I'm recommending a period of suspension from the programme. I believe you need to take some time to consider your readiness to counsel others. I want to offer you the time to reflect on how much of your personal relationship baggage you're bringing to your work, because if you can't admit your own challenges, then you certainly can't help others.'

Delilah stared, gobsmacked. She had absolutely no issues with her past relationships! In truth, she rarely gave the men she'd dated a second thought, so how could they possibly be a problem?

Polly raised a hand as if to forestall any protest. 'As professionals, we have to do the inner work that stops our personal experiences impacting our clients. I want you to re-engage with therapy to help you through this period of reflection. It will give you the opportunity to understand what's going on for you so you can ask for whatever help you need.'

Polly leaned forward, looking earnest. 'I believe in you, Delilah, and I want you to succeed. I'm referring you to Arne Bergen. He's one of the best therapists I know, and he has agreed to work with you.'

'*What*? I mean... pardon?' Delilah couldn't disguise her horror. 'But I've already done therapy, Polly. I'm fine!'

'I wouldn't be doing my job as your supervisor if I didn't encourage you to take time out and use the support systems we have in place. Arne is brilliant at helping his clients see their patterns of behaviour, explore their places of discomfort and draw on those insights to benefit their clients. We all have issues, Delilah, and I want you to use the time I'm giving you and the support on offer to reflect on your life and relationships.'

'Seriously, Polly, why don't you just kill me now?' Delilah's voice rose into a wail. What fresh hell was this? *For God's sake, all I'm trying to do is help people!*

Her relief on learning she hadn't been fired was draining away in the face of Polly's ultimatum.

But despite Polly's sympathetic tone, the steely glint in her eye made it clear she wasn't budging. 'Trust me, I don't enjoy doing this, but if you're not prepared to go through *all* the remedial steps I've just outlined, I'm going to have to let you go. If you're willing to do the work, then I can consider bringing you back.'

'And how long exactly am I suspended for?' Delilah asked, annoyed by the whimper in her voice that made her sound like a sulky teenager being sent to detention.

'It's not a punishment, Del. Work with Arne, and when he thinks you're ready to resume counselling clients, he'll sign you off and you can come back.'

7

'You can't be serious! She actually said that?' Salome's eyes were wide with disbelief.

'You heard me.' Delilah glared moodily at the screen of the TV Salome had put on mute, barely registering the panel of animated women who seemed to be furiously talking over each other. After leaving Polly's office, too upset to stop and update Armenique, Delilah had picked up her bag from her desk and fled the building to find refuge in Salome's house. Maya was at nursery and safely out of earshot, and Farhan was using his lunch break to take Arin to the park.

'So, wait, are you fired or not?' her sister demanded.

'If keeping my job means going back into therapy, then I guess I'm fired,' Delilah said with a bitter laugh. In frustration, she kicked her heel against the sofa, wincing as a dart of pain shot through her foot.

'Oh come on, Del, you *love* your job!' Salome shifted on the couch to face her. 'What's going on, sis?' Her voice switched to the sympathetic, concerned tone Delilah hated. Even more so when it came with sad eyes and a furrowed brow.

'Can you stop looking at me like I'm a sick puppy you've rescued from the side of a motorway!' Delilah snapped. 'I'll be fine. I've started over before and I can do it again.'

Salome hesitated, and then said, 'Well, you're not going to like this, but I think Polly has a point.'

'*Seriously*, Sal? Whose side are you on here?'

'Yours. Always,' Salome retorted, unmoved by Delilah's outrage. 'Which is why I think you need to take this seriously. You've worked so hard for this, and you can't just treat it like... like a bad date and walk out. I know it's a shock, but Polly gave you feedback to help you improve and you need to take it on board.'

'Look, I'm not saying I've been perfect at my job, but I do care about my clients, and I try everything to support them. Just because a couple of them haven't worked out—' Delilah shook her head and held up her palms in exasperation. 'For God's sake, Sal, it's not like every single couple is destined to stay together!'

'True,' Salome acknowledged. 'But isn't the whole point of relationship counselling to fix people's problems?'

'No, it isn't!' Delilah said heatedly. 'It's to get people to a place of honesty with each other and if that means they discover they're not compatible, then they shouldn't be forced – by me or by *anyone* – to feel like they have to stick with their situation!'

'Fair enough, but you've also said truth can be distorted by emotions, so shouldn't you be helping these couples challenge what they think is true?'

Delilah stared in exasperation at her sister. Had Salome been listening to a single word she'd said? And how exactly did she think quoting her own words back at her was supposed to help?

'What I'm saying is I'm not prepared to push women who aren't getting what they need from their partners to just suck it up. We both know where that can lead.'

She'd already said too much, Delilah thought, getting up from the couch and walking over to the window. After a few moments, with her back to her sister, she said in a low voice, 'The bottom line is Polly's not changing her mind unless I agree to all her conditions. The woman is heartless – she really had me fooled with her smiley, happy-clappy, long hair in bunches, fluffy hearts vibe.'

When Salome made no comment, Delilah turned around and leaned back against the wall with her arms folded. 'D'you know she had the nerve to accuse me of not being impartial because I'm, quote, carrying relationship baggage? Talk about inappropriate! I have *never* discussed my love life with Polly, and I haven't got a clue where she got that idea.'

'She's not wrong, though, is she?' Salome murmured. Delilah looked aghast but her sister shook her head. 'I said what I said. Let's be honest, sis. You have dumped every single man you've dated, bar none.'

'And for good reason!'

'Really?' Salome sighed. 'Sweetie, you've been in and out of relationships since you were seventeen and you've always got an excuse for why it didn't work out. I'm not being funny, but have you honestly never considered that you're the only common denominator?'

'What does that mean?' Delilah demanded, beginning to regret not going straight home from the office. So much for this being a safe refuge. Why the hell was everyone suddenly ganging up on her?

Salome tucked her legs under her and gazed intently at her sister. 'Like Polly said, she has a duty of care to you as well as your clients, and it sounds to me like she's trying to do right by both sides. Del, you can't be an effective relationship counsellor if you're in denial about your own relationships. Instead of throwing in the towel, show her you're ready to work on yourself.'

'How exactly am I supposed to do that?'

'Well, first of all, agree to therapy! I don't get why you are so resistant to the idea.'

'Because I don't need someone else to tell me what I already know about my life and there's nothing to be gained by constantly raking things up. What's done is done and talking about it endlessly won't change anything! Who knows what bringing up the past will do? Think about it, Sal! What... what if it means they don't think I'm fit to do this job?'

Salome's voice softened. 'Hon, nobody understands better than me how hard it is to open up to someone about what happened. We've had it tough, but we need to deal with it. I've told you a hundred times how much it helps me to practise mindfulness and check in with Alison every two or three weeks. Del, you haven't made peace with the past – you've just buried it, and when you squash things down, they pop up somewhere else. Please listen to me. Therapy will help you *and* make you a better counsellor.'

As if she sensed Delilah weakening, Salome persisted. 'Alison says that when we don't deal with the unresolved issues in our past, they will keep haunting us and driving how we feel and behave.'

Delilah stared in silence at the floor, absorbing her sister's words. Whether or not she agreed with Salome – and she didn't – there was no denying that she was fast running out of options. Was it worth opening up to a stranger and risk losing her job? On the flip side, if she didn't show willing to meet Polly's conditions, she'd be out of a job anyway.

'If I agree to therapy, do you think that might swing it?' she said slowly.

'It's possible.' Salome sounded dubious. 'But therapy's required as part of your training, so just doing what you're supposed to do isn't going to impress Polly. If you ask me, you need to come up with something major to show her you're serious.'

Delilah frowned. 'Like what?'

'Let's think about this logically,' Salome mused aloud, twisting her wedding ring round her finger. 'Polly's concerned you're letting your relationship history get in the way. So, you need a plan that says you agree that's a real possibility and you're taking steps to address it. You know, like in an interview when they ask you about your weaknesses and you pick something and then immediately say what you're doing to improve it.'

'Um, hello! This is not an interview, and I have no idea where you're going with all this.'

Salome fell silent, and her brows knitted together in thought. After a short while, her face lit up and she pumped a fist in triumph, looking more animated than Delilah had seen her in ages.

'I've got an idea! You know how whenever you dump a man – which we've established you do regularly – you block his number, totally ghost him, and never *ever* give him a reason why – which even you must admit is not only weird but deeply unfair. Well, here's the thing. You can prove your emotional maturity to Polly by apologising to these poor blokes you've hurt and explaining properly why you dumped them. It will be a fantastic learning experience *and* prove you're taking accountability for how you've handled your relationships.'

She beamed at Delilah, who was staring at her in horror.

'You must be out of your frigging mind!'

'It makes perfect sense,' Salome argued. 'If a guy broke up with me without a word of warning, I'd be mortified and probably blame myself. So, you can also look at this as doing the poor men a kindness while you're showing your supervisor you are serious about your career.'

'First of all, it's a ridiculous idea, and secondly, what makes you think I'm sorry for dumping them? Even you've called some of my exes weird.'

'Some, yes. But not all. At least think about it.'

'*No!* And even if I am sorry about one or two of them, apologising after all this time would be humiliating and make me look weak!'

Salome shook her head. 'No, hon. Like I'm always telling Maya, being able to say sorry when you're wrong is a sign of strength.'

'Yeah, well I'm not five years old,' Delilah said swiftly. 'You can't seriously be suggesting I go looking for every man I've ever dated?'

'You're right, that could take a while,' Salome conceded. 'Okay then, we'll focus on the boyfriends who lasted at least six months. There's only a handful who made it that far and they're much more likely to have got emotionally invested in you.'

Delilah suddenly felt deeply uneasy, and she studied her sister with narrowed eyes. 'Who exactly are we talking about here?'

'*Delilah!* Do you want your job back or not?' Salome demanded.

Delilah nodded reluctantly, and Salome beamed and bounced on the sofa excitedly. 'Excellent! I'm going to write a list of the exes I think you need to speak to. You find them and explain why you dumped them, make a sincere apology, and then move on. Report back to Polly, do your therapy, win/win all round, job done!'

'Do you actually hear yourself?' Delilah scoffed.

'You can mock all you want, sister dearest, but your boss isn't taking you back until you prove you're on top of your own relationship dramas,' Salome pointed out. 'If you really love that job—'

'You *know* I do! I've trained for ages and it's the only career that feels right for me.'

'Then put aside your pride and do whatever it takes to get back on track. If you're so sure you ended all your relationships for good reasons, then here's your chance to prove it. Think of this as, um... Alcoholics Anonymous – you know, find everyone you pissed off when you were pissed and make amends. Except, this will be relationship AA. Admit you have a problem, say sorry to the poor bastards, and get closure.'

8

Delilah pulled the front door shut behind her and stomped down the garden path, muttering under her breath. Salome needed her head examined if she thought her stupid plan stood a snowball's chance in hell of happening. She had seized on Farhan returning home with a grouchy Arin as her excuse to escape, although not before Salome had extracted a promise to at least consider her suggestion.

Lost in thought, it took Delilah a few moments to notice the man stooped over a flowerbed in the adjoining front garden. The familiar figure straightened and pulled off a worn pair of gardening gloves to scratch his head. Looking over the low dividing fence, he caught her eye, and she froze. For a long moment, they observed each other in silence and Delilah could have sworn there was a faint smile on his rugged mahogany-brown face.

Their paths rarely crossed, and it was almost two years since Delilah had laid eyes on him. There was perhaps a little more grey visible in the tufty dark hair than she remembered, but his expression was as warm and kindly as it had always been. Seeing him in his staple uniform of baggy chinos and checked shirt sparked a kaleidoscope of memories: howling with laughter over Jenga, blatantly cheating at Monopoly, dancing to the reggae tracks from his impressive music collection, sampling his famous lamb curry, and, most of all, long, quiet conversations in which she felt safe enough to tell him things she had never shared with Noah. For a time he had been a father figure to her, and she missed him more than she allowed herself to admit. But those days were gone, and today there was much more than a wooden fence separating Delilah from Noah's father.

'*Neville!* Why have you left the front door open? I don't want no creatures scurrying into the place!' The sound of the woman's voice from inside the house next door broke the spell and jolted Delilah back to reality.

Unwilling to risk another run-in with Mrs West, Delilah gave Neville a tentative smile and, when he nodded in reply, she hurried down the path, almost breaking into a run in her haste to get away.

9

Delilah frowned at the number on the scuffed door, looked up and down the busy high street, and then checked her phone again. It was definitely the right address, but the shared offices above a general household goods shop was not where she'd expected to find Polly's highly recommended therapist. She squinted at the labels alongside the two buzzers: 'Sadie, Tarot Specialist' and 'Arne Bergen'.

The harsh November wind and gloomy grey skies didn't help Delilah's mood. It had just started raining and the doorway offered no shelter, but she still hesitated, hovering her finger over the buzzer beside Arne's name. Although Polly had made it clear that therapy was non-negotiable, it had taken a week of Salome's relentless nagging before Delilah had reluctantly agreed to make an appointment. Even the idea of opening up to a stranger's prodding and probing felt exhausting, but if she was to avoid a repeat of her experience with Verity, Delilah knew she would have to play the game. This time, instead of stonewalling, she decided, she would answer the therapist's questions but reveal only what he needed to hear to confirm her readiness to return to work.

Armed with a strategy, she had booked a slot in Arne's calendar, but now she was actually here, she could feel her stomach twist into a spasm of anxiety and couldn't shake off an uneasy sense of foreboding. *Pull yourself together, Del.*

You've got this! A cold gust of rain-soaked wind blew over her, and she gritted her teeth and pressed hard on the buzzer.

Hearing a click, she pushed the door open and walked into a narrow hallway. Inside, the building was as dingy as the exterior had promised, with stacks of letters and junk mail on the shelf behind the door, tired mosaic floor tiles and faded floral-patterned wallpaper, and a musty odour of damp walls. There was no sign of life, and when she closed the door behind her, the sound of traffic was replaced by silence. She slipped off her damp puffer coat and shook her braids free before wiping her boots on the worn doormat and walking down the corridor.

At the foot of the stairs leading up to the offices, Delilah's nerves kicked in again. Taking a moment to remind herself of her gameplan, she climbed up to the first floor and continued down the passageway past a door stencilled with a pack of black and white playing cards. Although she wasn't normally one for spiritualists, at that precise moment Delilah would gladly have traded Polly's revered Arne Bergen for Sadie the Tarot Specialist.

Arne's name was on the door at the end of the corridor, and Delilah knocked softly. Moments later, the door was opened by a very tall man with a striking mane of red curly hair and piercing electric-blue eyes. His oversized Argyle patterned jumper and baggy corduroy trousers had clearly been designed for comfort rather than style, and with dark bushy eyebrows, saggy under-eye bags, and a scruffy beard, he looked like a rumpled, middle-aged Viking.

'You are Delilah, yes?'

'Um... yes,' she said hesitantly, shaking the hand he had extended. While his height was imposing, his voice was deep and gentle with an accent Delilah couldn't place, but assumed was from somewhere in Scandinavia.

'I'm Arne. Please come in.' He stood back and she walked in, immediately struck by the contrast between his warm, brightly lit office and the run-down interior of the building.

'Will you take some coffee?' Arne enquired, and when Delilah nodded, he walked over to a coffee machine in a tiny kitchenette at the end of the room.

While Arne busied himself, Delilah quickly scanned his office. The high ceilings and pale blue walls were decorated with black and white framed photos of snow-topped mountains and forest scenes that seemed a world away from the depressing grey November morning. Judging from the number of books crammed onto shelves that lined an entire wall, Arne liked to read. The room was plainly furnished, and a woven chocolate-brown rug with a cream geometric design brought a touch of style to the parquet flooring. There was no sign of the proverbial therapist's couch, and other than a desk in the corner, the room was furnished with three large armchairs, one of which was occupied by a sleek tabby cat who briefly opened one eye to scrutinise Delilah before closing it again.

Arne carefully placed a full mug of coffee on a side table and gestured towards a chair. 'Please, sit.'

Delilah took a seat and clasped her hands in her lap, while he sat in the chair across from her. He leaned forward and rested his forearms on his long legs, and Delilah tucked a braid behind her ear and cleared her throat, suddenly self-conscious under his scrutiny. She picked up the mug and took a tentative sip, almost scalding her tongue, and quickly set it down. She glanced at Arne with a nervous smile, and when he didn't seem inclined to break the silence, she nodded in the direction of the sleeping cat.

'What's her name?'

'His name,' he corrected. 'Sigmund. As in Freud. An inside joke, you might say,' he added with a straight face.

Delilah regarded him quizzically, not quite sure what to make of him. She hadn't given much thought to what the therapist would look like, but she certainly wouldn't have pictured this shaggy-haired giant with his calm, almost hypnotic voice and disdainful cat. There was a twinkle in his eye that made Arne seem less intimidating than she had initially thought, and despite his unorthodox appearance and the run-down premises, he appeared to be very much in demand. She had struggled to find a time in his online calendar, and in the end she'd been forced to book a Monday morning slot, which wasn't exactly when she was at her best.

'Thank you for coming. As you know, Polly Danbury contacted me to request that I work with you,' Arne said. Despite his strong accent, he was easy to understand. 'I believe you are on a leave of absence, and that you started personal therapy sessions in the past which you then discontinued. Am I correct?'

Delilah nodded. *So far, so true.*

'Was there a particular reason why you stopped attending your therapy sessions? It will help me understand if this process is one you will find useful and how committed you are to doing the work.'

Delilah gnawed her lip for a moment and then reached for the mug, taking a few cautious sips of the hot coffee while she gathered her thoughts. *Tell him what he needs to hear*, she reminded herself.

She put down the mug and said carefully, 'Yes, I am committed.'

Before she could help herself, her deep sense of frustration took over and she blurted out, 'But if I'm completely honest, I find this all a bit unnecessary. I don't know how much Polly told you, but you should know that I passed my counselling exams with flying colours. Is there room for me to improve in my work? Yes, of course! But that's what training is for, isn't it? I just don't get why I need to go through this... this...' *Don't say sham!* '...process,' she finished lamely.

'Is that why you stopped your previous sessions – did you also consider them unnecessary?'

Uncomfortable with Arne's calm questioning, Delilah shifted in the armchair and crossed her legs. 'I wasn't getting anything out of it, and there was absolutely no chemistry with my therapist. Frankly, I think she was just as relieved as me when I stopped going.'

'I see.' Arne nodded and gently tugged his full beard. 'So tell me, Delilah, what motivates you to be a relationship counsellor?'

Delilah blinked, thrown off by the sudden switch in topic. She scrabbled for a response that might impress him, and when none came to mind, she reached for her mug and swallowed a large gulp of coffee.

Arne gave her an encouraging smile, and she forced a laugh. 'Well, I've had loads of relationships myself, so there isn't much I don't know about them, haha!'

Cringing at her own pathetic attempt at humour, Delilah uncrossed her legs and sat up. 'I enjoy helping people and supporting couples to navigate conflict. You know, help them to improve how they communicate with each other and understand the other person's perspective, and... basically, develop more positive behaviours.'

'Anything else?'

'Well, I also think it's important to be aware of when couples can be a danger to each other—' She stopped abruptly, instantly regretting her choice of words.

'Danger?'

She felt a flash of annoyance that he'd picked up on the word, but it was too late to row back. 'Yes, you know – toxic relationships.'

Arne pondered on her words for a moment. 'Help me understand. Do you see your role as supporting couples to address their challenges or do you believe you should be saving people from holding on to poor relationships? I'm wondering what success looks like for you.'

Delilah shrugged. 'That depends.'

'On?'

'The safety of the woman – I mean, of the couple. If they're not good together, they shouldn't feel compelled to stay in a relationship.'

'Do you feel counselling encourages couples to prolong unhealthy relationships?'

Fired up by Arne's questions, Delilah had completely forgotten her game plan. 'Honestly? Yes, I think it can. I mean, we're so focused on helping people resolve their conflicts that sometimes we risk making them accept the unacceptable. I've had friends who've stayed with their boyfriends even when the men are literally the worst, and I don't believe my profession should be enabling that.'

She leaned forward, caught up in the discussion. 'Look, don't get me wrong. I'm not saying all men are bad. Take my sister, for example. Now she has the best husband in the world, but I've seen—' *Shut up, Del!* She broke off, clamping her lips shut to stop any more words from escaping.

In the sudden silence, Sigmund stretched and leapt off his chair. Padding across the rug, he hopped up onto Arne's lap and purred loudly when Arne stroked his back.

'Tell me, Delilah, do you find yourself drawn into your clients' problems during your counselling sessions?'

Not knowing what Polly might have told him, Delilah took her time to formulate a non-committal response. 'I like to think I'm empathetic but also very objective,' she said finally.

Arne raised a bushy eyebrow, and his droopy eyes lit up with a glint of humour. 'Then you must be Superwoman!'

She looked at him, nonplussed, and he smiled. 'I joke with you. Because you know we therapists and counsellors are only human. We develop empathy for clients we connect with and it's almost impossible to be objective when we see other people's pain, particularly if we feel helpless to alleviate it. But the question is whether we can recognise and address this before it hinders the counselling relationship.'

Delilah stayed mum, reluctant to be drawn into saying anything she might regret. The silence lengthened while Arne calmly stroked Sigmund and Delilah grew increasingly uncomfortable. *Okay, Del, you can give this guy the Verity treatment and never get your job back, or you can give him something to work with. Anything.*

'My sister thinks I need relationship AA to do my job better,' she blurted out before she could censor herself. 'She reckons I should go on an apology tour of my ex-boyfriends and make amends for dumping them.'

Arne raised his brows in surprise. 'That sounds like an interesting challenge. What makes this important to you?'

Already regretting her impulse to reveal Salome's mad scheme, Delilah waved a hand as if she could swat the topic aside. 'Frankly, I think it's a daft idea.'

'What was your sister's reasoning for this exercise?'

Arne clearly wasn't letting it go, and Delilah reluctantly added, 'She thinks I break up with boyfriends too quickly and that I'm never open with them about the reasons why.'

'And what do you think?' Arne leaned forward with interest, causing Sigmund to emit a miaow of protest and leap to the floor. Crooking his tail, he padded across the office and slunk under the desk.

Delilah wrapped a braid around her finger as she pondered Arne's question. 'I don't agree,' she said baldly. 'I know when a relationship isn't working, and I've always had perfectly good reasons not to stay with my exes. I admit I'm not great at having awkward break-up conversations and would rather just move on, but that's got nothing to do with my ability to be a good counsellor.'

'Who says it does?'

'Polly.' Delilah's mind went back to the last meeting with her supervisor, and she blew air out of her cheeks in exasperation. 'She seems to think I have relationship baggage which is affecting my ability to work with clients.'

Arne tilted his head as if weighing her words. 'Can we explore what you said earlier a little more? I'm curious to understand why you shy away from telling your partner your reasons for ending the relationship.'

Delilah shrugged defensively. 'I don't see the point in hurting someone's feelings just because I don't want to be with them any more.'

'I find this very interesting. Do you consider silence is less painful than the truth? Perhaps honesty would be a more generous response and offer them – and you – greater clarity as to why things didn't work out?'

Delilah hesitated, and then suddenly her game plan didn't seem quite so important. The nights of fitful sleep and the dark dreams that forced her awake put paid to her claim that she had moved on from the past. Salome's words flashed through her mind. *Have you honestly never considered that you're the only common denominator?*

'But what if the real reason it didn't work isn't about them?' she asked in a low voice. 'What if they're not the issue and it's me?'

Arne studied her thoughtfully. 'Isn't that more reason to be truthful about why you made the decision?' He paused, and when she made no comment, continued. 'Tell me more about this tour of apologies. What exactly will you be seeking? Do you want forgiveness to reassure yourself you are a good person or are you concerned about the person you have hurt and sincerely regret your actions?'

Delilah stared at him in dismay, trying to work out how they had arrived here. Despite her best intentions, Arne's questions had somehow provoked her into engaging with him, and she had a horrible feeling there was no turning back.

'Will you take up your sister's challenge?' His neutral tone made it impossible to gauge his opinion or ignore him.

'Truthfully? I don't know. Maybe. I mean, it's not like I've got a lot going on these days without work to go to.' She ran a hand through her braids and fell back in the armchair, rolling her shoulders to ease the tension building up around her neck.

'Who knows,' she mused aloud. 'Perhaps Salome's right – although there's no way I would ever tell her that. I still think the idea sounds mad, but if it shows Polly I've addressed my "relationship baggage"' – she raised her hands into exaggerated air quotes – 'then, why not?'

'Clearly, your job is very important to you,' Arne observed with a brief smile. 'Before we finish for today, let's talk a little more about your work. You mentioned earlier that couples who aren't good for each other should not stay together, which leaves me curious about how you know when you have done a good job.'

'I don't understand.' Delilah stared at him, puzzled.

'Do you feel a stronger inclination to see your clients stay together or is it success for you when they separate?'

When she continued to look baffled, Arne looked past her to a large clock on the wall and stood up, brushing Sigmund's hair from his trousers. 'Our time is up, so let's leave it there. I will reserve this time slot for you, and we can discuss this further next week.'

'But—'

Arne was already on his way to the door, and he opened it and waited while she gathered her belongings. 'Book your next session in my calendar, Delilah, and I'll see you then.'

10

It was freezing by the time Delilah left the cemetery. The anaemic rays of afternoon sun did nothing to warm the air and after several days of heavy rain, the grey clouds overhead threatened a further deluge. It was too early to meet Armenique for the sandwich lunch they'd planned, and Salome's house, which was a short walk away, was currently a hotbed of infection. Maya had brought home a streaming cold from nursery and passed it on to Arin.

With time to spare, Delilah decided to walk into the town centre rather than take the bus. While she waited to cross the busy high street, her gaze fell on to the purple awning of a tattoo parlour across the road. Suddenly, it was as if she had been yanked from her body as the noise from the heavy traffic faded away and the past roared back.

'Go on, then. Ladies first,' he announced with a grin.

Seeing the needle on the tray surrounded by pots of coloured inks and clear plastic cups sent Delilah's stomach into a nervous spasm. The bravado, fuelled by half a bottle of wine, which had spurred her to agree to this, was long gone, and she pushed Noah towards the black padded chair.

'No, no, you go first! That way I'll know what to expect when it's my turn.'

He looked sceptical but slid onto the worn leather chair without comment, deftly rolling up the sleeve of his shirt and laying the back of his exposed arm on the padded armrest. Delilah stood back, her mouth dry with apprehension, while Stan, the tattoo artist, wiped Noah's forearm and got to work. Instantly nauseous, she turned her head away, but that didn't stop the buzzing of the tattoo gun making her feel even sicker.

By the time Noah raised his arm to display Stan's handiwork – a stylish black crown topped with the initial D – it took every ounce of her willpower not to keel over.

'Hey, Del! Are you okay?' Noah's jubilant expression turned into a concerned frown.

Stan took one look at Delilah's face and disappeared, returning moments later with a glass of water. She gulped down its contents in one go and then wiped her lips and handed Stan the empty glass with a muttered thanks. Burning with embarrassment, Delilah reached for Noah's arm to inspect his new tattoo.

'Do you like it?' Hearing the doubt in his voice, she smiled at him, feeling guilty for her feeble reaction.

'Of course I do! It's – it's awesome!'

'You sure? You had me worried there for a minute.'

'Your arm's gone all puffy.' She hesitated. 'Was it really painful?'

'It wasn't that bad. Besides, it's worth it for my queen. Ready to do yours?'

A fresh wave of nausea washed over her, and she clutched his arm in panic, scarcely noticing him wince at the pressure on the tender patch of skin.

'I can't! I thought I could, but I can't handle the sound of that drill or having that needle stuck into me! I'm so sorry... Please don't be upset with me.'

Noah shushed her gently and swivelled round to pull her close with his good arm. 'It's okay, babe. You don't have to do it. It's all good.'

'I feel terrible! I love you so much and I wanted us to do this together.'

'It's fine. I promise. You don't need to prove anything to me.'

'Hey, lady! Are you planning to cross the road or what? I'm on the clock here!' The irritated shout from the red-faced van driver leaning out of his window jolted Delilah sharply back to the present.

Mortified, she wrapped her coat tightly around her and hurried over the pedestrian crossing, picking up her pace with each step as if hoping to outrun her thoughts.

11

'Okay, I'll do it.'

'Do *what*?' Salome sounded baffled, and Delilah stopped pacing up and down her living room and exhaled in irritation.

'Duh! What have you been nagging me to do since I got suspended?'

'*Oh!*' Salome exclaimed. 'You mean the apologies?' When Delilah remained silent, she added enthusiastically, 'That's *brilliant*, hon! It might feel a bit awkward at first, but once you've done the first one—'

'Sal, I hope you realise we're not talking about me learning how to paint a picture or – or knit a bloody jumper here! You're asking me to go out and find men I haven't spoken to in years and grovel. *Five* different guys, all of whom will probably want to kill me! Have you any idea how terrifying that is?'

Salome sighed deeply. 'Del, I know it won't be easy, but I really do think that having these difficult conversations will improve your self-awareness and give you closure.'

'I *have* closure,' Delilah started, and then stopped, hearing the lack of conviction in her own voice. The session with Arne had shaken her more than she was prepared to admit, and there was nothing like sitting around aimlessly in her flat to force some introspection about her past behaviour and drive home how badly she wanted to get back to work.

'What's changed your mind? Was it the therapy session?' Salome sounded curious and Delilah shrugged, not sure how to explain her decision to go along with a plan that sounded like walking into a lion's den without a single piece of armour.

'Maybe. Arne said it sounded like an interesting challenge. He also suggested I needed to be clear whether I was doing it for the benefit of the men I dumped or just to make myself feel good and impress Polly.'

'And?'

'And it's a good question. Obviously, I want my job back, but I was thinking about what you said – you know, about how you'd want to know why someone dumped you and that you'd blame yourself if you didn't have an explanation? If I'm honest, I'd hate it if a guy just disappeared on me. *Soo*, I'm thinking that as much as I hate admitting you're right – because you can never resist saying "I told you so" – maybe this time you've actually got a point.'

'*I told you so!*' Salome crowed triumphantly.

Delilah rolled her eyes in exasperation, only just resisting the urge to hurl the phone onto the floor. 'That's so mature,' she muttered.

Salome giggled, and then after a moment, her voice sobered. 'Seriously, hon, I'm glad you're ready to give it a try. I know it's a big ask, but taking accountability for hurting someone can only be a good thing, right?'

Can it? Delilah wondered grimly as she ended the call. She wished she shared Salome's optimism because from where she was standing, opening up the past to put things right was risking an awful lot more going wrong.

12

Delilah walked slowly up and down the short cul-de-sac of identical red-brick terraced houses, keeping a wary eye out for twitching curtains. It would be beyond embarrassing if a suspicious neighbour were to report her to the police for loitering – or worse, for stalking her ex-boyfriend.

When Salome had texted Delilah a list of her five ex-boyfriends a couple of days earlier, Desmond had been the easy first choice. It had been more than ten years since Delilah had ended their seven-month post-college romance, and while she had spotted him around town a few times over the years, not having any idea what to say to him, she had simply kept her distance. Now Desmond was happily married, she was hoping he would be amenable to accepting her apology.

After fifteen minutes, she pulled out her phone and sat on a low wall to scroll through his Instagram account. She knew she was in the right place because the white door with the number 23 directly across from where she sat was clearly visible in several pictures Desmond had posted of himself holding a little boy with the same square jaw and dark eyes. From the outside, his house looked exactly as she would have imagined: neat, conventional, and with nothing out of place. When she'd first met Desmond, his need for order and predictability had been a big part of his appeal. Until it hadn't.

Ten minutes later, Delilah's patience was wearing thin, and she checked her phone again. Today was Thursday, which meant that according to the humble-brag reel Desmond had posted on TikTok about the joys of fatherhood and doing nursery pick-ups on Tuesdays and Thursdays, Mr Predictable should have been home by now. She exhaled with relief when Desmond, wearing the fleece-lined jacket that featured in a number of his selfies, rounded the corner a few moments later pushing a stroller. Less predictably, a dark-haired woman, who Delilah could only assume was his wife, followed close behind, carrying the child featured in Desmond's photos.

Delilah got off the wall and brushed down the seat of her jeans, in two minds about her next move. She hadn't factored in the possibility of an audience while she tried to apologise, but, on the other hand, having mustered the courage to finally face Desmond, she didn't have much choice other than to go through with the plan. Neither Desmond nor his wife had noticed her, and they were now almost at the gate to his house. Before she could talk herself out of it, Delilah ran across the road and stood in front of him, blocking his path.

Desmond reared like a startled stallion and stepped back clumsily, almost bumping into his wife. He gaped at Delilah and then, as recognition dawned, his eyes widened.

'*Delilah!* What the hell—?'

'Calm down,' Delilah said breathlessly. 'I just wanted a quick word.'

Her cheeks were hot with embarrassment as she smiled apologetically at Desmond's wife, who was looking her up and down with open curiosity while she gently rocked the sleeping child in her arms.

Looking from Delilah to Desmond, the woman broke the tense silence. 'It's cold out here, Des. I'll take Damien inside and leave you two to chat.'

After a last quizzical look at Delilah, she turned and walked down the path, letting herself into the house and shutting the door.

Delilah turned her attention back to Desmond, who was staring at her as though in a trance. He hadn't changed much over the years, other than a few more lines around his eyes and a hairline that was starting to thin.

'What are you doing here?' he demanded. He didn't sound particularly pleased to see her, and now she was actually in front of him, the speech Delilah had rehearsed died in her throat.

'Um... okay, first off, I'm sorry for turning up out of the blue. I would have called you, but I don't have your number and—'

'How do you know where I live?' he interrupted brusquely.

After sheepishly confessing to tracking him online and wishing she sounded less like a stalker, she added defensively, 'You might want to rethink posting pictures of your house on social media. Any weirdo could come looking for you.'

'I only know one weirdo, and it looks like she's already found me,' Desmond said pointedly. He narrowed his eyes in suspicion. 'What's all this about, Del? It's been, what, ten years or so since I saw you last – or to be precise, since you ghosted me – and now you just show up outside my house without any warning?'

His eyes widened and he suddenly sounded panicked. '*Christ!* Please don't tell me you've secretly had my baby or something?'

'Of course not!' Delilah denied indignantly. 'You know I'd never do that.'

'I didn't think you'd just dump me without a word either, so who knows what you're capable of. Anyway, what are you doing here?'

When she hesitated, he shuffled his feet impatiently. 'Look, I'm not being funny, but it's bloody cold out here and my missus and my boy are waiting inside for me. So before we both end up with pneumonia, *what is it you want*?'

'I want to apologise,' she blurted out.

'You want to *what*?'

'I want – I want to say I'm sorry. I shouldn't have ended things with us the way I did. It wasn't fair and I'm really very sorry.'

Desmond stared at her with incredulity and then turned to scan the street before eyeing her suspiciously. 'Hold on, is this some kind of joke? Am I being filmed or something?'

Delilah closed her eyes and drew in a deep breath, trying to rein in her irritation. After all, she was here to apologise to him, not snap at him.

'No, I'm deadly serious. Yes, I know it's been years, but the thing is, I'm trying to work on myself and be a kinder person. What I did to you back then definitely wasn't kind, and I want to – well, make amends.' She stomped her boots on the pavement and blew into her hands, but her breath was so chilled, it made no difference to her icy fingers.

Desmond thrust his hands into his jacket pockets and stared at the ground. 'Okay, so why *did* you dump me, Del? I loved you and I really thought we had a future together.'

When he looked up, his expression was bleak, and she bit her lip and turned away. This was the difficult conversation she had disappeared to avoid having, and more than a decade later, she was as unprepared as she had been then. How could she hope to teach couples to improve their communication skills when she didn't have the courage to communicate properly herself? What would she have advised her clients in this situation, she wondered, and the answer was clear. To tell the truth.

She turned back to face him. 'I wasn't ready,' she admitted quietly. 'You kept talking about us getting married and having kids – four of them, if I remember right. It – it felt like you had our whole future mapped out without my say-so, and... well, it terrified me.'

'Then why didn't you say something? Was I so hard to talk to that the only way out was to disappear?' Desmond sounded so wounded that she wanted to shrivel up with shame.

'No, you weren't. That part was *my* fault! I was immature and didn't know how to handle the... the pressure. How I ended things is all on me, and I should have done it better and... and told you the truth. But, Des, be honest,' she added earnestly, 'I *did* try to get you to slow down on all the planning, but you'd get into a strop or just keep telling me how much you loved me and wanted to spend the rest of your life with me!'

'And was that such a crime?' he asked in a low voice.

She shook her head. 'Of course not. Like I said, it was wrong of me not to speak up about what was troubling me at the time instead of doing a runner.'

Desmond took a breath and blew the air from his cheeks loudly. 'Fine, you're sorry. So, now what?'

'Nothing, really,' Delilah said with a helpless shrug. 'We've both moved on with our lives, but I wanted to tell you that none of what happened between you and me was your fault and that I'm truly sorry for what I did.'

He gazed at her intently while considering her words and then nodded. 'Okay, then. Apology accepted.'

'So you forgive me?' she pressed, not wanting to leave any room for doubt.

'Yeah, I forgive you. It's in the past and done with. Besides, if you hadn't left me, I'd never have met Mollie or had Damien, so yeah, we're cool.'

She stifled the brief pang of hurt at being so casually dismissed by the man who had once called her the love of his life by reminding herself how ruthlessly *she* had dumped him. *Karma really is a bitch.*

13

The phone was answered with a high-pitched sneeze followed by a loud blowing of the nose, and Delilah grimaced. 'You sound awful, Sal!'

'I'm much better.' Salome sniffed, her voice thick with congestion. 'Arin's got it even worse than me, poor lamb.'

After two days of caring for her sick children, Salome was also down with the flu, leaving Farhan as the only one in the house still standing. It was typical of Sal to downplay her own needs, Delilah thought with a wry smile. If her sister was at death's door, she'd still insist someone else was worse off.

'Do you need anything? Should I bring over some medicine or food or anything?'

Salome cleared her throat. 'No need, hon, but thanks. Farhan's bought enough drugs to stock a pharmacy. At least Maya's back at nursery, thank God, and I'll have a lie-down once Arin gets off to sleep.'

'Where *is* Farhan?' Delilah demanded. 'You shouldn't be dealing with everything on your own, especially when you're not feeling great yourself.'

'He's been on video calls with his team most of today. They've got a new product launch next week and he's under a lot of pressure. Don't worry, I sound worse than I feel. How'd it go with Desmond?'

'Mortifying. He was with his wife who probably thought I was some kind of psycho.'

'Someone in your profession should know better than to use words that trivialise mental health,' Salome said huskily, and Delilah scrunched her nose sheepishly at the rebuke.

'Sorry,' she said contritely. 'It was just so embarrassing, and I felt like a complete idiot ambushing him in front of his family.'

'So what happened? What did he say?'

'Basically, even though I messed him up thirteen years ago, he's now with the love of his life so he forgives me and everything's cool between us.'

After a violent fit of coughing, Salome croaked, 'Okay, so it's one down and four to go. Who's next?'

* * *

The half-empty car park in front of Kwame's office wouldn't have been Delilah's choice of venue for a conversation, and particularly one as sensitive as she had planned. Unfortunately, as soon her ex-boyfriend saw her waiting on the sofa in his office reception, he had bundled her outside before giving her the chance to say more than hello.

Kwame was easily the best-looking man she'd dated, and during the course of their eight-month long relationship, Delilah had often wondered what it must feel like to be so beautiful. Ten years later, Kwame's long-lashed caramel-brown eyes, high cheekbones, smooth chocolate skin and full sculpted lips were just as mesmerising. Unlike his expression, which could best have been described as livid, and for a second Delilah wondered how quickly she could get away.

'What the *hell* are you doing here?'

No points for originality, she thought resignedly. This time, however, she'd come prepared, and she launched into a brief and heartfelt explanation, trying not to feel intimidated by the six feet and three inches of hostile ex-boyfriend looming over her. When she reached the part about asking his forgiveness for disappearing, Kwame's expression darkened further.

'Are you kidding me? You *told* me why you were breaking up with me!'

Delilah blinked in surprise. 'Really?'

Their final conversation was a total blank, but there was no question that even after all these years, Kwame was still furious with her. She could only assume that being so ridiculously gorgeous, he wasn't used to women leaving him, and she must have seriously dented his pride.

'You were supposed to come up to Leicester with me to meet my family. You didn't show up at the train station and I phoned your mobile,' Kwame said stonily. 'Does *that* ring a bell?'

Delilah had arrived ready to deliver her rehearsed apology and move on, but something in Kwame's expression stopped her cold. Behind his anger was an emotion which, she suddenly recognised, wasn't punctured pride at all, but a raw and intense hurt. Shaken, she forced herself to retrieve the buried memory.

'Del, where are you? We're going to miss the train!'

'I... I'm not coming...'

'What are you talking about? You promised. Mum and Dad are dying to meet you, and my grandparents are already waiting at the house!'

'I'm sorry...'

Kwame must have seen realisation dawning in her face because he took a half step back and lowered his voice. 'You accused me of being clingy and moving too fast. You said you felt suffocated – remember that? And now you show up asking me to forgive you...?'

He tailed off as a car drove into the car park and waited until the woman behind the wheel had exited her car and walked into the building before turning back to face Delilah.

'I remember that day like it was yesterday,' he said bitterly. 'You were the first girl I'd ever wanted to take home, and yet somehow you thought it was okay to dump me in the middle of a packed train station. Do you have *any* idea how that felt?'

14

'What happened next?' With Sigmund curled up on his lap, Arne sat back in his chair, his blue eyes bright with interest.

Delilah stared silently at the patterned rug on the floor, too humiliated to recount the intense guilt and the self-disgust she had experienced during her exchange with Kwame.

'Were you able to make peace with him?'

Delilah looked up to meet Arne's gaze and gave a half-shrug, pulling her legs up under her in the cocoon of the armchair. It was only their second therapy session, and Delilah had already forgotten her game plan involved *not* giving away any more information than was necessary to get her job back.

'We talked for a while. I let him vent and took all the blame and explained I was the one with commitment issues. In the end, I think he was just desperate to get rid of me. But yes, he said the magic words. So, I'm forgiven, apparently – even though he clearly still hates me.' To her horror, her voice cracked, and she rubbed her hands over her face as she tried to regain control.

'I do believe there is a path to redemption if someone makes amends and takes accountability, but Delilah, let me ask you again. Are you seeking this redemption for your own purposes or for the sake of those you have wronged?' Arne's neutral tone conveyed no judgement, and Delilah fixed her gaze on the slumbering cat while she considered the question. She hadn't seen Kwame in ten years, and yet there was no denying the pain she had seen in his eyes.

'You know, at first, Salome's stupid challenge was just a big gesture to convince Polly I've become much more self-aware about my behaviour. But after seeing Des and Kwame, I'm starting to realise just how badly I've hurt other people and then not given them a second thought.' Delilah shook her head and returned her gaze to the rug. 'Sal warned me to take this seriously, and it's so clear I've got work to do.'

'You often talk about your sister,' Arne observed, 'but you don't mention other family members. Can you tell me a bit about your family?'

Startled, Delilah jerked her head up and she looked at him guardedly. 'What do you want to know?'

'Well, in therapy we explore our past so we can improve our present. Tell me about your mother. Are the two of you close?'

Delilah hesitated. 'We were, but she died when I was seventeen.'

'I'm sorry to hear that. Losing a mother is very painful at any age but even more difficult, I imagine, when one is so young. What about your father?'

'He's dead, too,' she said shortly. 'It's just Salome and me – and Farhan and the kids, of course.' Eager to change the subject, Delilah straightened her legs and bent to stroke Sigmund, who had left the comfort of Arne's lap and was slinking past her chair. He responded to her half-hearted attempt to pet him with a disdainful miaow and hopped into his blanket-lined basket.

Arne waited until he had her full attention and then continued. 'I'm sure you learned about attachment theory and styles in your studies, so you will know that our early childhood can shape how we subsequently build relationships, yes?'

Delilah nodded dumbly, and Arne went on. 'Then you appreciate that childhood experiences can help us understand why we might choose to invest less emotion into a relationship or indeed put emotional distance between ourselves and our partner to avoid getting hurt. As adults, we often model our approach to relationships on what we saw as children – or indeed, what we didn't see. What do you recall of your parents' relationship?'

She drew in a sharp breath and balled her fists. *Relax, it's okay. You can do this.* Her lips felt as stiff as cardboard, but she forced her voice to sound normal. 'The usual married couple ups and downs, I suppose... Mum really loved being married.'

'Tell me more.' Arne pressed his fingertips together, his head tilted to the side attentively.

Delilah nodded, but when she tried to speak, her breathing suddenly felt shallow. She could feel her pulse racing and she pushed her hair back from her face, fighting the overwhelming urge to jump out of the chair and run from Arne's office. She took in several deep breaths before she could trust herself to continue.

'Th – they went to school together. He asked her out when they were fifteen and they stayed together until – until the end.'

As if sensing her distress, Arne moved on. 'You mentioned earlier your realisation that you have hurt people's feelings but then not given them a second thought. Why do you think that is?'

At the change in topic, the pounding in Delilah's chest began to ease, and intensely relieved, she answered before she could catch herself. 'I don't remember bad things that happen – or at least I've learned not to. So, it's surprising to me that other people don't do the same. I was shocked when I realised how upset Kwame still is with me even though it's been years since we were together. And Des—' She broke off and shook her head. Delilah hadn't dared admit, even to Salome, just how desperately remorseful she'd felt after her encounter with Desmond, and how hypocritical she'd felt for criticising clients like Ross for not pulling their emotional weight.

'What about Desmond?'

'He looked so incredibly hurt when he asked me why I'd left him. It's beyond ironic that I dare to give people advice about their relationships when I've messed up so many of my own.' Her eyes welled up as a wave of sadness engulfed her.

There was a long silence, and then Arne said gently, 'That's a big step, Delilah. Let's stop there for today.'

15

The club was heaving when Delilah walked in, with a queue two people deep pressed up around the bar. The multicoloured strobe lights and thumping eighties disco music were an immediate turn-off and under normal circumstances, she would have walked straight out again. But Armenique had chosen the venue, and Delilah was desperate to see her friend and catch up on the office gossip – most of which she suspected was about her – and frankly it was a relief to get out of her flat. At the end of the day, even Kool & The Gang at full blast was better than another night in watching reality TV and property makeover shows.

She looked round the dimly lit bar, and spotting Armenique's shiny silver headwrap, Delilah weaved her way through the crush to where her friend had snagged a table and was scrolling through her phone, her head bobbing in time to the music, and tapped her shoulder. Armenique sprang up, hugging her so tightly that the huge silver star-shaped brooch pinned onto her clingy black one-shouldered jumpsuit almost took Delilah's eye out.

'*Girl*, you look stunning!' Delilah stepped back to eye Armenique's outfit with a raised eyebrow. 'You should have said we were dressing up!' she said plaintively, gesturing towards her own black trousers and plain white crop top.

'Ah babe! With those curves, you're gorgeous whatever you wear.' Armenique smiled. 'Turn around – I'm *loving* the hair!'

Delilah obliged with a grin, shaking her head from side to side to show off her new shoulder-length twists. 'Thanks. I needed a change.' Bored to distraction and with nothing but time on her hands, she had spent half a day earlier that week undoing her long braids followed by a further two hours hanging around in the local salon waiting for her nimble-fingered hairdresser, Eunice, to style her hair. Taking the empty chair at the table, Delilah looked up and wrinkled her nose at the multicoloured lights spinning across the ceiling in time to Donna Summer.

Armenique followed Delilah's gaze and shuffled her chair forward. 'I swear I had no idea they were doing an eighties night,' she said apologetically. 'I got this table cos it's furthest away from the speakers, so at least we can hear ourselves. I've ordered us a bottle of Prosecco—'

She broke off as a harried-looking waiter appeared with an ice bucket and two glasses. He twisted off the cork in one swift movement and filled the glasses, and as soon as he'd gone, Armenique raised a glass and clinked it against Delilah's.

'Cheers, Del! It's so good to see you. I can't tell you how much I've missed not having you at work.'

'I've missed you more! Trust me, I'd give anything to be back.' Delilah took a long sip of the chilled wine and leaned back happily in her chair. After Farhan had finally succumbed to the flu, she had been avoiding Salome's house all week, and it was great to spend time with Armenique, who had grown into a dear friend. Tonight was exactly what Delilah needed after days of near isolation and nights punctuated with disturbing dreams about Noah and waking up in a cold sweat, drenched in vivid memories of the past.

The music changed, and Delilah put down her glass and leaned forward to make herself heard above Rick Astley.

'How's everything at the office?'

Armenique grinned wickedly and arched her perfectly shaped eyebrows, clearly unconvinced by Delilah's attempt to sound casual. 'I think you mean how's Polly and what's she said about you coming back?'

Delilah pulled a face and braced herself. 'So, what *has* she told everyone about why I'm not at work?'

Armenique sipped her wine and waved an airy hand. 'There's nothing to stress about, Del. You know Polly's discreet. She sent out an email to everyone saying you were on a leave of absence, and that she'll be handling your client list until you get back.'

Delilah tossed back the rest of the wine in her glass, relieved her reputation was still intact but also frustrated that Polly's communique gave no clues about how long Delilah was suspended. 'Yeah, well I wish her luck with the Hendersons. Who knows – maybe *she'll* be able to get through to Brian!'

Grabbing the bottle from the ice bucket, she refilled their glasses while singing along as Gloria Gaynor belted out 'I Will Survive'. Already lightheaded from the first glass, she pushed caution aside and swallowed a large gulp of Prosecco. There was nothing she could do about her job situation and tonight was the first time she'd been out in ages. *Forget about Polly and enjoy yourself!*

Armenique echoed her thoughts. 'Let's not talk about the office. What I really want to hear about is how your apologies are going!'

Delilah had spilled the beans about Salome's infamous list in an unguarded moment over lunch. Having to revisit the awkward encounters with her former boyfriends wasn't top on her list of preferred conversations, but knowing Armenique would prise the details out of her one way or another, Delilah filled her in while they worked their way through the rest of the bottle – and ordered a second.

'Good for you, Del. God, you're so brave!' Armenique exclaimed. 'There's no way I'd have the guts to confront my exes. Ugh, you must have felt so vulnerable, not knowing how they were going to react. But I do think your sister's right. When Polly hears you've taken her advice to heart, I bet it makes all the difference.'

The waiter arrived with another bottle of Prosecco and when he'd refilled their glasses, Armenique took a sip of her drink and smacked her lips loudly before eyeing Delilah curiously. 'So who's next, then?'

'Please don't remind me. I'm breaking into a cold sweat just thinking about him,' Delilah said heavily. She put down her glass and sighed. 'Salome's only gone and put Carl on the list.'

'Carl... *Wait!* Isn't that the guy you were seeing when we first started the course? But that's ludicrous!'

Delilah nodded with a pained smile and picked up her glass again. The alcohol was rapidly numbing her brain, but it was going to take more than two bottles of Prosecco to blot out her time with Carl. She'd kept his number in her list of phone contacts, but only so she'd know not to answer if he ever tried to call.

'It *was* Carl who—?' Armenique started, and Delilah cut in emphatically before she could finish.

'Yep.'

'Jeez! He was such an arse – no offence. I remember how he'd crack these really bad jokes and then laugh like a drain. He was okay looking, but definitely not boyfriend material. What on earth did you see in him?' Armenique asked bluntly.

Delilah screwed her face up in bewilderment and held up her palms. 'I wish I knew! I met him long before I started the counselling course. He used to come into the café for a cup of tea and a chat when I was still waitressing. I'd just finished a relationship and was going through a bit of a bad patch, so I suppose having someone to banter and have a bit of a flirt with took my mind off things. He took it way more seriously than me, and if I'm honest, we only lasted so long because he worked on a cruise ship and only flew back for the odd weekend. By the time I started the course, he'd finally clocked that I wasn't into him, which was when—'

'—he started sending you flowers at college every day. I still remember those rambling poems and love letters he'd send with words he'd cut out of magazines. God, that was *so* creepy! No wonder you cut him loose.' Armenique shuddered. 'What was your sister thinking putting him on the list?'

'She says it's because *technically* we lasted longer than six months and that ghosting him when he was desperately in love with me wasn't "compassionate" – which is bollocks because Carl deserved to be dumped and I'm not sorry at all!'

Delilah frowned into her wine glass while her foot tapped along to Cyndi Lauper shrieking 'Girls Just Wanna Have Fun'. Salome was seriously out of order for making her contact a man who'd already proved he couldn't take no for an answer.

Another hour and three more glasses of Prosecco later, the world looked a lot rosier. The small dance floor was packed with people boogieing to popular eighties disco tracks and Delilah, merry from the booze and flushed from singing along with the crowd, was feeling on top of the world. So much so that when an equally sozzled Armenique suggested they call Carl so Delilah could stop stressing and take him off the list, any resistance on her part quickly slipped away.

'If you don't want to speak to him, just send him a text,' Armenique urged, trying not to slur her words. 'Go on! Do it now before you bottle it again.'

'Okay, *okay*!' Delilah giggled. 'But what if he—'

'You'll never know if you don't try,' Armenique said, speaking slowly and deliberately, and wagging a finger in Delilah's direction. 'Right, let's go. First off, knock back the rest of that glass.'

Delilah dutifully obliged, and Armenique instructed, 'Now, take out your phone.'

Delilah pulled her phone from her bag and frowned dubiously at the screen. 'Hold on, isn't there a law against drinking and texting?'

'Don't worry, girl. I've got you.'

Hi Carl, it's me, Delilah. I need to talk to you.

She typed the words and glanced up at Armenique, who nodded reassuringly. Drawing in a sharp breath, Delilah pressed send, immediately dropping the phone on the table as if she'd been burned.

They stared intently at the phone and less than a minute later, it pinged with a text.

Why, what do you want?

Delilah picked up the handset as gingerly as if she was handling a rabid dog and tried to focus on the words. She thought for a moment through a haze of alcohol and then typed.

Can we meet?

I'd rather not.

Taken aback by the abrupt response, Delilah's hackles immediately rose. After everything Carl had put her through, the least he could do was consider her incredibly polite request. Feeling no more prepared to take no for an answer than Carl had been two years earlier, she jabbed out another message.

> Why not? I just want a few minutes of your time. That's all.

> No! I'm working through healing myself and SETTING BOUNDARIES! You know your trouble, don't you? Women like you say you want a man who can open up and share his feelings and then when he does, it's TOO MUCH for you!! I spent a fortune on flowers, and it took me ages to make you those letters! I literally poured my heart and soul out to you. For what?? For you to block my calls and just disappear. No explanation??? No NOTHING???

Jolted, Delilah read Carl's furious message twice, the high from the Prosecco slowly seeping away like air from a deflating balloon. Was there *anyone* she hadn't messed up? Too much alcohol combined with the vitriolic text brought sudden tears to her eyes.

Armenique leaned over and gently prised the phone out of Delilah's hand, her lips forming a silent 'wow' as she read the message.

'Not much sign of any healing going on there.' She looked up at Delilah with raised eyebrows.

'What should I say?' Delilah pleaded, and Armenique shrugged and handed back the phone.

'Just say sorry and cut your losses, Del. You can't win them all.'

But Delilah was too weighed down with guilt to leave it. She might not be able to force Carl to meet her in person, but she *could* tell him what he clearly still needed to know. Before her friend could stop her, Delilah tapped furiously on the phone keypad.

> I'm truly sorry. Please believe me. It was incredibly immature of me to behave that way, and you didn't deserve it. I don't expect you to forgive me, but as part of your healing maybe you should at least consider if you can?

She waited with bated breath. Then:

> If I say I forgive you, do you promise never to contact me again?

She hesitated, and then quickly typed:

Yes

While 'Don't Leave Me This Way' played loudly in the background, Delilah watched the three dots that showed Carl was still typing move around for what felt like forever. Finally, a message landed.

I forgive you.

16

'Who's next?' Salome asked brightly.

'Why do you sound like you're enjoying all this?' Delilah asked waspishly. Twenty-four hours after consuming more alcohol than she'd had in months, she was curled up on the sofa in her sister's living room with gritty eyes and a pounding headache.

'Well, it's not like I've got much going on in my own life, is it?'

Delilah looked up in surprise at the aggrieved tone in Salome's voice. She had put Sal's tired eyes and the dull pallor of her usually flawless skin down to the after-effects of flu and the toll of nursing her sick household, but the uncharacteristically sour comment was an immediate red flag. It suddenly struck Delilah that almost every conversation since she'd been suspended from work had centred on Delilah's problems, and not once had it occurred to her to ask Sal if she was okay. When had she become so self-absorbed that she'd stopped checking in with her sister? Had she become so selfish that she didn't notice other people's troubles?

'What's going on, Sal?' she asked tentatively. 'You look exhausted.'

'I don't know, hon.' Salome's normally upbeat voice sounded bleak. She massaged her temples with her fingers and then sat up straight and exhaled noisily. 'I'm so lucky I can be at home with my children, and don't get me wrong, I'm really grateful. It's just sometimes my life feels like an endless round of cooking, cleaning, changing nappies, and wiping snotty noses.'

Delilah's mouth fell open as she stared at Salome in shock. *What the hell is going on?* If there was anyone on the planet who was born to be a wife and mum, it was her sister. Salome was *the* ultimate Earth mother – from her spotless, perfectly decorated home to her love of cooking huge, freshly made meals for her family. For as long as Delilah could remember, Salome had loved nothing more than taking care of everyone – including her younger sister.

'Okay, I'm so confused. Sal, where's all this coming from? I thought you loved staying at home with Arin?'

Salome turned her face away. 'I do love having this time with Arin, but it can get soul destroying being stuck at home, and we can't afford to put both kids into full-time nursery. I know it's not forever, and the children will be grown in no time, but—' Her voice cracked, and she broke off mid-sentence, keeping her eyes fixed on the ground. 'It gets to me sometimes, that's all,' she confessed in a low voice.

Salome was the most positive person in the world, which made her hunched posture and dispirited tone not only astonishing, but completely baffling.

'I know you've had a lot on your plate lately but... but *why* have you never said anything?' Delilah asked carefully. 'I had absolutely no idea you've been feeling like this. Have you talked to Farhan?'

As if she'd already said too much, Salome pasted a smile on her face that didn't quite reach her eyes. 'Look, ignore me, okay? It's just one of those days and I'm being silly and having a moan.'

Delilah shook her head, refusing to be fobbed off. 'I'm serious, Salome. What's going on? Please talk to me.'

Salome's smile faded, and she leaned back into the cushions, her eyes resting on the large family portrait hanging over the mantelpiece. 'I sound *so* ungrateful! I love Farhan and adore my kids, but I'm desperate to do something for *me* for a change. I miss the buzz of work and, yes, I know PR isn't rocket science, but at least back then, before I had kids, I was able to talk to other people and use my brain.'

'Could you look for a job, then?' Delilah suggested, trying to make sense of the revelation that Salome, who was everyone's rock and the person whose strength they all took for granted, was herself floundering.

Salome looked disconsolate. 'I don't know. I've been out of the game so long, I'd have to take a salary cut – assuming anyone would even want to hire me – and then I could only do part-time because of the kids. Farhan says having both kids in full-time nursery would eat up whatever I earned and take time away from Maya and Arin. He has a point, but it feels like life's passing me by and the longer I stay out of the market, the harder it will be to ever get back in...' Her voice trailed into silence.

'But Sal, if you feel this strongly about it, you have to tell Farhan how important it is to you and then stick to your guns! The man worships the ground you walk on, and he'd hate knowing you feel like this.'

'I can't!' Salome burst out. 'He's carrying all of us financially at the moment, and I don't want him to feel bad. He's already chosen to work from home so he could help out with the kids when, quite frankly, it would be better for his career if he spent more time in the office. He's so keen to prove his value to the company that he's dragged himself back to work even though he's feeling rocky. Besides, even if Farhan agreed, I'd still feel guilty for leaving Arin so early.'

'Loads of kids of his age go to nursery. Arin would be fine!' Delilah tried not to sound exasperated. 'Putting your kids into nursery doesn't make you a bad mother, and it sounds to me like you're stressing yourself out when you don't have to. Why must you try so hard to have every single thing be perfect?'

Salome winced, and Delilah instantly felt remorseful. She knew only too well why her sister felt the need to control her environment, but suppressing her own needs and ambitions was clearly having a detrimental effect.

'I just want it to be different for my kids than it was for us,' Salome said quietly. 'You know what? Forget it! I shouldn't have said anything to you – that's what Alison's for,' she added.

Delilah looked sceptical but Salome shook her head decisively. 'I mean it, hon, don't worry about me. I'll be fine. Right then, change of subject. How're you feeling after what happened with Carl?'

When she put her mind to it, Salome could be twice as stubborn as Delilah on a good day, and judging from the look on her sister's face, Delilah knew nothing she said would make her talk if she didn't want to. Making a mental note to find another opportunity to return to the conversation, she went along with Salome's wishes.

'You read Carl's messages – take a guess how I'm feeling after finding yet another man who hates me! After all *his* antics, apparently I'm the one who's so toxic that he refuses to meet me. So it looks like I have to settle for forgiveness by text this time.'

Delilah couldn't help the slight tremor in her voice, and it was Salome's turn to study her sister.

'Del,' she started hesitantly. 'Can I ask what you're learning from all this? I mean, about how you've managed your relationships?'

'Christ, you sound exactly like Arne!' Delilah groaned. 'Well, if you really want to know, my biggest takeaway is finding out every man I've dated thinks I'm a first-class bitch.'

'Don't talk about my sister like that!' Salome said with a loud tut. 'I do like the sound of your Viking therapist, though, and he must be doing something right if you're still seeing him.'

'It's not like I have a choice, is it?' Delilah said moodily. 'It's either Mondays with Arne or never getting my job back. To be fair, he's not awful. He's actually starting to grow on me, but he definitely does not shy away from asking some tough questions.'

'Good,' Salome said briskly. 'So put your back into it and finish the job. Who's next on your list?'

'*Your* list, you mean. I tried Remi's number a couple of days ago, but I couldn't get through, so I called his office. Don't look at me like that – you wrote that stupid list! Anyway, turns out he's travelling on business. Brazil, apparently.'

'Which leaves you with the final name on the list. *And*, as you've just pointed out, I wrote the list, so we both know who that is. So, tell me, exactly how long are we going to keep ignoring that massive grey elephant in the room – and when are you going to call Noah?'

Delilah trained her gaze on the floor, contemplating the question. Since the day she had seen Noah's name on Salome's list, scarcely a night had gone by without him showing up somewhere in her dreams. No matter how hard she tried not to think about him, her mind appeared to have other ideas. The sleepless nights and troubled dreams couldn't continue indefinitely and, deep down, Delilah knew it was time.

'He changed his number after we broke up. I know that, because I tried calling him a few weeks after – well, you know – and it was disconnected. There's no chance his witch of a mother will give me his contacts, so I've got no idea where to find him or—'

'I've got his number,' Salome cut in. 'And his home address.'

'*What?*' Delilah's eyes bulged in disbelief. '*How...?*'

'He gave it to me a few months ago. Well, not gave it to me exactly...' She ruminated in silence while Delilah bounced up and down on the sofa with frustration.

'*Salome!*'

'Okay, *okay*! I bumped into him outside the house one day and asked if he could put me in touch with the gardener that cuts the grass in his mum and dad's garden. He texted me Ben's number – and the man's been a godsend! Farhan never has time to mow the lawn, and at one point we had so many weeds, I was terrified of letting the kids out.'

Delilah held up a hand to cut off the rambling. 'I get it, you've got his number. But how the hell did you get his address?'

'I asked Mrs West. Told her I wanted to send him a thank you card. Like I said, Ben's been an absolute godsend.'

Delilah was still trying to make sense of Salome's admission. 'You mean, you've known all this time... but... but *why* didn't you say?'

Salome shook her head. 'That's not important,' she said impatiently. 'What matters is you know how to contact Noah, so get on with it! You'll have to face him at some point to ask his forgiveness, and the sooner you do it, the sooner you'll get your job back.'

17

'What made you decide to become a therapist, Arne?'

Arne sat back, contemplating Delilah's question, and a ray of sunshine through the window blinds crossed his face, highlighting glints of gold in his fiery-red beard.

'Perhaps for the same reason you turned to counselling,' he said eventually. 'I wanted to help people. Help them understand what they want for themselves and what drives them into decisions and behaviour that sabotages that success.'

She studied him curiously. 'And has the job been what you expected?'

'You wish to ask all the questions today, Delilah?' He raised a bushy eyebrow and cracked a rare smile, and she grinned back from where she sat curled up in the oversized armchair.

The winter sunlight flooding through the room made her feel calm and safe, and after only a few sessions together, it felt like she had known Arne for ages. She had become less tense under his scrutiny and super intense attentiveness and had grown accustomed to how he stroked his beard while he was reflecting or tilted his head when she spoke, as if making sure he captured every word. Sigmund, on the other hand, continued to barely acknowledge her and was fast asleep in the other chair.

'Yes, I would say it has been a very satisfying career so far,' said Arne. 'Therapists often get – how do you say it... a poor rap? There is sometimes a perception that we profit from other people's misery to make a living, whereas we are professionals who only wish to help those living with deep unhappiness or trauma they don't need to experience.'

Delilah mulled over his response. 'The reason I ask is because I've been thinking a lot about your question in our first session – you know, about my motivation to be a counsellor.'

'Is that so?'

'Hmm... and I think the biggest reason is wanting to help couples who can't communicate properly to work through their issues. I've still got a lot to learn but it's incredibly rewarding when you see people using the tools you've taught them to build strong, healthy relationships. But then...' She paused, and Arne leaned forward.

'Go on.'

'When I'm dealing with a couple who obviously shouldn't be together – you know, like if one person is manipulative or trying to control the other person or seems emotionally abusive, that's where I struggle to stay impartial.'

'Because you want to save the person you see as a victim?'

Delilah nodded. 'That's what Polly was furious about. But it's not because I'm trying to be the hero... well, at least I don't think I am, although I can see why it could come across that way.'

'You mentioned the satisfaction of giving your clients tools so they can resolve their difficulties themselves. How can they put these into practice if you swoop in to save them?'

Delilah pulled a face and wrapped her arms around her knees. 'I get it. Instead of empowering them, I'm doing the exact opposite.'

'Have you wondered why that is?'

'I feel like I identify with what someone is going through, which is frustrating because then I can't stop myself wanting to do something about it. Empathy is supposed to be a good thing, but I'm starting to wonder if there's such a thing as *too* much empathy.'

Arne's hands were clasped loosely in his lap while his piercing blue eyes studied her. 'If by too much empathy you mean you absorb people's emotions instead of observing them, then my answer would be yes. If we fall back on our own experiences and use that to advocate actions for our clients, we have shifted the focus from what the client needs in order to heal. When you tell your client "I feel your pain", it puts you at the centre and sends a different message from "I see you are in pain and I'm here to support you". The second approach is compassionate and offers comfort, but it also acknowledges their challenge without bringing it back to yourself. Do you see?'

'It makes sense,' she said slowly. 'I suppose that's why we spent so much time in training learning about maintaining boundaries and not getting burned out from absorbing everyone's issues.'

They sat in comfortable silence for a while, and then Arne asked, 'How are you progressing with your tour of apologies?'

Delilah had deliberately avoided bringing up the topic, unwilling to revisit the painful episode with Carl. Since the night out with Armenique, she'd found herself re-reading Carl's texts obsessively and feeling worse about herself each time. Reluctantly, she related the events at the bar to Arne.

'Isn't it weird how I apparently feel too much empathy for my clients and yet I didn't seem to have any for the men I dumped,' Delilah ended wryly.

'Why do you think that is?'

'I know it sounds ridiculous,' she said hesitantly, 'but it's like I don't even remember what I've done. Somewhere inside me, I know I've hurt someone, but because I don't know how to make it better, I think I blank it out or bury it and move on.'

'That's interesting. And how does admitting this make you feel?'

'Guilty – and awful about myself!'

'Do you think there is some way you can change this pattern?'

Delilah stretched her arms above her head and rolled her neck gently to relieve the stiffness from slouching in the chair. 'I'm not sure. I've got two more people to go, so we'll see. One of them is away for a couple of weeks, which leaves the other one. I'm dreading it, and I've been dithering for days. But I'll just have to pull up my big girl pants and get on with it.'

'Is there a reason why this particular man represents such a challenge?'

Instead of answering, Delilah looked around the room, taking in the photographs on the walls. The black and white images were so sharp and vivid that the forest appeared to teem with life. She could imagine the intense green of the leaves on the majestically tall trees and picture the vibrant colours of the flowers and birds circling overhead.

'Did you take those pictures?' she asked, suddenly curious to know more about the man who knew so much about her.

Arne followed her gaze. 'Yes. In Norway. I grew up in a rural area close to the forest and the wilderness. Even now, being outdoors is my therapy. I find the natural world helps me feel more connected to everything around me.'

Delilah turned back to him, struck by how his droopy eyes had lit up.

'Whenever I am home, I like to walk somewhere beautiful in nature,' Arne added. 'It reminds me that despite everything we humans do to each other, the world is still a beautiful place. Even here in England, when the weather permits, I walk to the top of a hill and take in the views.' He contemplated the photographs for a few moments and then turned back to study Delilah, who was hunched in the armchair, playing with a twist of her hair.

'Do you find it uncomfortable to talk about the next person on your list?'

'Maybe,' she said quietly.

'Can you tell me why?'

Delilah gnawed on her lip and twirled her hair around her finger. How did you ask forgiveness from a man you hadn't spoken to for three years and yet who still had the power to keep you awake at night?

'He's the one who—' Her voice broke, and she stopped and shook her head.

Arne observed her in silence, saying nothing while she composed herself. Then he rose to his feet with a kindly smile.

'I think that's enough for today, Delilah.'

18

Delilah shoved her hands deep into her coat pockets to protect them from the late November chill. The fresh flowers she had just arranged into the brass vase brought a splash of colour to the white headstone.

'I miss you so much, Mum.' The silence swallowed her whispered words, and she crouched down to perch on the edge of the marble slab, letting her thoughts wander in the peaceful surroundings of the cemetery.

Salome's challenge had started as a means to get her job back, but instead it had opened her eyes to a pattern with her relationships she had never appreciated before. After the conversations with Desmond and Kwame, followed by Carl's bitter text messages, she had to wonder if she was so damaged that she could throw grenades into people's lives and then move on without any accountability for her behaviour, much less any consideration about how the men might feel. If she had so little self-awareness, what hope was there of her ever becoming the skilled relationship counsellor she aspired to be?

She wasn't a sociopath, Delilah thought sadly. She cared about the feelings of others, and she knew right from wrong. And yet, avoiding emotionally charged situations and burying unpleasant memories had been her survival strategy for years. Sometimes, memories were best left forgotten, but it seemed that between Salome's list and the probing sessions with Arne, the past was being dragged from a blurry distance into an uncomfortably sharp present.

She ran her hand along the smooth marble of the tombstone and said aloud, 'Sal's been on my case for days and I can't put it off any longer, so I'm going to contact him – Noah, I mean,' she added, in case her mother needed clarification.

Leaning forward, she tweaked the stems of the colourful blooms. 'I'm dreading this, Mum. I know I have to do it, but facing the others was tough enough – and I didn't care about them the way I did about Noah.'

She sat still, letting the chirping from the birds on the branches overhead fill the silence. Dusk was falling and the gates to the cemetery would soon close, but she was reluctant to leave the comfort of her mother's side.

'You'll be fine, Del. You are stronger than you know.'

Delilah closed her eyes and concentrated hard, straining to hear more. But the only sound was the rustling of leaves as the breeze moved through the trees.

19

'What are you doing here?'

His voice was as arctic as the weather, and Delilah shivered from where she stood at the top of the stone steps of the converted Victorian terrace.

Noah was literally inches away, his broad shoulders blocking the entrance to the front door. He was in jeans and a grey sweater that clung to his broad chest and toned body, and she had clearly caught him unawares as his feet were bare. Although he towered over her, she was close enough to see the charcoal flecks in his light brown eyes and smell the faint tang of the familiar lemon cologne.

When she couldn't answer, Noah stepped back and made as if to close the door, and Delilah impulsively stuck her booted foot into the space to stop him. She scoured his face hungrily, and seeing only contempt in his eyes, she felt the heat of humiliation clawing its way up from her chest and into her face. She felt wretched knowing she was the one who had caused her funny, loving and affectionate fiancé to look at her in this way. She had hurt him badly and he had every right to hate her, but he *had* to hear her out.

'Please, Noah. I need to talk to you.' The air felt trapped in her chest, and she sounded breathless, but she was determined not to move her foot and let him get rid of her.

'How did you even find me?' The minute he spoke the words, realisation dawned, and he shook his head with a groan. '*Salome!*'

Delilah nodded. 'I swear I didn't know she had your address until a few days ago. I tried and tried to call you after... well, after—'

'After you broke up with me literally twenty-four hours before we were supposed to get married? Is that what you're struggling to say?' he said harshly.

The reality of confronting Noah was far worse than she had anticipated, and the heat flooding her face intensified as she stared at him dumbly. In the scenarios she had rehearsed, not once had Noah looked at her with such fury and scorn, and she felt her heart cracking. The pressure of tears building behind her eyes was a warning that she would lose whatever self-control remained if she stayed a moment longer.

'I'm sorry,' she whispered. 'I – I shouldn't have come.' She removed her foot from where she had wedged it inside the door and turned away.

'Wait!'

She kept her back to him and blinked back the gathering tears before slowly turning around.

For a long moment, Noah simply stared at her, and then he exhaled as if he had just run a marathon. 'You're three years and four months too late but, for whatever reason, you've come all this way so I suppose the least I can do is listen.'

While his words proved he'd been keeping track of the time since their break-up, nothing in his expression indicated that it was for positive reasons. Grateful Noah was at least prepared to let her say her piece, Delilah gave him a half-smile, which he didn't return. Opening the door wider, he went up a flight of stairs with long strides, leaving her to shut the front door and follow.

The door to his flat was ajar, and he walked in without turning to see if she was behind him. Following Noah through a narrow entrance hall into a large airy lounge with a square bay window and high moulded ceilings, Delilah looked around curiously. Other than a large TV screen which dominated one wall of the room, the only furniture was a sofa and a couple of squashy armchairs. Noah's extensive collection of CDs and vinyl records filled the length of open shelving beneath the bay window but, unlike the untidy studio she remembered, Noah's new flat was surprisingly uncluttered. She couldn't help wondering what else had changed.

When she turned, Noah was staring at her. His expression was unreadable, and she flushed under the scrutiny. It was surreal to be finally face to face with the man who had haunted her dreams for weeks, and yet here she was. But while he hadn't yet thrown her out, she had no guarantee he wouldn't change his mind.

'Thanks for giving me the time of day and I won't keep you long,' Delilah started. He remained silent, and she bit her lip nervously. 'Look, I... I know I'm the last person you would ever want to see, and—'

She stopped. It was no use. She couldn't think straight with him looking at her, and she was mortified by how inarticulate she sounded. *Get on with it, Del!* She took a breath and tried again.

'I've wanted to talk to you for such a long time, but you... you disappeared and – well, your mum hates me and refuses to speak to me. I was too embarrassed to call any of your friends to find out how you were and, I suppose if I'm honest, I was scared of what they'd say to me. Sal told me where to find you and I decided to come over rather than ring you because... because I wasn't sure you'd take my call.'

Still, Noah said nothing, and Delilah ploughed on. 'The thing is, I wanted to let you know how much I regret the way I behaved towards you.'

'*Regret...!*' Noah burst out angrily. 'Christ, Delilah, you sound like a bloody politician! Are you serious right now? Is this why you came over here? To get this – I don't even know what to call it – off your chest and then vanish again?'

That wasn't a question that had come up in her imagined scenarios, and she stared at him dumbly. Her legs felt unsteady, and even though Noah hadn't invited her to, she sat in one of the armchairs, perching on the edge to avoid looking as if she was making herself comfortable.

'Noah, what can I do?' she pleaded, looking up at him with wide eyes.

'You can start by being honest,' he said stonily. 'There's no point showing up here with some half-arsed apology if you can't give me a good reason why you ditched me and cancelled our wedding with a day's notice.'

It was the question anyone in his shoes would have asked, and yet it was impossible for Delilah to explain what she still didn't fully understand. *You should really have thought this through better before coming.* Why couldn't Noah just accept she felt awful about what she had done instead of making this harder for both of them, she wondered miserably.

Noah dropped into the other armchair, and feeling slightly less intimidated, Delilah fell back on her script. Glossing over the details, she filled him in on her new job and her goal of becoming a better counsellor by making amends for her past behaviour.

'...and that's it. I came here to apologise. I really am sorry, Noah.' She bit her lip and stared searchingly into his face. 'You didn't deserve what I did to you and if there was any way I could make it up to you, I would.'

His silence was unnerving, and she added earnestly, 'Please forgive me.'

'No.'

'What?'

'I said no.'

Delilah stared at him in dismay. 'I swear to you I meant *every* word I've just said.'

Noah's eyes were as hard as flint and they skewered her without mercy as he leaned forward, his elbows resting on his knees. 'No, Delilah, because, yet again, this is all about you. Let's be honest, you're not here for me – the only reason you've shown up today is so *you* can feel better about what you did to me. Absolving yourself at someone else's expense is bullshit and pure selfishness. So no, I don't forgive you.'

It was hard to argue with him, but she wasn't ready to give up. 'I get that you're angry with me and, believe me, I know what I did was unforgiveable, but—'

'Good word, that. Unforgiveable. Yes, it was, so I don't know how you have the gall to ask me to let it go.'

'Noah, I'm trying here. I know I can't make up for what I did to you—' She couldn't stop the tremor in her voice and she turned her head away before he could see the tears filling her eyes. Who was she kidding? He was well within his rights to hate her, and she was wasting her time and his by hoping time had softened his anger.

'Actually, maybe you can.'

Delilah turned to find him eyeing her speculatively.

'Really? How?' she asked hopefully.

'You said you're a relationship counsellor now, is that right?'

'Ye-es,' Delilah said slowly, wondering where this was going.

Noah chewed on his lip in silence for a moment and then he sat back in his chair. 'Leaving aside the obvious irony, are you any good at your job?'

'I'm not yet fully qualified, but yes, I do counsel clients,' Delilah said carefully. Instinct told her this wasn't the time to get into the technicalities of her current situation.

'Alright, if you're serious about making things right with me, then I need you to help me make things right with Zazie.'

'Wait, *what*? Who's Zazie?'

'My girlfriend.'

The words sent a sharp stab of pain through Delilah. This had definitely not been part of her imagined script, and she couldn't help wondering if Noah was deliberately trying to hurt her, which would be understandable after what she had done to him. But then, Noah being involved with someone else shouldn't have come as a surprise. It was over three years since she'd walked away, and he was a very attractive man who had never lacked for attention from women. Reminding herself that she had no right to feel betrayed, Delilah rallied quickly, determined not to show her hurt feelings.

'I see. What's the problem?'

'We've been going out for a while and it's serious – or rather it could be, if she and my mum would just get along.'

Delilah had dubbed Noah's mother the Wicked Witch of the West for good reason and despite her mixed feelings about Noah's new girl, she felt a pang of sympathy for the unknown Zazie. But that didn't mean she wanted to get involved.

'I'm sorry,' she said firmly. 'I don't see how I can help with that. I work with couples on their own relationships.'

'Exactly. My relationship with my *girlfriend*' – Delilah tried not to flinch at the emphasis Noah seemed to enjoy placing on the word – 'is messed up because of her relationship with my mother. I don't want to lose my girlfriend, and you're a relationship counsellor. It's simple: you help sort us out – me and Zazie, and Zazie and Mum – and then maybe I forgive you for what you did to me.'

Delilah jumped to her feet. 'That's outrageous!' she gasped, dropping any attempt to be conciliatory. 'And it's also blackmail!'

When Noah looked unmoved, she took a breath and tried to speak calmly. 'There's no way I can counsel you and your' – she tried, but she couldn't get the word out – 'um, Zazie, when you and *I* used to be a couple. It would be completely unethical, and I could get fired.'

'I don't see how that's a problem since you and I are ancient history,' said

Noah in an indifferent tone that set Delilah's teeth on edge. 'But I suppose you have a point.'

'Thank you!' Delilah breathed in relief.

'So we won't tell Zazie we used to go out.'

Delilah opened her mouth to argue, but Noah stood up and placed a silencing finger on her lips to stop her. It was the first time he had touched her since her arrival at his door, and it was as if her body had suddenly gone up in flames. She looked up into his eyes and their gaze locked for what felt like an eternity. Then she shook her head, freeing her lips from his touch and breaking the spell.

Despite herself, her eyes darted towards his arm. Was the tattoo still there under the sleeve of his sweater? If Delilah was ancient history, it was very likely he'd had it removed or – worse – had tattooed Zazie's name over it.

The idea that she had been so easily replaced shifted Delilah's emotions from sadness into the safer territory of anger. She knew it was irrational to be upset that he'd moved on, but that didn't stop her silent fuming. Even if Noah was in love with someone else, how *dare* he demand that she help him with his relationship? She might have behaved badly towards him, but what he was asking of her was simply cruel.

'You're being unreasonable,' she snapped at him with blazing eyes. 'I can't force your mum to like someone she doesn't. In case you've forgotten, I couldn't even get her to like *me*!'

'I'm not changing my mind, Delilah, so it's up to you. Help me fix things with Zazie and then I'll forgive you. That way, we can all move on.'

His tone was uncompromising, and Delilah turned away in frustration. She had come to apologise, not to land herself in an impossible dilemma. She might need Noah's forgiveness to complete her mission and prove to Polly that she had gained enough self-awareness to get her job back, but if she was daft enough to agree to his outrageous request, she would be jeopardising the very job she was desperate to save.

20

'Oh no, he didn't!' Salome breathed.

'Oh yes, he did,' Delilah echoed grimly.

'But that's ridiculous!'

'No, it's *beyond* ridiculous! It's absurd, asinine, laughable, outrageous—'

'Calm down, Ms Thesaurus, and let's think this through logically,' Salome cut in impatiently. 'I totally get that he's still furious with you – and for good reason – but he surely can't expect *you* to be his counsellor. What if you... I don't know... deliberately tried to break them up?'

'He knows I wouldn't do that!' Delilah protested. 'Besides, it would be unethical.'

Salome arched a sceptical eyebrow. 'At this point, I think we've moved way past ethical and into la-la land. Anyhow, what makes Noah so sure this Zazie woman would even agree to bare her soul to a woman he was once engaged to?'

'That's what I asked, and he says he'll introduce me to her as a friend of a friend. For obvious reasons, we'd have to keep our past a secret.'

Looking flummoxed, Salome reached for the coffee she'd just brewed for Delilah and absently took a sip, immediately setting the mug back on the kitchen table with a shudder.

'I don't know how you can drink that stuff. Coffee smells a lot nicer than it actually tastes.' She walked over to take a bottle of water from the fridge and swallowed half the contents in one go before turning to Delilah, who sat with elbows resting on the table, holding her face between her hands and looking miserable.

Salome was quiet for a few moments. 'Why do you think Noah's asking you to do this?' she probed. 'I mean, if the man needs relationship advice, there are a hundred other counsellors he could turn to. No offence, but why's he picking *you*? Especially as you told him you're still in training *and* that what he's demanding is unethical?'

'First off, he doesn't give a toss about whether or not it costs me my job. Why me? Because how else is he going to hurt me like I hurt him? I think he just wants to punish me so badly that he's not thinking straight.' Delilah gave a bitter laugh. 'Look, I get it, and I'd probably be a petty bitch too if this was the other way round. But seriously, just how pissed off do you have to feel to expect your ex to help you repair your relationship with your... your...' She huffed in frustration at the word that simply wouldn't come. 'You know what I mean!'

Salome screwed the cap back onto the bottle and eyed her sister shrewdly. 'So, what did you tell him? Please don't say you've actually agreed to this bonkers plan?'

'*No!* At least, not yet. I honestly didn't think anyone could top you for daft ideas, Sal, but Noah's giving it a good try.'

Salome ignored the sarcasm and came back to the table, taking a seat directly across from her sister. 'Help me understand this, hon. If it's unethical to counsel someone you've had a relationship with, why are you even considering going along with it when you're trying to keep a job that's so hot on ethics?'

The irony wasn't lost on Delilah. 'Again, I told him that, but Noah is as stubborn as a bloody mule!'

'He's not the only one,' Salome murmured, taking another sip from the bottle.

'I argued with him for ages, but he won't budge. *If* – and that's a big if – I decide to help, he needs to agree that it'll be coaching rather than counselling.'

'So you'd be fudging it, basically?'

'If it comes to it, I prefer to think of it as a workaround,' Delilah said. She drank the rest of her coffee while she absorbed the enormity of what she was contemplating. If she agreed to Noah's demand, she would definitely be straying into dodgy territory – forget straying; what she was considering would be more like moving in and setting up home. To make matters worse, there was no way she could tell Arne what she was planning, which would be one more thing she had to keep from her therapist.

Salome looked unconvinced. 'If he's come up with this to hurt you back, why are you letting him? I wrote that list so you could apologise, not get involved in his messy love life. You don't have to do this, Del.'

Delilah sat for a moment absorbing Salome's words. Yes, of course she could refuse Noah's request or – more accurately – demand. At the same time, a tiny voice inside her wondered if she owed Noah whatever he needed as closure. 'Yes, I probably do. If I'm doing this challenge, then I've got to do it properly and get him to forgive me. Besides, I can't get the way he was looking at me out of my head. It was like he *detests* me. I know I'm risking my job, but I really hurt him, Sal, so how do I say no?'

'Noah's really making you pay for what you did to him,' Salome said in a voice filled with pity. She hesitated and then said baldly, 'I know you hate me bringing this up, but why *did* you run away that day?'

Delilah shrugged. 'Bad timing, bad decision, who knows. He rang just as I was looking in the mirror in your room and thinking I didn't recognise myself. The white dress... the whole get-up – it didn't look like me, it didn't feel like me. I felt like I was playing a part. But it wasn't even that... I don't know. I remember I was feeling excited, but then when he rang and – and said... suddenly I just *knew* that marrying him would be a huge mistake.'

Salome's eyebrows drew together in a frown. 'Every bride gets nervous. Remember I threw up three times the morning Farhan and I got married? But you – you were absolutely fine until you took that call. What did Noah say that spooked you so badly?'

'I've just told you! I suddenly realised that marrying him would be a mistake. Oh my God, Sal, why can't you just let it go!'

'But you loved him!' Salome persisted. 'Anyone could see that.'

'Well, love makes people do stupid things,' Delilah said tightly. 'Love certainly isn't enough reason to walk into a situation you'll have to stay in for the rest of your life.'

Farhan walked into the kitchen holding a drooling Arin, and Salome pushed back her chair and reached for the child.

'Come to your mummy,' she cooed.

'This kid oozes more liquid than a sponge,' Farhan muttered, handing Arin over and swiping the back of his hand down the side of his trousers. 'Maya's having her nap so I'm going to pop down to the shops. Do you need anything?'

'No thanks, my love.' Salome turned to her sister. 'Del?'

Delilah shook her head. 'No, I'm fine,' she muttered, giving Farhan a pointed look. He frowned, looking puzzled, but Delilah held her peace.

Salome still looked exhausted and, recalling her recent tearful admission, Delilah knew her sister wasn't happy. While she didn't doubt Farhan loved Salome, someone needed to remind her brother-in-law that his wife also had needs. If Sal wanted to make changes to her life, then it was her husband's job to know that and to help make it happen. While she had no intention of saying anything in front of Salome, Farhan certainly had a case to answer, and Delilah intended to make sure he did.

21

'You seem quiet today, Delilah. Is something troubling you?'

Startled, Delilah looked up to find herself the focus of Arne's gaze. 'No, no, of course not. I'm just a bit tired,' she replied, shifting in the chair and trying not to sound defensive.

Arne made no comment and after a moment Delilah burst out, 'Fine, the truth is I'm fed up with being off work! I have too much time on my hands and too much time to think.'

She knew she sounded sulky, but she was sick of spending her days parked in front of the television, re-reading books from her course or beating the worn track between her house and Salome's. Christmas was fast approaching and while the entire country seemed obsessed with mince pies and shopping, she simply felt depressed. She was desperate for intellectual stimulation from people other than Maya and Arin, and while at the time she'd been shocked by Salome's frustrated outburst – one which her sister subsequently downplayed whenever Delilah tried to bring it up – she had a new-found respect for Salome's willingness to stay at home full-time.

'When you do all this thinking, what do you find yourself reflecting about most?' Arne's question dragged Delilah back to the present and the predicament that was never far from her mind. It had been over a week since the encounter with Noah and it was hard to think about anything else. She squashed the temptation to spill the beans to Arne about the unholy bargain her ex-fiancé was offering. There was little point inviting a lecture on the obvious conflict of interest when she hadn't yet agreed to Noah's terms.

But Arne was waiting for an answer, and so she blurted out the first thing that came into her head. 'I find myself thinking a lot about relationships and wondering why some couples work so well while other people seem to, well – suck at them, frankly.'

'And why do you think that is?'

'No offence, but somehow I don't think I'd be sitting here with you if I knew the answer,' she said with a wry smile. 'Why do *you* think some people are lucky enough to have found "the one"' – she crooked her fingers into air quotes – 'while the rest of us stay broken or have to fix ourselves and make do with whatever we can get?'

'That sounds rather depressing – and perhaps a bit reductive, no? Do you consider love to be a random win of the lottery? That there are a few winners and everyone else settles for second best?'

Trust Arne to answer a question with a series of questions, Delilah thought in amusement. 'Well, quite often relationships *are* depressing,' she countered. 'That's why people like me exist – to help couples find the joy that vanishes as soon as people become crutches for each other.'

Arne arched an eyebrow, and Delilah broke into a laugh. 'God, I really sound like a doom merchant, don't I? Don't get me wrong, I *like* seeing people happy in their relationships and if I can help them get there, then so much the better.'

'Since you posed the question, how much of people's success in their relationships do you think is down to luck and how much comes from healthy or unhealthy patterns of behaviour and emotional baggage from childhood?'

'There's definitely an element of luck,' Delilah said slowly. 'I mean, how many of us actually get to find our soul mate? But if you're asking whether people replicate toxic or one-sided relationships, then, yes. I've been going back over some of the papers I studied for my counselling exams and a lot of them link dysfunctional adult relationships to emotional scars from childhood.'

'So you would agree that an adult who was exposed to unhealthy relationship dynamics as a child can struggle with maintaining meaningful relationships?' Arne probed.

'It's possible,' Delilah said carefully. 'But it can also strengthen someone's survival instinct.'

'In what way?'

'Well, by putting up boundaries and keeping enough emotional distance to protect yourself from being sucked into situations you can't control,' Delilah shot back.

'That is very interesting.' Arne leaned forward, his eyes boring into hers. 'And when you reflect on your own relationships and those you observed in your childhood, what do you think taught you to be vigilant and to avoid getting too close to someone in case you are hurt?'

Arne spoke calmly but his words hit Delilah with the suddenness of an assassin's bullet to the brain. Her heart rate accelerated, and it was as if the breath had been sucked out of her chest. She shook her head violently and squeezed her fists so tightly she felt her nails cutting into the softness of her palms.

'Delilah, I assure you this is a safe space for us to explore your experiences and try to understand how they have impacted you,' he said softly. 'Can we try that?'

She nodded dumbly, not sure what she was agreeing to, and Arne continued, his deep voice as gentle as if speaking to a child. 'We all carry wounds from our childhood, but with self-awareness and compassion, we can heal. However, any healing requires acknowledging what, perhaps, you have already indirectly admitted. Being willing to recognise your vulnerabilities can only make you a more effective counsellor and I want to support you in this. Is that okay?'

Delilah closed her eyes, slowly breathing in and out to steady the riot of emotions Arne had unleashed. She knew he was trying to help, but the harder he pounded at her defences, the more afraid she was to let them go.

'I think the apology exercise is helping me take a more mature approach to relationships,' she said quietly. It wasn't what he'd asked, but it was all she was prepared to tell him.

If Arne was disappointed at her for avoiding his question, it didn't show, and his expression remained neutral. 'In what way?'

'Coming clean to my exes and seeing things from their perspective has made me grow up a bit and take more accountability for my actions.' She pulled her knees up to her chest and pondered her next words. She hadn't planned to tell him, but she also needed to distract Arne – whatever it took.

'Well, even a few weeks ago, I couldn't have imagined speaking to my ex-boyfriends, let alone trying to help them out. Did I mention Noah asked for my advice with some issues in his relationship? Strictly as a friend, of course!' she added, injecting a casual note into her voice. 'Obviously, I'm aware that counselling someone I've had a relationship with *could* be seen as breaching ethics, but I've been very clear that this is more like coaching – you know, just giving him and his... his girlfriend a few ideas to help her navigate a bit of awkwardness with Noah's mum.'

Arne's bushy brows knitted into a frown as he tugged gently on his beard, a sign Delilah had come to know meant he was deep in thought.

'Delilah, there is a good reason why we are required to abide by a code of ethics as counsellors and therapists,' he said eventually. 'Do you consider yourself able to remain fair and impartial in your advice and avoid causing inadvertent harm, given your history with Noah?'

'I might have ended the relationship, but I still care about him, and I would never do anything to hurt him or Zazie,' Delilah said earnestly, aware she had boxed herself into a corner and was now defending a decision she hadn't even made yet. But if she did help Noah – and it was still an *if* – she would do everything in her power to put aside their past history. Besides, the man was madly in love with Zazie now, so how hard could that be?

'I am struggling to understand how inserting yourself into Noah's relationship will help you. Have you reflected on your motivations here and is it possible you may be trying to sabotage your own success in learning from your past choices and making better decisions?'

Was it her imagination, or did she detect a note of disappointment in Arne's voice?

'Noah and I finished years ago, and the way I see it, if Noah's willing to forgive me and I can help him – *them* – then surely it's proof I'm able to stay objective – which is what Polly seems to have a problem with,' she said defiantly, not sure which of them she was hoping to convince.

Arne paused and thought for a second. 'Help me understand your end goal here, Delilah,' he said eventually. 'With the other men, you accepted what they offered and moved on, so what is different this time? Are you seeking redemption, or is what you are suggesting founded on a desire to prolong contact with Noah?'

At a loss for words, Delilah lowered her gaze and stared at the floor in silence.

22

The doorbell tinkled as Delilah opened the café door and walked in. Although the warm shop with its tantalising aroma of freshly brewed coffee and warm pastries was a welcome relief from the sharp December chill, the décor left a great deal to be desired. While she was no fan of Christmas, the decorations – if that was the right word to describe three strings of coloured tinsel wrapped around the counter and a bunch of plastic mistletoe sellotaped onto the wall behind the cash register – were paltry and uninspiring. It was quiet for a Saturday morning, and other than a man wearing headphones and sitting cross-legged on a sofa typing furiously on his laptop, there was only a handful of people enjoying a mid-morning coffee break, making it easy to spot Noah seated towards the back of the café. Much to her relief, he was alone. Despite her breezy assurances to Salome and Arne, Delilah couldn't deny the tension that had been building up inside her at the prospect of coming face to face with Zazie. At least she still had a bit of time to gather her composure and, despite finally and reluctantly agreeing to help, maybe persuade Noah to change course or, preferably, abandon ship altogether on his ridiculous idea.

Noah stood up and waved her over, and Delilah navigated a path between the empty tables, squeezing past a weary-looking woman sipping a cup of coffee while gently rocking a double buggy with two sleeping babies.

When she reached Noah's table, she hesitated, unsure whether to attempt a friendly hug. He solved her dilemma by pushing a chair in her direction and taking his seat again, and Delilah slid onto the chair without comment. She hadn't expected to be greeted with open arms, but Noah's boot-faced expression was unnerving. While she was thankful that he wasn't looming over her with rage like the last time they'd met, it was still tough to reconcile the laughing, spontaneously affectionate Noah of old with the emotionless man sitting across the table.

'Have you been waiting long?' she asked brightly.

'About three years, give or take,' he replied shortly, and she squirmed at the sarcasm. While the curt tone suggested it was unlikely she could persuade Noah to ditch his idea, Delilah tried anyway.

'Noah, I—'

'Save it, Del.' He cut her off abruptly and glanced at his watch. 'Zazie's late, as usual, but it gives us time to get our stories straight. Listen, don't mess this up because she's super smart and she'll sense any bullshit straight away.'

Instantly bristling at the implication that she would be the one to mess up his stupid plan, Delilah nevertheless held her tongue. *Focus on why you're here!* Noah had made it clear he'd moved on, and her only goal was to make amends for dumping him without explanation. If that meant listening to him sing Zazie's praises from morning till night, she would just have to sit and take it. This was not a competition, she reminded herself, although she couldn't squash the inner bitch voice that wondered why the supposedly super smart Zazie couldn't arrive anywhere on time.

'There isn't a lot to mess up,' Delilah said crisply. 'You've explained that I'm a friend of a friend who suggested you talk to me because I'm a relationship counsellor, because I might be able to give you and Zazie some tips to improve her relationship with your mum.'

She glanced at Noah's half-empty cup. 'I'm going to need some coffee first,' she added, making as if to stand, but he beat her to it.

'My bad. I'll get it. Latte, right?'

She nodded, trying to ignore the rush of joy that he still remembered. Watching him walk towards the counter, she couldn't help the sad sigh that escaped her. *What have you got yourself into, Del?* Maybe Arne was right, and she was lying to herself. Without Salome's challenge, she might not have gone in search of Noah, but it was hard to deny the potent effect he still had on her.

Lost in thought, she didn't notice Noah until he suddenly appeared beside her and set a steaming mug of milky coffee on the table before sitting down.

Picking up the mug, Delilah cradled it between her fingers, suddenly feeling shy. After a few moments, she peeked up at him through her lashes and when their eyes met and he didn't look away, she felt her face flush with a heat that rivalled her coffee. She wrenched her gaze away and looked around the quiet café, desperate to break the tense silence.

'Do you come here often?'

As soon as the words emerged, she cringed and braced herself for a sarcastic response. But he didn't comment and when she looked at him, Noah's shoulders were shaking and his lips twitching as he dissolved into silent laughter. After a few moments, he shook his head and wiped under his eyes.

'Seriously, Del. "*Do you come here often*?" Is that the best you can do?'

This was the Noah she knew, the *real* Noah, and Delilah smiled ruefully. 'Sorry, I'm a bit nervous. It's weird sitting here with you like this after... after everything.'

Noah's expression sobered, and he picked up his cup and took a long sip before leaning back in his chair with a speculative expression. 'Yeah, I know. I appreciate it's all a bit awkward, so thanks for agreeing to this. I wouldn't have asked if it wasn't important. The honest truth is, if you can help sort out Zazie and my mum, it would mean the world to me.'

Arne's warning flashed through her mind and Delilah said quickly, 'I know I said I'll help, but please remember I won't be counselling you or Zazie. I'm only offering suggestions because—'

'Oh good, here she is!' Noah exclaimed as the café door bell sounded, cutting off her feeble attempt to establish an ethical boundary. Delilah had her back to the door, but she immediately felt her heartbeat accelerate. Steeling herself, she turned around in time to see a girl with long legs and a mane of copper corkscrew curls race across the room and launch herself onto Noah.

'*Hi babe!* Sorry I'm late – the Tube was a nightmare!'

The breathless greeting was followed by a kiss so passionate that Delilah was forced to avert her gaze. When she dared to look, Zazie was smiling at Noah with her arms linked around his neck. Her black knit maxi dress accentuated a reed-slim figure, and wearing a pair of lilac, high-heeled ankle boots, she was almost as tall as Noah. Trying not to compare Zazie's casual chic to her own worn jeans and scarlet polo-necked jumper, Delilah cleared her throat, and Noah unclasped Zazie's arms and steered her around by the shoulders to face Delilah.

'Zaz, this is Delilah, the friend I told you about. Delilah, meet my girl, Zazie.'

Delilah pasted on a bland smile, which she hoped hid her inner turmoil at seeing Noah kiss another woman, and stuck out her hand. Zazie seized it and immediately pulled Delilah into a smothering hug, which left her struggling to breathe through the mass of hair in her face.

When Delilah eventually managed to escape her embrace, Zazie clapped her hands excitedly. 'Oh my God, thanks *soo* much for agreeing to do this!'

'Um, hi. It's great to meet you,' Delilah said weakly. She hadn't known what to expect, but it definitely wasn't this tall beauty with the energy of an exuberant puppy. With a long oval-shaped face, razor-sharp cheekbones, huge hazel eyes, and flawless skin, it wasn't hard to see why Noah's girl was a model. Even her voice – husky overlaid with honey – was alluring. She was undeniably gorgeous, and Delilah felt short and dumpy in comparison. It was just as well there was no competition at play here, she acknowledged, because Zazie would win hands down.

'Why don't we all sit down,' Noah suggested, pulling out a chair for Zazie, who slipped onto the seat with a lithe gracefulness Delilah could only dream of.

'What are you drinking, Zaz?' he asked.

'Green tea for me, babes,' she replied cheerfully, crossing long slim legs and gazing up at him with a loving smile that tore at Delilah's heart.

As soon as he'd left to fetch the tea, Zazie leaned across the table and lowered her voice. 'Noah reckons you can help his mum and me get along, but I can't lie. That woman is the *devil*! She's so sarky when she even bothers to talk to me, and I can't seem to do anything right with her.'

Zazie's accent was pure London and despite the unfairness of the woman winning the lottery on looks *and* bagging her ex, Delilah found it impossible to dislike her.

'You know what they say about mothers and their sons,' she said with a genuine smile. 'No one's ever good enough for their precious boy, and—' She stopped before she said too much and blew her cover. As a friend of a friend, she couldn't possibly have met Noah's mother. 'What I mean is some mothers take a bit more persuading when it comes to accepting their son's girlfriends, but I'm sure you can win her round.'

'I hope so. Noah's so close to his mum that if she doesn't like me, I know he won't – you know – set a date,' Zazie confided, her dazzling smile dimming at the prospect.

A frisson of shock passed through Delilah. '*Oh!* So you two are that serious, then?' She tried to sound nonchalant despite the sharp stab of pain between her ribs.

'Well, we've been going out for over a year, and I'm not getting any younger. Don't want to be stuck on the shelf at thirty!' She chuckled throatily.

Noah reappeared, balancing a full cup, which he placed carefully on the table. Zazie looked up at him with a teasing smile. 'Thanks, babe. Delilah said she didn't realise we were serious… I thought you'd told her everything.'

Noah hesitated and then said gruffly, 'Well, yeah, we've talked, but I was waiting for you to get here so we could explain everything properly.'

Zazie took a quick sip of tea and turned her attention to Delilah, who was trying to absorb the crushing news.

'So, how do you two know each other again?'

Noah jumped in before Delilah could speak. 'I told you, Zaz. Delilah's a good friend of…' He paused for an agonising moment and Delilah quickly interjected, 'Martin.'

'Chris!' Noah exclaimed at the same time. He glared at Delilah while Zazie looked from one to the other curiously.

'Silly me, of course it was Chris!' Delilah said apologetically. 'I always get him mixed up with his brother.' She cleared her throat. 'Um, Zazie, why don't you tell me more about your relationship with Noah's mum?'

For a moment Zazie's dubious expression had Delilah convinced she'd messed up just as Noah had warned, but it was soon clear his girlfriend had other concerns.

'What relationship? His mum *hates* me! Noah introduced me to his parents after we'd been together a few months and right from the off, it was like she had it in for me, wasn't it, babe?' She looked appealingly at Noah, who shrugged, looking uncomfortable.

Come on, Noah! This is what we're here for, isn't it? Delilah pleaded silently. She watched his hands play with his empty mug, and her eyes lingered on his forearm, wondering once again if the crown tattoo was still there under his long-sleeved shirt. She looked up to find him watching her and her heart picked up its pace.

'Noah, you know your mum best,' she asked, trying to keep her voice even. 'What do you think is holding her back from welcoming Zazie?'

'What do *I* think?' he echoed mockingly. 'I think Mum's seen me get hurt in a past relationship and, in her own way, I suppose she's trying to protect me.'

Delilah's chest constricted, and she struggled to get her words out. 'What do you think you can do to help your mum know Zazie better so she can appreciate how' – she gritted her teeth – '*different* she is from the women you've dated?'

'I've tried really hard to be nice to her, haven't I, babe?' Zazie chimed in. 'I even offered her the sample designer bag I got from the B.B. Cartwright people after the fashion shoot.'

'*B.B. Cartwright!*' Delilah raised a brow in astonishment. Even she knew their bags cost hundreds, if not thousands of pounds. 'That was very generous. What did she say?'

'She looked at it like I'd offered her some cheap tat from Primark and then she goes, "Oh, that's very nice of you, dear, but it's not really my style."' Zazie sniffed. She sipped her tea delicately, somehow managing to make the green water look delicious.

'It sounds to me like you and Noah's mum need to find some common ground to build your relationship on,' Delilah said tentatively. 'But before I say any more, Zazie, and just so you know, I've told Noah I'm not allowed to officially counsel you because it's against the rules for me to work with a... a friend. But I am happy to offer a few suggestions for you two to consider, if you think it would help?'

Hoping against hope Zazie would respond with a 'thanks but no thanks', Delilah groaned silently when the girl's face lit up.

'Honestly, Delilah, anything you can do will be amazing!' She knocked back the last drops of tea and pushed her chair back. 'I'm really sorry but I've gotta dash. I'm running late for a photo shoot, but I'll get your number off Noah and call you so we can have a proper heart to heart, yeah?'

Before Delilah could reply, Zazie gave Noah a lingering kiss and then grabbed her coat and bag from the back of her chair. Blowing a cheerful kiss in Delilah's direction, Zazie raced out of the café.

23

'So you finally met Zazie! Okay, go on then, spill the beans. What happened after she left?' Salome demanded.

Delilah absently stroked Arin's fine baby hair as he sat quietly on her lap with his thumb stuck in his mouth. 'Nothing. Absolutely nothing. Noah and I sat there for about five minutes in an awkward silence you could have cut with a knife. Then I got up and left.'

'Well done, hon.' Salome reached across the kitchen table to squeeze her sister's hand, her eyes brimming with compassion. 'Meeting your ex's girl can't have been easy for you.'

'Especially when she looks like a bloody supermodel *and* seems like a lovely person,' Delilah agreed with a wry smile.

'Thank God you don't have feelings for Noah any more.'

When Delilah made no comment, Salome tilted her head and scrutinised her sister through narrowed eyes. 'Hold on, you *don't* still have feelings for him, do you?'

Delilah sighed. 'I don't know – maybe?' She buried her face in Arin's curls. 'Seeing him again is bringing up all these weird emotions, but maybe that's just a normal reaction to meeting an ex's new partner.'

'It didn't bother you when it was Desmond,' Salome observed dryly, reaching across the table to stroke her son's cheek.

'True, but then he wasn't asking me for marriage counselling, was he?'

Salome's hand stilled and she stared at her sister with wide eyes. '*Marriage?* Are you serious?'

Delilah nodded. 'Yup. And so, it appears, are they. Once they get mummy dearest onside, they'll be setting a date.'

Salome looked stricken as she took in the information. 'I'm starting to regret making you go through this apology exercise. I didn't realise you were still into Noah. I'm sorry, sis – what are you going to do?'

'There's nothing I *can* do except finish what I've started. I owe him, Sal, and if I can help him get his happy ever after, maybe he'll stop hating me and I'll stop feeling guilty. When they get his mum's blessing, and I get Noah's forgiveness, hopefully then we can all move on with our lives. I'm meeting up with them on Tuesday to talk through some strategies – I mean, suggestions.'

Salome's sympathetic expression was beginning to jar, and Delilah quickly changed the subject. 'Guess who's back from Brazil?'

'Really?'

'Yup. I called him yesterday. Do you know, Remi's the first man on your stupid list who actually sounded pleased to hear from me.'

'Why?' Salome asked bluntly.

'I didn't ask! Anyway, I'm meeting him on Thursday evening, so I suppose I'll find out.'

Arin squirmed on her lap and Delilah sniffed, screwing up her nose as the tell-tale aroma hit her. 'Eww, *Arin*! I wondered why you were sitting so still! Sal, your child needs changing.' She stood up and held Arin under his arms, dangling him above the table.

Salome didn't move. 'Well, I'm knackered. Delilah, you do know that you could change him yourself.'

'Haha. You know I don't do poopy nappies. Seriously, Sal, take him before he leaks all over me!'

Reluctantly, Salome pulled herself up from her chair and reached for her son. 'Come on, little man. Let's go upstairs and get you cleaned up.' She glanced at Delilah. 'Can you make me a cuppa, hon? I'm parched.'

Delilah had just switched on the kettle when Farhan wandered into the kitchen. Walking over to the fridge, he took out a half-empty packet of sliced cheese and glanced over at her. 'Where's Sal?'

'Upstairs, changing Arin. Actually, if you've got a minute, I've been wanting to have a word.'

'Oh? Why, what's up?' He folded a slice of cheese into quarters and crammed it into his mouth and then opened a cupboard and took out some crackers.

'Have you noticed how tired Sal looks lately?'

Farhan lowered the cracker that was halfway to his mouth and swallowed hard. 'What do you mean?'

'I *mean* my sister looks absolutely shattered and needs more support than she seems to be getting from you,' Delilah said.

A flash of anger crossed his face. 'What exactly are you trying to say, Delilah?'

Delilah ignored Farhan's terse tone and stuck to her guns. Salome's unguarded confession about feeling frustrated with her life had been weighing on Delilah. Her sister's upbeat demeanour couldn't hide the dark shadows under her eyes, nor had a new air of restlessness escaped Delilah's notice. Salome worked extraordinarily hard to make everyone happy and ensure everything around her was perfect. Any cracks in the flawless image her sister chose to project meant something was very wrong, and her husband should have been the first to spot it.

'Listen, it's your job to take care of her and, if you ask me, I think she's doing too much,' Delilah said firmly. 'I know you've been busy with work, but you must have noticed she's run off her feet.'

Farhan flushed and dropped the cracker he was holding on to the kitchen counter. 'Are you serious?' he said, his voice rising with incredulity. 'You think I don't know how hard Sal works to take care of the kids and me, not to mention looking after the house? Not that I need to justify myself to you, but I've been begging her for months to let us get a cleaner in to help out, and she won't have it. If you can take a minute to climb down from your high horse, maybe you can ask yourself what's taken *you* so long to notice! Instead of having a go at me, look in the mirror and ask what you're doing to help.'

'I'm always over here keeping her company, aren't I?'

'And how's that helping?' Farhan scoffed. 'It's not like you offer any hands-on support, is it? You might be in and out of here, but have you ever asked if you can help out with the kids – or with anything? When we all got hit with the flu, where were you? Bloody hell, you won't even change a flaming nappy, so don't you dare insinuate that I don't care about my wife!'

As Farhan's verbal blows landed squarely on their target, Delilah's face burned with humiliation. Furious at him for twisting her legitimate concerns about her sister into a damning indictment of her own failings, she couldn't stop herself.

'If you care so much, then how come you're blocking her from getting back into her career? Do you know how utterly *bored* she is of just being a housewife?'

'*Delilah!*' Salome's shocked voice cut into the tense silence.

Standing in the doorway with Arin in her arms, Salome shook her head in bewilderment as her gaze swung from Farhan to Delilah. 'What the *hell* is going on? I've literally been gone for five minutes! What's happened?'

Ashen-faced, Farhan put the packet of crackers back into the cupboard before turning to face his wife.

'Is it true?' he asked quietly. 'What she said – that you're bored of being at home with me and the kids?'

When Salome hesitated, Farhan shook his head, his expression suddenly so deeply hurt that Delilah's anger fizzled out like a damp firework. If she knew one thing for sure, it was that Farhan idolised Salome. So much so that he had never questioned Delilah's importance to his wife or queried the open-all-hours access she had to their home.

She opened her mouth to apologise but Farhan's attention was focused on Salome. 'Why didn't you say anything?' he asked.

'Because it's not how I feel all the time,' Salome whispered, rocking Arin gently in her arms. 'I'm so grateful you're here at home with us, and you know I love being with the kids. It's just that at times I want to – to do something else for a change. I miss work. Not every day, but there's times when I need contact with people who aren't mums and who talk about something more than whose kid is teething or walking or whatever. I know you say we don't need the income from me going to work, but I still feel guilty that you're carrying the financial burden of all of us.'

Salome sounded close to tears, and Delilah looked on aghast.

Farhan ran a hand through his hair and shook his head. 'Darling, you don't have any reason to feel guilty,' he said gruffly. 'You do so much every day. Why was it so hard to talk to me about this? I really wish you had told me instead of —' His voice unexpectedly cracked, and he gestured towards Delilah, who gasped, horrified at what she had provoked. *Why couldn't I keep my big mouth shut!*

'I'm sorry, Farhan. I'm so, so sorry,' she pleaded. 'I was being a total bitch. What I said was horrible and uncalled for. Please forgive me. I should never have said that.'

'No, you shouldn't,' he said flatly. Without another word, he walked past Salome and out of the kitchen.

Delilah looked at her sister in panic. 'Sal, I'm so sorry! I shouldn't have—'

'Why, Delilah? How in the world could you say that to him?' Salome sounded so stricken that Delilah could have wept.

She raised her hands and then dropped them down by her sides again, only too aware she had no excuse that didn't make her sound like a petulant child. 'I had a go at him for not taking better care of you, and he called me out on my own behaviour. I saw red and said the first thing that came into my head to hurt him back. I was angry, but I should never have thrown that in his face.'

'I spoke to you in confidence!' Salome looked devastated. 'I thought I could trust you.'

'You *can*, Sal. Come on, please. I made a mistake and I'm sorry.'

Salome's expression hardened. 'Do you think saying sorry is going to take the pain away? You saw his face! *That's* why I haven't said anything to him – and now look what you've done.'

Delilah took a deep pained breath and closed her eyes, unable to bear the reproach in her sister's eyes. How had she managed to get it so wrong, she thought wretchedly.

'I'm sorry... I swear I was only trying to look out for you. I overstepped and —' She broke off in horror as Salome's face crumpled and tears streamed down her face.

'How could you, Delilah?' she sobbed. 'I need you to leave our house. *Now!*'

Cradling Arin's head against her shoulder, Salome turned away from her sister and followed Farhan out of the room.

24

They had been in the café for almost half an hour and, so far, Zazie had done most of the talking. Arriving fifteen minutes late, she had launched into a list of grievances against Noah's mother in between sips of hot water flavoured with a slice of lemon. It didn't take a genius to pick up on Zazie's deep-seated resentment of her boyfriend's mother and, in Delilah's opinion, the couple who really needed counselling was Zazie and Mrs West. But, seeing as she had herself never conquered that particular mountain, Delilah was hard pressed to suggest an approach that could work.

'*Only child syndrome*,' she had teased Noah mercilessly after he had finally coaxed her into the house next door to meet his parents. Her initial impression of Noah as the golden child smothered by his overbearing mother's attention was reinforced when she started joining him on his weekend visits home. The Sunday routine in the West household rarely varied. Church for his parents (a practice Noah had long sworn off) was followed by a huge meal cooked by his mother. After that came a couple of hours listening to Neville's extensive collection of vinyl records while the family caught up with the events of their week, before wrapping up the day with board games.

From the moment they arrived, Mrs West would fuss endlessly over her son, paying no attention to his obvious discomfort. The fussing had never been extended to Delilah and, in stark contrast to Neville's immediate and warm acceptance, Mrs West's frost-tinged formality towards

Delilah had never quite thawed. It shouldn't have come as a surprise then to learn Noah's mother was giving Zazie a hard time, although Delilah struggled to understand why. Surely even the most protective mother in the world would find beautiful, charming Zazie utterly enchanting.

Eventually Zazie ran out of steam and Delilah glanced at Noah, who sat across from her. Despite the occasional pained expression she had seen creeping onto his face, he had let Zazie speak without interruption.

'What's on your mind, Noah?' Delilah asked quietly.

Staring into his coffee, Noah shook his head without comment, and Delilah felt her hackles rise. Was she supposed to influence his sceptical girlfriend by herself? Irritated by his lack of support, Delilah suppressed the strong temptation to remind him she was only here under duress and kept her tone even.

'Noah, it's important you're honest with Zazie because you're going to need to show a united front when it comes to your mum. If she gets how important it is to you that Zazie feels welcomed, and that her being hostile towards your – your girlfriend' *Dammit, why was it* still *so hard to get that word out*! – 'risks alienating you, I'm sure she would make the effort.'

Noah exhaled loudly and ran a hand over his head. He opened his mouth and then paused, clearly struggling to articulate his thoughts. Zazie put down her cup and squeezed his hand affectionately.

'Yeah, babe. What are you thinking?' She gave him an encouraging smile. Noah gazed down at her hand clasping his for a moment and then cleared his throat.

'Look, I don't really know how to say this...'

'Say what, sweetie?'

Noah's eyes remained downcast as his voice dropped into a murmur. 'Don't take this the wrong way, but the thing is... and I know you mean well, but sometimes you can come across as a bit...'

'A bit what?' Zazie frowned.

'Well... a bit full-on. I know it's your personality and I don't think anything of it, but Mum is a very reserved person and sometimes – well, I'm just saying that sometimes less is more.'

'Noah!' Delilah stared at him in disbelief. How could he possibly hold Zazie responsible for his awful mother's stand-offish treatment?

Zazie clearly thought the same. Stricken, she pulled her hand away, looking as wounded as if someone had just slapped Bambi.

Noah studied the table intently and tapped his fingers in a silent tattoo. 'Zazie, I know you mean well. Really, I get it. But – seriously, who gives an expensive designer bag to someone you've only met twice! You can't buy a person's affection.' He looked up at her, his face unsmiling. 'Come on, you must admit that was over the top.'

Delilah shook her head slowly, shocked that he was doubling down on his harsh comment instead of apologising to an obviously hurt Zazie. When had Noah become so cruel? And why was he doing his best to sabotage Delilah's efforts to help them?

Zazie sprang to her feet so abruptly she almost knocked over her half-empty cup of lemon water. Her face was flushed, and her chest rose and fell rapidly beneath her white cashmere sweater as she pointed a trembling finger at Noah. 'I actually cancelled a photo shoot today that my agent set up weeks ago, because I thought we were all here to work out how to get your mum to treat me right,' she hissed. 'But instead of taking my side, you have the bloody nerve to attack *me?* What's that about, hmm?'

Noah sighed. 'Zazie, sit down and stop making a big deal about this. I'm not attacking you. I'm just trying to be honest. That's what you want, isn't it?'

'What I *want* is for you to support me for a change. You've seen how your mum is with me, but no matter what she says, you always find a way to defend her! Instead of taking my side, you want to make me the problem here. So it's okay for her to talk to me like dirt and if I have a problem with it, I'm a flipping drama queen?' She flung the angry words at him, oblivious to the heads turning at a nearby table.

'That is not what I said,' Noah replied doggedly. 'Don't put words in my mouth. Can you sit down so we can talk about this like adults?'

The tension at the table was so thick Delilah could have cut it into chunks. Zazie's eyes shot daggers at Noah but, to Delilah's relief, she took her seat without a word.

Delilah leaned forward and tried to keep her voice down, only too conscious of the people nearby openly watching the drama. 'Okay, let's take a step back and acknowledge it's possible to have different perceptions of a situation and different feelings as a result. Noah.' She looked across at him, trying hard not to get lost in the gaze he directed back at her. *Why exactly am I doing this again?*

Giving herself a mental shake, she continued. 'Noah, you've admitted your mum and Zazie don't get on, which is why you asked for my, um... input. Zazie has just shared – at great length – how your mother's attitude towards her makes her feel, and she's given loads of reasons to back that up. It's important that she knows you're hearing her and not dismissing her feelings.'

'Of course I'm not dismissing them!' Noah shook his head, sounding impatient. 'Believe me, I know my mother can be hard work at times. That's why we're here, isn't it? All I'm saying is Zazie could try a bit harder to meet her halfway. It can take Mum a bit of time to warm up to someone and—'

'A *bit of time*?' Zazie spluttered. 'We've been going out for almost two years, and whenever she sees me, she acts like it's the first time we've met!'

For the love of God, Noah, stop talking! Delilah begged silently as Noah persisted. 'Like I said, Mum can be hard work, but maybe you can help by toning it down a bit. If you come across as desperate, you'll never win her over.'

Zazie's expression darkened. 'Oh! So now I'm *desperate*?'

'Once again, that is not what I said!'

It was hard to tell if Noah was here to support or to sabotage but, other than entertaining the folks at the nearby table who were now openly eavesdropping, the discussion was going nowhere. Between Noah's obstinate stance and Zazie's short temper, Delilah could feel herself flagging, and she cleared her throat loudly. Two pairs of angry eyes turned towards her, and she paused for a moment to let the tension subside.

'We're getting off track here, so let's just take a minute to cool down. Both of you should consider framing your communication in a more constructive way – remember the goal here is to protect your relationship. Noah, although you didn't call Zazie desperate, she *feels* like the words you used amount to the same thing, and you can acknowledge her feelings as legitimate without putting her down.'

Zazie huffed in vindication and picked up her cup to sip the colourless lemon water. No one spoke for a while, and the observers returned to their conversation.

Noah finally broke the silence. 'I'm sorry if what I said came off as me putting Zazie down. Believe me, it wasn't my intention. However' – he spoke slowly as if choosing his words with care – 'we can't work out a decent plan of action to sort out this situation if Zazie continues overreacting.'

'*I'm* overreacting!' Zazie gasped, visibly flushed beneath her smooth brown skin. 'Well, if you ask me, you're *underreacting*!'

Delilah closed her eyes and drew in a deep breath. 'Noah, you can't know how something feels to another person, so you don't get to decide how they should respond. You need to take more responsibility for your language because it sounds like you're belittling her concerns and that's not helpful. Can't you understand how upset Zazie feels and just give her your unconditional support?'

Noah raised his hands in surrender. 'Okay, fine, I take it back! Zazie, I'm not trying to piss you off, I promise. I know my mum gives you a hard time and I totally get how it makes you feel.'

'Good!' Delilah said firmly before turning to a still fuming Zazie. 'Given what Noah was trying, in his own clumsy way, to say, is there anything you're willing to change in how you interact with his mum that could make her behave more warmly towards you?'

Zazie folded her arms and crossed her legs, her skinny jeans outlining toned thighs Delilah would have killed for. 'No offence, Delilah, but I'm starting to realise there's no point in me trying to be nice to that woman. I don't think any of this is actually about me. I could be as sweet as pie – and God knows I've tried – but the bottom line is she hates the idea of someone taking her precious son away. This isn't down to me – *she's* the one who needs to get over herself.'

Noah sat bolt upright, and a muscle twitched in his jaw. 'You're right, Del, we're not getting anywhere here. My mother is who she is, and I don't see her changing for anyone. Zazie has to be the bigger person and do whatever it takes to make things right with her.'

Zazie snorted in disbelief. 'Why do *I* have to be the bigger person? Your mum's a grown arsed woman! *You* need to talk to her and tell her what's what. I can't win here if you're always going to put her feelings before mine. D'you know what? I bet she's the reason why none of your relationships have lasted!'

Noah's expression froze, and Delilah winced. She was about to leap to his defence when she caught his eye. His expression dared her to speak and make a mess of things, and she bit her lip hard to stop the words fighting to escape. Why, why, *why* had she agreed to this terrible idea? She could pretend as much as she liked, but there was absolutely no way she could be a neutral party in this situation. She and Noah had way too much history for her to help him and Zazie in good faith.

Zazie stood up and reached for the short faux-fur jacket on the back of her chair. 'I've had enough of this,' she declared. This time, Noah sat in stony-faced silence and made no attempt to dissuade her.

'When you're ready to accept that your attitude to your mum is the real problem, call me. Delilah, thanks for trying to help.' Zazie's smile looked forced and there was a faint wobble in her voice. 'You've been brilliant.'

Without giving Noah a second glance, Zazie stalked off, her long strides quickly eating up the short distance to the door.

'What the hell was that about?' Delilah turned on Noah in disbelief. 'Is it really more important for you to be right than to sort out a problem you claim really matters to you?'

Noah shrugged off the question. 'It's not that big a deal. She'll come around when she's calmed down.'

'You *do* understand that telling someone they're overreacting isn't going to get you anywhere? What the hell, Noah! All you had to do was acknowledge she was upset and suggest talking it over when you've both had a chance to reflect.'

'Yeah, well you're the counsellor, not me,' he said shortly. They sat in silence while Delilah toyed with her empty coffee cup, debating whether to speak out or mind her own business. Noah and Zazie's relationship wasn't about her, but it was hard not to feel a sense of obligation to help him find happiness and stop him sabotaging his own relationship.

'The way you were just now...' She forced herself to say the words. 'You were harsh and unkind. That's not the person you were before – when you were with me.'

It was like watching a statue come to life as Noah's face lit up with fury and his eyes blazed with resentment. 'You think I don't know that? Well, here's a newsflash. *You* destroyed the person I was with you, and if you think I was unkind to Zazie, then what you did to me was a hundred times worse. Did you ever think about the consequences of your actions? Did you seriously think you could just trample over my heart, and I'd bounce back like nothing happened?'

Delilah's eyes filled with tears at the unexpected tirade, and she shook her head dumbly. But as if her words had opened the floodgates, there was no stopping Noah.

'You broke things off between us with no warning – and on the bloody phone, of all things! How did I deserve that?' he raged. 'No, I'm sorry but you don't get to sit here and call *me* unkind. When you bailed on me, I couldn't get out of bed for a week, didn't talk to anyone for a month. My mother was so freaked out, she had everyone from the doctor to her pastor round to stop me from doing something stupid...'

Horrified by the picture Noah had just painted and the raw pain in his voice, Delilah hung her head, too ashamed to look at him.

'It's no wonder she hates me,' she said brokenly. 'I'd hate me too if someone did that to my son.'

'She doesn't hate you,' Noah said quietly. He exhaled deeply and his shoulders slumped as though he was exhausted. 'She's just hurt for me. They both liked you. Dad – Dad loved you almost more than I did!'

Delilah couldn't help the tremor that ran through her at his admission – even if he had framed it in the past tense. She owed him the truth, or at least as much of it as she could contemplate.

'Maybe it was too much,' she said haltingly.

'What was too much?'

'All that love. I think I got scared because it felt like a lot.'

When Noah still looked puzzled, Delilah swallowed hard. 'Well, it's obvious I didn't deserve all that love, isn't it? Look at what I did to you! It might sound like a weird thing to say, but I'm glad you met Zazie. You're a good man and you deserve to be happy.'

Delilah tried, but she couldn't control the tremble in her voice. 'What I did to you was the absolute worst thing anyone could do. I let you love me and then I literally ran out on you. I don't expect you to forgive me, but I hope one day you will. I know it sounds selfish, and I don't mean it to be, but maybe if you can forgive me, you'll stop feeling so angry and give yourself a chance to properly move on with Zazie.'

25

Inside the bustling Nigerian restaurant, the lively Afrobeats music combined with the aromas of spicy food transported Delilah back to the days of sitting in the kitchen while her mother cooked up large pots of Ghanaian food and played African music on full blast. As she waited for Remi to join her, the mix of English and African languages interspersed with loud laughter around her was a bitter-sweet reminder of the boisterous get-togethers with her mother's extended family – before they all drifted away and eventually lost touch with her and Salome.

Delilah mentally shifted gears from the perilous path her thoughts were taking and returned to her discreet people watching. The restaurant was almost full, but the waiting staff – a grand total of two, as far as she could tell – didn't appear under pressure and instead joked with customers as they distributed plates and bowls loaded with steaming rice, pounded yam, and piping-hot soups and stews. No one seemed in a hurry, she concluded, watching a waiter carry a pile of menus over to a table of eight people who had arrived before her and were only now, after two rounds of drinks, ready to order.

The restaurant had been Remi's idea and with everyone busy in the lead up to Christmas and little else to do with her time, Delilah had arrived early. But after almost half an hour alone at her table surrounded by groups of people having a whale of a time, she was starting to feel awkward and more than a little self-conscious. Remi was running late, and there was only so much toying with her phone she could do. She briefly wondered if he intended to stand her up as revenge for her dumping him, but then quickly dismissed the idea. Not only was he the most transparent person on earth, but he, unlike her other exes, had sounded genuinely pleased to hear from her and had readily agreed to meet.

Delilah took a sip of the pineapple juice she had been nursing since her arrival and picked up her mobile once again to check if Remi had sent her a text. It was far too noisy in the restaurant to attempt to call anyone, and besides, other than Armenique, who was out with her new man, the only person she wanted to speak to was giving her a wide berth. Simply thinking about Salome set Delilah's heart aching. Sal was more than a sister; she was her best friend and closest confidante. On the rare occasions they fell out, they always made up quickly and moved on. But this time was different. By attacking Farhan, Delilah had forced Salome to choose between her sister and her husband, and the day after Delilah's argument with Farhan, Salome's text asking her to stay away and give them space to sort things out had made it clear where she fell in the pecking order.

'Hey, Del!'

Startled, Delilah looked up to see Remi in front of her. She had been so lost in thought that she hadn't noticed him walking in.

'Sorry I'm late,' he said with a broad smile. 'I've been driving around for twenty minutes trying to find parking.'

Still clean-shaven and stocky with short natural locks, Remi literally hadn't changed since the last time she'd seen him – the beige shirt with wide brown stripes he wore over his chinos was one she instantly recognised. She stood up and let him pull her into a hug, which she returned awkwardly. When she stepped back, he ran admiring eyes up and down her short knitted dress and knee-length boots.

'You are looking *good*, girl.'

The open inspection was unnerving, and Delilah slipped back into her seat and gestured towards the chair opposite. He sat down and immediately leaned forward to look her straight in the eye.

'I've been thinking about you a lot since you called, Del. I can't tell you how excited I am to see you.'

While Remi's friendliness made a pleasant change from the outright hostility she'd encountered with her other ex-boyfriends, his intensity was unsettling, and she tried to distract him by handing him a menu.

'We should probably order. It looks like it takes ages to get served in here.'

He took the menu from her without breaking eye contact. 'The food's great, though. It's a popular joint and they're really chilled. You can hang out here, eat, and relax for hours without being hassled.'

Delilah dropped her gaze and made a show of studying the menu. Perhaps she should have been clearer on the phone about why she wanted to meet up because she definitely hadn't come here to relax. On the flip side, Remi's was the first friendly face she'd seen in days, and she was the one who needed his forgiveness.

'Everything on here looks incredibly yummy,' she observed, genuinely intrigued by the variety of dishes. She'd studied the menu at least three times while she was waiting, but she ran her finger down the list of options once again. 'I was thinking of getting the jollof rice but maybe I should try the *eforirio* – I love spinach stew. What do you reckon?'

'Go for it. It's spicy but very tasty. I'm going to have the *egusi* soup with pounded yam. Should we order some fried plantain on the side?'

'Of course!' Delilah exclaimed. 'What's African food without plantain?'

Remi laughed and gestured to a passing waiter. After a quick exchange, he placed their order and when the waiter left, he leaned forward and shook his head slowly from side to side.

'Honestly, Del, I can't believe I'm sitting here with you,' he marvelled. 'I never thought I'd hear from you again. What made you decide to call me?'

Delilah shifted uncomfortably under his gaze. This was going to be a tricky conversation but while she was keen to say her piece and wrap things up with Remi, she was also ravenous and craving the meal she'd ordered.

'I'll tell you everything, I swear,' she said quickly. 'But first, why don't you catch me up on what you've been up to. You were in Brazil recently, is that right?'

Remi nodded. 'Yeah, my company has a branch over there and I travel every couple of months to check on my team.'

'I've never been to South America but it's definitely on my bucket list to visit one day.'

'You'd love it!' he raved. 'The country's amazing and everyone is incredibly friendly. Brazilians are such a diverse people, and their food is unbelievable.

My team take me to a new restaurant every time I'm there.' Remi grinned and tapped his fork on the table. 'And it's paradise for a plantain addict like you. There's no shortage of the stuff.'

Their meal arrived surprisingly quickly, and Delilah tucked into her rice and the spiced spinach stew while Remi dug into his soup with eager fingers, expertly scooping up chunks of meat and fish. Whether it was the food, the wine he'd ordered, or the cheerful atmosphere in the restaurant, Remi's soulful glances grew less irritating, and Delilah found herself relaxing and enjoying their friendly banter.

Remi finished his pounded yam and excused himself to wash his hands before returning to finish his soup with a spoon. When he reached across the table to spear a couple of slices of fried plantain, his shirt strained against his muscular biceps.

'From the look of those arms, I bet you're still a gym bunny,' she teased.

Remi laughed and flexed his arm to show off an impressive bulge. 'Yep, five days a week, no excuses.' He chewed enthusiastically on a mouthful of plantain and swallowed. 'I've always loved working out! Really gets the juices flowing and gives me a ton of energy. You know how it is – get into a habit, and it's hard to break.'

Delilah nodded. 'Tell me about it. I'm trying to break my own habits – and not necessarily good ones. That's why I called you,' she added impulsively.

'Oh?' He raised an eyebrow.

She put down her fork and took a deep breath. 'Okay, so I'm really grateful you agreed to meet. I honestly wouldn't have blamed you if you'd told me to get lost.'

He frowned. 'I'd never do that!'

'I know, and that's because you're a much better person than I am,' she admitted with a rueful smile. 'Breaking up with you the way I did wasn't kind, and I wanted to say I'm sorry.' She hesitated and he looked at her enquiringly.

'Go on.'

'Like I told you earlier, I'm a relationship counsellor now' – *or at least I hope I still am*, she thought, mentally crossing her fingers – 'and part of my training is understanding my own history, and my biases and triggers when it comes to relationships.' She paused and then continued, choosing her words carefully.

'If I'm being honest, Remi, it's been brought to my attention that I haven't behaved very well, to say the least, in my relationships. I've been selfish and thoughtless, and I've treated people who cared about me very badly. That's why I reached out to you – to apologise for ending things so abruptly and without explanation and then making things worse by not taking your calls.'

She looked at him expectantly, but Remi swallowed another spoonful of his soup without comment. Then, putting down his spoon, he studied her for a moment.

'So tell me, Del. Why did you end things with us? I really liked you – no, I'll be honest too. I *still* really like you. When I heard you'd called the office and then when you rang me again last week, I was hoping it was because you wanted us to try again and—'

She cut him off, groaning softly at his pained expression. 'I'm *so* sorry! I didn't mean to give you the wrong idea. When I – I disappeared on you, I didn't believe we were right for each other, but I owed you a grown-up conversation, not just running away and cutting off contact in the way I did.'

'But that was then,' Remi persisted. 'Is there any chance we could give it another go? We got on so well and – Del, the truth is I haven't stopped thinking about you.'

Delilah bit her lip, stunned that he still had feelings for her after she'd let him down so badly. 'I know it sounds like a cliché, but what I did – it – it wasn't your fault. I was immature and scared of—'

'Scared of what?' Remi interrupted, sounding frustrated. 'I *loved* you and I'd have done anything for you.'

'I know,' she muttered, feeling guiltier by the second. 'That was the problem. I couldn't handle being loved so intensely – by *anyone*. Look, it's my issue to deal with, and believe me, I'm trying. I'm seeing a therapist and everything.'

'Then, maybe things would be different with us this time? I still love you, you know.' He stared at her intently as if willing her to confess the same, but she shook her head. She'd had no idea Remi would feel this way. He had been so kind and generous to her all evening, and the guilt she'd already felt was compounded by the knowledge that she was about to hurt his feelings once again.

'I'm sorry, but I don't feel the same way and I don't want to lead you on by pretending we would work as a couple.'

Remi's face clouded over, and Delilah stared down miserably at her plate, feeling like she had just kicked a defenceless puppy.

'So, what now?' he asked with a resigned sigh.

'I don't deserve it, but I'm asking – no, begging – for your forgiveness. I've had a lot of time to think about my past behaviour, and I'm trying to do better.'

Remi picked up his spoon and continued his meal. 'How's your sister? She was pregnant when we were going out. What did she have in the end?'

Delilah blinked, thrown off by the sudden change of topic. 'A boy. Arin.' She hesitated. 'Sal's fine, although she's not talking to me.'

Remi looked up in surprise. 'Are you serious? The two of you were always super close. I can't imagine you falling out.'

Delilah shook her head dumbly, suddenly perilously close to tears.

'What happened?' Remi sounded so genuinely concerned that Delilah found herself confessing to the argument with Farhan and how Salome had barred her from their home.

'It was all my fault,' Delilah admitted sadly. 'I broke my sister's trust, and I hurt Farhan who's been like a brother to me ever since he started going out with Sal. Like I said, I'm crap at relationships and at treating people who care about me properly.'

She drummed her fingers nervously on the table. 'To tell you the full ugly truth, I've been suspended from work to figure myself out, and I'm starting to think I should give up trying to counsel other people when I've made such a mess of my own relationships.'

To her surprise, Remi reached across the table and the reassuring warmth of his hand over hers stilled her jumpy fingers.

'I'm sorry to hear that,' he said gently. 'Sounds like you've been going through a tough time.'

She blinked back the tears pricking her eyes, overwhelmed by the undeserved kindness. 'I wish I knew how to make things right with Sal,' she said finally.

'It's Christmas in a few days. I'm sure she'll want to spend it with you.'

Delilah shook her head. 'Christmas has never been a good time of year for us, and Sal and I must be the most un-Christmassy people in the universe. If it wasn't for the kids, we wouldn't bother with it. No, Christmas is definitely not going to make her change her mind.'

'Then maybe give it some time, like she asked. Let everyone have some space to cool down and then call Farhan and ask if he's okay with you coming over to apologise.'

'*He's* probably the one keeping her away from me in the first place,' Delilah remarked bitterly, knowing the accusation wasn't true even as she said it.

'Well, you did put yourself in between him and his wife,' Remi pointed out. 'I know Salome's important to you, but she's married and has her own family to protect. Don't blow things out of proportion. As I remember it, you and Farhan have a great relationship, so tell him you understand why he's annoyed with you, and you are really sorry.'

Delilah exhaled in frustration. 'God, all I seem to do in my life is apologise!'

Remi raised an eyebrow, and she shook her head. She had already said far more than she'd intended. 'You're right. I'm just being defensive, but it's been so *hard* not seeing Sal.'

'I'll bet she's missed you as well, but it sounds like she's caught in the middle, so do the right thing with her husband and I'm sure it'll all work out.'

Delilah wrinkled her nose at him and then smiled wryly. 'It's sweet of you to say that, especially after the way I screwed things up with us.'

Remi shrugged. 'Life isn't predictable, and things don't always go the way we'd like. It hurt like hell when you finished with me, but I guess if we were never going to work, it's probably better we didn't drag it out and make things worse. Look, Del, I want you to be happy and if it's forgiveness you need from me, then you've got it.'

Delilah felt deeply humbled by Remi's kindness. 'That's really generous of you,' she murmured.

He released her hand and gave her an exaggerated wink as he reached for his glass. 'See what you passed up? A sweet, generous guy with great muscles!'

She laughed and their eyes locked, and, for just a second, Delilah felt a pang of regret. Remi had always been caring and considerate and had left her in no doubt that he adored her. But she had learned enough about herself over the past weeks to know it was that very intensity she had run away from. She was only grateful that, despite everything, Remi refused to hold a grudge.

'Maybe we can be friends,' she suggested hesitantly, although as soon as she'd spoken, she knew friendship wasn't what either of them wanted. Remi's 'Yeah, maybe' response sounded equally unconvinced.

An Afrobeats song started to play, and a loud cheer immediately went up in the restaurant. The song was clearly popular, and the waiter grinned and cranked up the volume so loudly Delilah felt their table vibrate. The party atmosphere made any serious conversation impossible, and she and Remi exchanged wry smiles. Delilah raised her glass and after the briefest hesitation, Remi picked his up and clinked it lightly.

'Thanks for coming out tonight,' he said, raising his voice to be heard above the music. 'It's been fantastic to see you.'

Putting her glass down, Delilah tilted her head and flashed a cheeky grin. 'Would it be really bad to order another side of fried plantain?'

26

Christmas was over, much to Delilah's relief, and she could breathe again. Staying safely cocooned in her flat watching action movies on Netflix during the chilly winter days and nights and taking the occasional walk through the nearby parks had got her through a time of year she had long struggled with. But without Salome and her family, Christmas Day had felt bleaker than ever. Not even downing an entire bottle of wine and eating her way through a huge Chinese takeaway had numbed the pain of being separated from the people she loved.

Today was their first meeting after Arne's Christmas and New Year break, and Delilah was pleasantly surprised to realise quite how much she had missed their sessions. Taking the steaming mug of coffee Arne had prepared, she cradled it for a few moments to warm up her cold fingers before setting it down and easing off her trainers. She tucked her legs under her, feeling relaxed and marvelling at how far her dread of therapy had receded. While Arne continued to challenge her, for the most part he seemed content to let her push the boundaries of their conversations at her own pace. Rather than worrying about being blindsided or caught out, Delilah now found herself wanting to share thoughts she had never admitted to anyone, including herself.

'You're looking well, Arne. Did you have a good Christmas?' She picked up her mug and settled back in the armchair.

Arne crossed his legs and leaned back in his chair. He wore a brushed cotton shirt with blue checks she hadn't seen before and which he'd tucked into his uniform brown cords. Despite having had a trim, his mop of curly red hair still gave the impression of growing in several different directions at once.

'I did, thank you,' he replied genially. 'It was very cold, but I enjoyed visiting my hometown and spending as much time outdoors as possible. And you?'

'It was great, if you don't count falling out with my sister and her husband just before the holidays,' Delilah sighed.

Arne looked taken aback. 'Is the disagreement serious?'

When Delilah made a non-committal noise and took a sip of coffee, he didn't push it, instead picking up a lined notepad by his side and skimming through its handwritten pages.

'From my notes, I see it's close to two months since we started working together,' he announced.

'Makes sense. I haven't been at work since the beginning of November, so...' Delilah shrugged, as if she wasn't painfully aware of every week that had passed since Polly's edict. Waking up each day with no job to go to had been tougher than Delilah could have imagined. She was lucky to still receive her salary, but her small flat had never been so tidy, and she was running out of ways to fill the endless empty days. Taking a trip somewhere just to break the monotony was out of the question as she was required to show up for her weekly sessions with Arne – not to mention the task she'd signed up for with Noah, she thought glumly.

'How are things progressing with your apology tour?'

Not for the first time, Delilah wondered if Arne could read minds, and she took a few sips of coffee while considering the question. She thought back to the evening she'd spent with Remi and the unconditional forgiveness he had freely offered. They had stayed in the restaurant enjoying the music and working their way through two more portions of fried plantain before eventually going their separate ways, and that night, for the first time since taking on Salome's challenge, Delilah had felt a sense of peace.

Sigmund miaowed loudly as he slunk past Delilah to leap up into the empty armchair beside her, and she forced her mind back to Arne's question.

'I guess I've finished now – well, almost,' she corrected herself as she remembered the very much unfinished business she still had with Noah. 'I met up with the final person on the list while you were away, and it went really well.'

She recounted the details of her meeting with Remi, and Arne listened intently. 'So that was that. We said our goodbyes and parted with no animosity on his side,' she concluded with a pensive smile.

'And how do you feel now you have his forgiveness?'

'Happy. Really happy. Also relieved that someone actually accepted my apology without throwing what I did back in my face.'

'And how does it feel to know Remi is still in love with you?' Arne probed gently.

She stared up at the ceiling and cast her mind back to the conversation in the restaurant. 'I was surprised although, looking back, maybe it shouldn't have been a shock given how keen he was for us to meet up. Actually, if I'm honest, I also feel a bit sad. He's a sweet guy and it would be amazing if I felt the same way about him, but I don't. It feels a bit like I'm throwing away something good.'

'Did you ever love him?'

'No, not really,' she admitted slowly. 'I've been thinking about how messed up my expectations of relationships are.'

'Can you tell me more?'

'Well, it's a bit like Goldilocks.'

Arne still looked puzzled, and Delilah grinned at his blank expression. 'You know. The girl in the fairy story who broke into the house with three bears. When she tested their beds and food, everything was either too hot or too cold. Anyway, the point is, Goldilocks had a set idea of what she wanted, and didn't compromise until she found the right fit.'

'In what way do you see this fairy tale applying to your past relationships?'

Delilah stretched out her cramped legs and wiggled her toes. 'I feel like I have certain expectations with relationships and if things go off-script, my first instinct is to shut it down.'

Arne leaned forward slightly as if keen not to miss a word. 'Go on, Delilah.'

Delilah hesitated, distracted by the intense attention. But her curiosity to explore feelings she had never articulated before overcame her uneasiness.

'I – I do want to be loved,' she said hesitantly, 'but not too much. Otherwise, it gets really uncomfortable.'

'And what is it that makes love feel like too much?'

The words spilled out before she could censor them. 'When I feel smothered. When I'm not in control. When – when love can really hurt me...'

The stark silence that followed felt so painful Delilah could have groaned. Why the *hell* had she said that? Suddenly, she felt so exposed that she wanted to melt into the depths of the armchair, and her mind raced through a hundred scenarios in seconds. What would Arne think of her admitting such a thing and how could he ever recommend to Polly that it was safe to send Delilah back to work?

It was as if a shrill voice in her head was screaming at her. *Nobody in their right minds wants a messed-up relationship counsellor*. She pulled her knees up to her chest and clasped them tightly, hiding her face as if that would protect her from the vicious words she was directing at herself.

When she eventually looked up, it was to find Arne watching her. He didn't appear shocked, and his eyes reflected only warmth and concern.

'It took courage to admit this, Delilah. Opening up with honesty and showing your vulnerability is a strength, particularly when you seek deep and authentic connections with those you are supporting.'

Arne's voice held no hint of judgement, and Delilah slowly released her grip and tried to focus on his words.

'I hear you recognise that intense love can feel overwhelming for you. How do you think this might show up when you work with clients?'

Intrigued by the framing he had placed on her unguarded admission, Delilah tried to quiet the internal voice berating her so she could mull over Arne's question.

'I suppose it might trigger me if I think someone in the couple is being controlling or exploiting the other person's love for them...' she started, and then sat bolt upright as realisation dawned. 'Oh my God, that's what I did with Janine and Brian!'

'They are your clients?'

Delilah nodded absently as her mind raced to connect the dots of a pattern she could see for the first time. 'They've been married for a long time, and Brian is really fixed in his ways. He's used to laying down the law and he knows Janine worships him, so he gets away with it. He only agreed to counselling because she watched a YouTube show about being more assertive in your marriage and then threatened to leave him if he didn't change.'

'How do you think your biases came into play with this couple?'

'I should have been facilitating their communication, but I took over...' Her voice tailed off as things came into focus.

'Polly was right,' she breathed, shaking her head in disbelief. 'I was so bent on getting Brian to admit he was in the wrong that I didn't hold Janine accountable or even encourage her to explore her part in why their relationship had become so toxic.'

Arne stroked his beard thoughtfully. 'That's a very insightful observation. If we take the "I think *you* are at fault and you need to fix yourself" approach because we think someone is wrong, then we are of no use to our clients. What would have been a more effective approach in that situation?'

Feeling like a student being put to the test, Delilah massaged her temples and thought back to the training material she'd been re-reading. 'I should have done more to build better rapport with Brian right from the start so he would trust me and see me as impartial. Then, instead of painting him as a bully, I could have asked questions that gave him a chance to articulate his fears about his wife suddenly changing the rules after decades of marriage.'

When Arne smiled, she grinned with relief. Even his tacit approval made her feel like she'd won the jackpot.

'I suggest you reflect on this further, and we can discuss it in our next session. On a different note, how do you propose to heal the rift you mentioned with your sister?'

Arne's unwelcome reminder of the dire state of relations with her family instantly crushed Delilah's sense of elation. Christmas had come and gone with no word from Salome except a brusque 'I'm not ready yet' in response to Delilah's text on New Year's Day pleading for a chance to talk. As the days went by, Delilah was feeling increasingly hurt and sorry for herself. She had only confronted Farhan because she cared about Salome, and now she was being punished for doing what any loyal sister would have done.

'Sal won't even speak to me,' Delilah muttered, not even trying to hide her resentment. 'I can't believe she's treating me like this. We've never spent this time of year apart since – well, for ages. I made a mistake, but she won't let it go! It's either that or Farhan's making her do it.'

'You sound like you feel she has abandoned you when she appears to be dealing with her own needs. Even if her husband is part of the decision, it may be that he is trying to protect her while they tackle this challenge in their relationship.'

'Protect her from *me*? Her own sister?'

'Delilah, you have spoken to me of how heavily you leaned on your sister after the shared trauma of losing your parents. Is it hard to imagine her husband might want you to support your sister in the same way she has done for you? Perhaps if you can show him your readiness to minister to Salome's needs as she does to yours, he will take a different view.'

She recognised the picture Arne painted of her big-hearted, generous sister, and there was no way Salome would have cut her out of her life unless Farhan was insisting on it. Her sister loved him, and he was counting on that to keep Delilah out of the picture. Delilah set her jaw stubbornly, ignoring the voice of reason in her head reminding her of the many ways Farhan had always loved and supported her, and focused instead on her own pain.

'You talk about one mistake, Delilah. What do you believe was your one mistake?' Arne asked.

'I told you. I should have kept my mouth shut about what Sal said about wanting to go back to work and feeling like she was in a rut at home. She did play it down afterwards, and I should have let it go. But I held up my hands to that and apologised to Farhan right in front of her! Besides, it's not as if she hasn't mentioned going back to work before, so it shouldn't have come as a massive shock to him.'

'Hmmm. I hear you saying you are sorry and yet I also hear you justifying what you are apologising for. *Are* you sorry?'

Delilah looked at Arne in exasperation. 'Of course I am! All I'm saying is that Farhan shouldn't be forcing Sal to stay at home if – *oh*!' She broke off and covered her hand with her mouth, her eyes wide with horror as her words struck home.

'Oh my God! I'm doing it again, aren't I?' she whispered. 'I'm doing it *again*. I'm judging my own brother-in-law just like I was judging Brian!'

Arne stroked his beard, and his silence confirmed what Delilah already knew. He glanced up at the clock. 'Our time is almost up, but I notice you haven't mentioned Noah.'

Delilah shook her head, shell-shocked from the barrage of truth missiles that had struck her during the session. It would be far too humiliating to admit now that Arne's reservations about her impartiality when it came to helping Noah and Zazie had been fully warranted. In any case, she still couldn't back out of her ex-boyfriend's absurd plan while she needed Noah's forgiveness to complete the challenge which might change Polly's mind.

'Nothing to report on that front,' she said quickly. Before Arne could probe further, Delilah jumped to her feet and picked up her handbag. 'Same time next week?'

27

Lying in bed staring up at the ceiling, Delilah felt like a prisoner. Two days of heavy rain had kept her trapped indoors and restricted from the long walks she had started taking to get out of her flat and out of her own head. She hadn't heard from Noah since his spat with Zazie in the café and she wasn't sure whether to be annoyed at the silence or relieved to be spared further involvement in his love life. Without a job to distract her from the monotony that had become her life, the ongoing separation from Salome was ratcheting up Delilah's levels of anxiety, and even the long chat earlier that morning with Armenique hadn't managed to ease Delilah's frustration or motivate her to get out of bed.

Just as she was contemplating ringing Polly and begging her to reconsider, her phone rang. Sending up a silent prayer that it was Salome calling to make up, Delilah picked it up and frowned at the unknown number on the screen. Curiosity overcame her instinct to cut the call, and she tapped the green icon.

'Hello?' she asked cautiously.

'Delilah?'

It took a minute for the voice to register.

'Zazie?' Caught off-guard, Delilah scrambled upright, her guilty conscience immediately sending her into a panic that Noah had told Zazie the truth about her.

'Yeah. You all right? I got your number from Noah. Look, I know you're probably really busy with work and I'm sorry to drag you out in such crap weather, but is there any chance you can meet me today?'

Zazie didn't sound like someone ready to murder her for lying about her past relationship with her man, and Delilah slowly released her breath and leaned back against the headboard. She cleared her throat and gave it a few seconds while she consulted her empty calendar.

'I might be able to make some time this afternoon. Where are you?'

'I'm in the middle of a fashion shoot, but it looks like I'll be stuck here all day cos we can't do the outdoor shots until this sodding rain stops. Listen, I really need to talk to you. If I text you the address, can you come over as soon as you're free?'

* * *

The large building with peeling blue paint on the edge of an industrial park didn't look like an obvious venue for a fashion shoot, was Delilah's first thought while carefully picking her way up a path of cracked paving stones. But then, what she knew about the fashion industry wouldn't fill the back of a postage stamp.

The rain was still bucketing down, and she huddled under the portico to close her drenched umbrella before pressing hard on the intercom. A crackly voice answered and buzzed her in before she could say a word, and she pushed open the door into what looked like a vast, empty warehouse. The large windows, dirty white walls and stained concrete floor were grimy rather than glamorous, and there was no sign of Zazie or anyone else. Making out the faint strains of music coming from down a long corridor, Delilah slipped off her wet puffer jacket and followed the sound, eventually tracking the source of the music to a room at the back.

She tapped on the closed door and when no one answered, knocked harder. Seconds later, the door flew open, and Delilah blinked in stunned surprise at the sight of Zazie in skintight denims and a silver bra top that left nothing to the imagination. Silver streaks ran along the model's sculpted cheekbones and under the arches of her eyebrows, while her shimmering metallic lipstick complemented silver highlights in her thick corkscrew curls.

The silver theme extended to glittering high-heeled sandals that added more inches to her already impressive height.

'Oh good, you made it! Come and meet the guys,' Zazie said cheerfully, grabbing Delilah's arm and pulling her into the room.

Momentarily disorientated by the pounding rap music blaring and a bank of dazzling spotlights angled around white canvas screens, it took her a moment to notice the two men in the room poring over a digital camera. They glanced up, and one of them turned a knob on a console to cut the music.

'Tony's the photographer for the shoot and Marc's his assistant,' Zazie announced with a casual wave in their direction, adding loudly, 'Guys, this is my mate, Delilah.'

Delilah returned Tony and Marc's friendly nods with an awkward smile before turning to Zazie. 'I hope I'm not interrupting, only you did say to come whenever...'

'No, it's fine. We're pretty much finished with all the indoor shots, so we're just hanging around. I'm hoping the rain stops before we lose the light cos it'll be a real pain to get all togged up again tomorrow. I'm *soo* glad you came!'

It would have been so much easier to have hated Noah's girlfriend, but Zazie's bubbly, easy charm made it impossible.

'You look incredible, by the way,' Delilah said sincerely. 'It's probably a stupid question, but... um, what exactly are you modelling?'

'*Jeans!* Can't you tell?' Zazie exclaimed, pirouetting gracefully in the spiky heeled sandals Delilah would have struggled to stand in. 'It's a new brand of denims by an up-and-coming Black designer. Sinbad's just starting out after design college and can't afford much.' She glanced at the men and lowered her voice. 'Which is why we're filming his social media ad campaign on a crap budget in this crap building. My agent thinks it's good for my image to be seen supporting the community, but between you and me, I've told him we need to raise our game. There's loads of big brands trying to book me, and I don't want to waste my time doing shoots like this where they can't even afford a friggin' make-up artist!'

'Oh, right!' Delilah said weakly, trying to keep up with Zazie's rapid-fire explanation.

Zazie looped an arm through Delilah's and drew her further out of earshot of Tony and Marc. 'I really appreciate you coming all the way out here.'

'That's okay. What did you want to talk about?'

'Noah, of course.' Zazie sounded surprised by the question.

'Oh, yes, of course. Silly me. How are things going with you two, then?' Delilah asked, bracing herself.

'We're great! After that day in the café, he rang me and apologised for being such an arse. Then, he came over to mine that night and *really* apologised – if you get my drift.' Zazie's throaty chuckle and exaggerated wink had Delilah immediately suppressing a bout of nausea. It was surreal enough knowing that Noah loved someone else without being forced to hear the intimate details.

Zazie went over to a Styrofoam cooler on a nearby table and took out two boxes of fruit juice. Handing one to Delilah, she tore the straw off the other, punctured the carton, and took a long sip. With a satisfied sigh, she glanced across to where Tony and Marc were bent over a laptop scrolling through pictures and leaned in closer to Delilah.

'Thing is, Del, just cos me and Noah are good now isn't enough. I need to sort out this issue with his mum. It doesn't matter how much he says he loves being with me, that man's *never* gonna propose if the old cow doesn't give her seal of approval.'

Delilah made a show of pushing the short plastic straw into her juice box and took a sip, silently longing to be back in the boring yet peaceful cocoon of her flat. Frankly, anything was better than being forced into a ring-side view of Noah's love life. The situation was awkward and painful, but there was no way out. *Pull up your big girl pants, Del. The sooner you help this girl, the sooner you can exit Noah's life.*

'Zazie, why do you think Mrs West doesn't like you? At the café, you said something like she wouldn't accept any woman Noah brought home. That might be true, but is there anything you might have said or done that maybe she took the wrong way – apart from the handbag, that is,' she added hastily.

Zazie's silver eyebrows merged into a metallic frown as she pondered Delilah's question. Then she shook her head. 'Nope. Nothing.'

'Nothing that's made her pull that face that looks like she's just sucked a lemon?' Delilah persisted.

'How do you know she does that?' Zazie looked at her curiously and then her eyes narrowed. 'I thought you were friends with Noah's mate?'

'I – I don't... I mean, I am,' Delilah stammered. *Damn!* The girl was as sharp as a tack. 'It must have been something Noah said that stuck in my head.'

Zazie appeared to take Delilah's words at face value, because her brow cleared. 'Like I said, I've been on at Noah about this for months, but all he ever comes back with is *I* should be patient with *her*. You've heard him yourself. His mum always comes first!'

Zazie exhaled dramatically and then shrugged. 'Things need to change cos I'm not gonna hang around forever. I look good now, but I'm not getting any younger.'

Delilah smiled in sympathy. 'I get it. I really do. But you're still young and you've got loads of time to start a family.'

Zazie had started sucking thirstily on her straw, and she promptly choked. 'You *are* joking, right?' she spluttered. 'My body's my *career*, Delilah. I can't ruin it by having kids.'

'*Oh!*' It was Delilah's turn to be shocked. If she was sure about one thing, it was the fact that Noah loved children. In the past, they had always laughed at the weird baby names celebrities came up with, swearing that when they had their own children, any names based on fruits, days of the week, or star signs were off the table. Noah must really love Zazie if he was prepared to forgo having a family, Delilah thought, wondering why the thought made her feel so miserable.

'There's nothing wrong with not wanting children as long as you're both on the same page,' she said stiltedly, trying not to sound judgemental. 'So Noah's okay with not having kids?'

Zazie's silver-framed eyes glinted with a shrewdness Delilah hadn't seen before. 'Let's just say I'm not making a big deal about the whole kids issue until I've got Noah locked in.' The sudden steeliness in her voice was in marked contrast to the earlier bubbly sweetness.

'Don't get me wrong,' she added. 'I don't have a problem with other people's kids, but my career's taking off and I'm in high demand. I'm bloody good at what I do, and my agent swears I'll be making big bucks modelling, especially abroad. When Noah and I are married, I'm gonna be travelling all over the world, and I want him by my side. He'll see for himself it makes no sense to even think about kids. But, until then, mum's the word, Delilah. Alright?'

She giggled at her own pun and then put down the juice box she had sucked dry. 'So listen, that's why I asked you to come over. I want this sorted out asap and I need your help. What do I have to do to get the old cow onside?'

Stunned by Zazie's casual attitude to telling such a monumental lie, Delilah was about to protest, and then stopped, reminding herself that this was none of her business. Zazie's bouncy puppy façade was doing a great job of hiding her inner bitch, but it didn't change the painful truth that she was the woman Noah had chosen. Delilah's only job, she told herself grimly, was to help the girl mend fences with her mother-in-law to-be and secure Noah's forgiveness. With that, she could persuade Arne and – by extension – Polly, to allow her back to work and finish her counselling qualification.

Delilah tamped down ruthlessly on the voice in her head telling her Noah deserved better. Even if she was mad enough to risk telling Noah that Zazie was lying to him, there was every chance Noah wouldn't believe her or – worse – accuse her of being jealous of his girlfriend and deliberately causing trouble between them. Whatever she thought about Zazie's behaviour, it wasn't Delilah's responsibility to act on it. *Focus on what you're here for, Del!*

Zazie was waiting for an answer, and Delilah forced a smile. 'Well, first of all, it would help if you didn't call her an old cow. Words are powerful and affect our thoughts and emotions. Here's my advice: try not to see her as an obstacle... Think of her as a concerned mother who's just trying to do her best for her son.'

Zazie pouted prettily, but Delilah ignored it. She was completely over the other girl's superficial charm. 'I know it's hard, Zazie, but you have to put your ego aside and try to empathise. Unless you make the effort to see where she's coming from, you'll keep getting resistance.'

The irony of her own words wasn't lost on Delilah, who had made no effort to put her advice into practice. For the past three years, it had been easier to hate Noah's mother for rebuffing her attempts to apologise, rather than put herself in the other woman's shoes.

'I could try, I suppose,' Zazie said dubiously.

'Here's an idea, let's try an exercise in positive affirmations.'

'What's that mean?' Zazie stared at her blankly.

'It's about framing how you communicate in a positive way,' Delilah said patiently. 'Now, imagine yourself arriving at Mrs West's front door. You're walking in and she's coming forward to greet you. What can you say to her?'

'That she's a stuck-up snob?'

'No! You're only allowed to say something positive. Think of a compliment you could give.'

Zazie's expression screamed scepticism. 'D'you know what? If you'd ever met the woman, I swear you wouldn't make this all sound like a piece of cake.'

'I *have* – I mean, I have a good idea of what she's like from what you've described. Look, you have to try something different if you want a different outcome, right? Trust me, it's a tried and tested exercise. If you lead with positive statements, it'll give Mrs West the incentive to reciprocate.'

'Hey, Zazie!'

Startled, both Zazie and Delilah turned to see Tony holding up his arm and tapping his watch. 'We'll have to call it a day, love. Even if it stopped raining now, there's no way we can set up outdoor shots today. It's just as well Sinbad paid for two days.'

Marc nodded in agreement. 'We'll pack up the equipment now and hit the road. See you back here tomorrow morning at eight, yeah?'

Zazie's face clouded, and she stamped a sandalled foot on the concrete floor. 'It took me ages to do this make-up, and I wanted to wash this stuff out of my hair tonight,' she grumbled. She turned to Delilah and her face lit up. 'Hey, Del, me and you could go for a drink now, if you like? It'll be fun and we can practise the whole affirmations thing.'

Hanging out with Zazie was the last thing Delilah wanted to do. She had seen a different side to Noah's girl today and there was no guarantee she'd be able to hide her feelings if she was left alone with her too long or avoid any more slip-ups. Walking across the room to pick up the damp jacket she had draped over the back of a chair, she slipped it on and gave Zazie an apologetic smile.

'I'm really sorry, but I have to go. I've... um... just remembered I have to call a client before the end of the day, and it'll take at least an hour to get home. Maybe another time?'

Before Zazie could object, Delilah picked up her umbrella from the floor and waved at Tony and Marc, both of whom were too preoccupied with packing their equipment to notice. Flashing Zazie a brief smile, Delilah backed out of the room and closed the door. Turning, she ran through the building, only slowing when she was outside the main door.

The rain was still pelting down as Delilah hurried down the uneven pathway, afraid to stop and catch her breath in case Zazie caught up with her. Despite her frustration with Noah, her heart ached at the idea that the woman he loved could deliberately deceive him about something as important as having children. Knowing how much damage she herself had inflicted on Noah, was she really prepared to stand by and watch another woman destroy him?

28

'Can I come in? Please?' Delilah could hear the quiver in her voice, and she cleared her throat and took a breath to calm the butterflies in her stomach.

Farhan studied her in silence, and then nodded. Stepping back, he held the door open, and Delilah crossed the threshold into the house. It was only three weeks since her last visit, but it felt more like three months as she scanned the familiar hallway nervously.

'Um... where's Sal?' she asked hesitantly. Salome's text had been brief, asking her to come over, but there was no sign of her, and it was hard to read her brother-in-law's expression.

'She's taken Arin out for a walk,' Farhan said flatly. 'She won't be long, but she wanted to give us a chance to talk alone.'

Delilah slipped off her jacket and slowly hung it on a peg while her mind raced through a succession of worst-case scenarios. What if Salome was still so angry with her, she'd left it to her husband to break the news that she didn't want to see Delilah again? Wiping her suddenly damp palms down the sides of her jeans, she turned back to stare at Farhan in mute appeal.

He sighed and scratched the rough stubble on his cheek, and then ran a hand through his hair, clearly uncomfortable.

'D'you want a cuppa?' Without waiting for an answer, he turned and walked towards the kitchen.

Delilah nodded before realising he couldn't see her. 'Yes. Please.'

She hovered in the doorway of the kitchen while Farhan filled the kettle and rummaged in the cupboard for mugs. He glanced over to where she stood and raised an eyebrow. 'I'm not going to bite. Have a seat and I'll bring the tea over.'

He didn't sound like someone getting ready to sever a close relationship, and Delilah sat down at the kitchen table as instructed. Neither of them spoke while they waited for the water to boil, and Farhan swiftly made the tea, pouring a generous splash of milk in both mugs before carrying them to the table and sitting down opposite her.

Murmuring her thanks, Delilah wrapped her hands around the warm mug while sneaking a surreptitious peek through her lashes at her brother-in-law. Three years behind Salome and Farhan at school, she still remembered how the girls in her class had swooned over Farhan's soulful eyes and curly black hair. But even then, Farhan had only been interested in Salome. This morning, he looked exhausted; the soulful eyes had deep shadows, and the black curls were sprinkled with grey strands she'd never noticed before.

'So, how've you been?' Farhan took a sip of his tea, his impassive expression making it impossible to guess his thoughts.

'Not great,' Delilah admitted. 'You look tired. Has work been busy?'

He shrugged. 'No more than usual. Arin's teething, and it's a struggle getting him to sleep through the night, but he'll grow out of it.'

'I've missed him – and Maya. All of you, actually. Thanks for agreeing to see me.'

Farhan grimaced and put down his mug, looking straight at her. 'Okay, I'll get to the point. What you said when you were here – about me not caring about Sal... well, I was beyond furious with you, because if anyone knows how much she means to me and what I'm prepared to sacrifice for her, it's you. But what you were accusing me of made me – us – face some hard truths. I've been so wrapped up in work that even though I knew Sal was struggling, I thought working from home and helping with the kids was me showing support. She always puts me first, and I should have done the same and asked her what she needed, but I didn't. What's worse is whenever she tried to tell me, I – well, I suppose I shut her down or just chose not to hear her.'

Delilah's tea sat untouched while she listened in wonderment. Having arrived more than ready to eat humble pie and do whatever it took to make things right with her sister and brother-in-law, this bald confession was the last thing she had expected.

'I don't know what to say,' she said slowly. 'I came to apologise to you and Sal. I was totally out of order that day, and it certainly wasn't my place to say anything about your marriage. The last thing I wanted was to come between the two of you. Sal loves you so much and she took back what she'd said to me as soon as the words came out, and—'

'Del, it's fine,' Farhan cut in, shaking his head emphatically. 'After you left, Sal and I had a long talk about – about everything: how she feels about staying at home, feeling isolated, what she'd like to do with her life... literally everything. We hadn't realised quite how disconnected we'd grown, but we've kept talking, which is why we asked you for space. If I'm honest, it's been a tough few weeks with more than a few tears on both sides, but we're in a good place now. So, I suppose I should thank you,' he finished with a wry grin.

Delilah looked at him, feeling at once overwhelmed by what Farhan and Salome had gone through as a couple and guilty for causing the conflict between the people she loved the most. But from Farhan's explanation, it was clear he and Salome had found a way to communicate through their crisis and strengthen their relationship.

'Maybe I'm not such a crap relationship counsellor after all?' she ventured.

'I never said you were,' he pointed out.

'I know.' Delilah sighed. 'It's just...' She paused, too ashamed to admit she was effectively unemployed again and had pleaded with her sister not to share her troubles at work with Farhan.

'So, when are you going to tell me what's going on with you?' he asked, tilting his head questioningly. 'You're here on a Friday morning, so you can't be working. Sal won't let on, but from the way the two of you have been huddling and speaking in hushed voices for God knows how long, something's obviously going on.'

Delilah took a long swallow of tepid tea, feeling guilty at the tinge of hurt in Farhan's voice. It was hard to remember the last time she had sat down for a heart to heart with him, and yet for years, the two of them had been as thick as thieves. Whether it was bypassing the payment gate to sneak into the local tennis courts and bat around balls with Farhan's old tennis racquets, teasing Salome about her obsessive neatness, or taking the kids to play in the park to give her sister a break, she had always enjoyed hanging out with him. While Farhan never let an opportunity pass to wind Delilah up, there was no question that he had been a rock for her and her sister. After their mother's death, and without ever being asked, he had stayed up with Delilah during the long sleepless nights she had sat mute with pain, making her endless cups of tea. When she eventually felt ready to live alone, it was Farhan who had hired a van to take her stuff to her new flat and built the flatpack bed and bookcases she had no clue how to assemble. For years, he had treated her like the sister he'd never had while she'd taken him for granted, casually dismissing his generosity and kindness. Yet another relationship she had messed up and needed to apologise for, she acknowledged sadly.

'You're right, Farhan, and I'm sorry. I've behaved so badly towards you and there's stuff I should have told you weeks ago.'

Putting down her mug, she recounted everything that had happened over the past several weeks, starting with her conversation with Polly. Farhan listened intently and when Delilah stopped talking, he reached across the table and covered her hand with his.

'I'm sorry you've had to go through all this. I wish you'd told me what was going on.'

'I was embarrassed,' she said quietly. 'I didn't want to admit you were right when you were joking about how I can't hold down a job. I've made such a mess of things and at this point, I honestly don't know if Polly will ever give me my job back.'

Farhan mulled over her words and looked at her thoughtfully. 'D'you know what, Del. Most people run and hide rather than face up to the damage they've done to other people. So, big respect to you for going and finding these guys and owning your mistakes.'

'It's definitely been a journey,' Delilah conceded with a humourless laugh. 'I've learned a lot about myself, and a lot of it isn't good.'

'But you're holding yourself accountable. And therapy… really?'

'Well, it was either that or get the sack. But actually, Arne's been amazing. He's intimidating at first glance, like he's this super-tall Norwegian with big, flaming-red hair and a thick beard – but he's the gentlest soul. He's very empathetic and he really gets it when I feel uncomfortable or ashamed and doesn't judge me. It can get a bit tricky sometimes, especially when he starts down the "What were your parents like and what kind of childhood did you have?" line of questioning. But all in all, it's been good to have someone objective to help me reflect on my own emotional skills – or lack of them!'

Farhan shook his head. 'You going to therapy is something I never thought I'd see – and that should count for something with your boss, surely?'

'Maybe. But now I've got myself tangled up in this situation with Noah and – and Zazie. If I mess *that* up, Arne will never give me the go-ahead. He warned me that I couldn't stay impartial, and I made such a big deal about how my feelings for Noah were strictly in the past...' She tailed off miserably.

Farhan squeezed her hand reassuringly. 'Hey, give yourself some credit. I know it's been a lot, but you're strong, Del. Stronger than I think you realise – look how far you've come since... everything...' He sighed. 'I know I take the piss out of you at times, but I've got a lot of faith in you. You'll work this out.'

Before Delilah could reply, she heard the front door slam, followed by the sound of Salome's voice.

'Hello!'

'We're in here,' Farhan called out, and moments later Salome walked in carrying Arin. She looked apprehensive, her gaze darting from Delilah to Farhan.

'It's okay.' Farhan smiled. 'We've talked, and it's all good.'

Salome exhaled loudly. 'Thank God! I was terrified I'd come back and find you two trading blows in my kitchen.'

Delilah rolled her eyes. 'Seriously, Sal?'

Salome's grin lit up her face and she handed Arin to Farhan and rushed over to Delilah, who stood up and walked into her sister's open arms. They held each other tightly for a long moment, and then Delilah pulled away, wiping her eyes.

'I'm sorry I was such an awful pain,' she sniffed. 'You and Farhan have every right to hate me.'

'That'll never happen, hon,' Salome said gently, stroking Delilah's cheek. 'God, I've missed you *so* much! Farhan explained why...?' She turned to her husband, and he nodded.

'Yeah, but I'll leave you to spill the details you guys seem to share when I'm not around.'

Salome and Delilah immediately exchanged a guilty look and Farhan burst out laughing. 'Honestly, you should see your faces!'

He tossed a squirming Arin into the air and then snuggled his face into his son's neck, blowing a loud raspberry. 'Okay, my boy. Let's leave your mum and auntie to it and go and play wreck Daddy's computer, yeah?'

Delilah watched Farhan leave and then turned back to Salome. 'I've been such a selfish cow,' she said penitently. 'Honest, Sal, you've been a second mother to me since Mum died, and I wouldn't have survived without you. No,' she insisted as Salome tried to interrupt her. 'Farhan was right to call me out on my crap. I knew you were struggling, and I should have been there for you instead of judging him.'

Salome eyed Delilah suspiciously. 'Who are you and what the hell have you done with my sister?'

Delilah grinned and grabbed Salome into a tight hug, feeling lighter and happier than she had in weeks. Farhan was right: she *was* tough, and she would figure things out. But right now, she had her family back, and everything else paled into insignificance.

'Come on, then,' Salome said, releasing Delilah and rubbing her hands briskly. 'Let's get the kettle on. I need an update on *everything*!'

Two cups of herbal tea later, Salome sat back open-mouthed. 'What? *All* of this happened in the last three weeks?'

'I know, right?' Delilah grimaced. 'So now, I'm stuck with helping Zazie to work her charms on Mrs West so Noah can propose.'

Salome stared at her accusingly. '*Really?* Even though you still have feelings for him?'

Delilah ducked her sister's probing gaze and studied her nails intently. 'That's neither here nor there. Whatever I feel – or don't feel – doesn't alter the fact that I'm trapped into helping him to be with someone else.'

Changing the subject before Salome could delve further, Delilah said softly, 'I'm so glad you and me are okay again. I really do wish I'd been a better sister. Working with Arne has forced me to dig deep and think about the past and all the things I've spent so much energy trying to suppress.'

Salome leaned forward to take her hands between hers, and Delilah returned the pressure gratefully, not realising how cold her fingers were until she felt the warmth of her sister's hands.

Salome said softly, 'I'm happy you're seeing Arne, hon. We've been through a lot and asking for help isn't a sign of weakness.'

Delilah nodded. It was exactly what Arne had said, but after years of refusing to open up her past to scrutiny, convinced that it had no bearing on her present, it was still a challenge to acknowledge quite how wrong she had been. 'For years, I've pretended I'm over everything that happened, but finding my exes and apologising for treating them so badly has made me see how I'm still stuck in – you know, every time I feel a guy getting too close to me, it feels like I'm in danger and back there again. With Mum and... *him*.' Struck by the enormity of her confession, Delilah lapsed into silence while Salome gently rubbed her hands.

'I know this process is tough, hon, but I'm glad it's helping to bring you some clarity,' Salome said soberly.

'Okay, enough about me, how are *you* doing?' Delilah released Salome's hands, ready to change the subject. 'It was good to catch up properly with Farhan, and it sounds like you two have been through the mill.'

Salome smiled happily. 'I'm great and feeling really positive. Farhan and I have talked – and I mean, *properly* talked – more in the past three weeks than we have in years. I suppose that's what having kids does to your marriage if you let it. Neither one of us was communicating properly, and I know I should've been honest and articulated what I needed. I'm more focused about therapy, too, and Alison's helping me do better at letting go and not feeling like everything has to be perfect.'

'Thank God!' Delilah exclaimed with an exaggerated whoosh of relief. 'I know you think I'm all over the place but sometimes, sister dearest, it's okay to be a little messy.' She grinned and tilted her mug to pour a small splash of tea onto the pristine kitchen table.

When Salome instantly glared at her, Delilah widened her eyes innocently. 'What? It's just a tiny spill. Think of it as aversion therapy – you know, to help you get over your compulsion for perfection.'

Salome gritted her teeth, and Delilah cocked an eyebrow. 'Too soon?'

Salome stared at her for a beat, and then they both exploded into laughter, howling hysterically until they were bent over double and gasping for breath.

'Oh – oh, oh God!' Salome wheezed, clutching her stomach. 'I haven't laughed so hard in ages!'

Delilah wiped the tears under her eyes and tried to catch her breath. 'Where are you going?'

Salome was already halfway to the kitchen counter, returning seconds later with a strip of paper towel. 'To clean up your mess. I said I was working on it – I didn't say I was there yet!'

Delilah chuckled softly as she watched her sister wipe the spilt tea. Sometimes you had to know when to cut your losses.

Tossing the tissue into the bin, Salome sat down again, and her expression sobered. 'So what are you going to do about Noah?'

The kitchen door opened, and Farhan stuck his head through the gap. 'I'm going upstairs to change Arin.'

Delilah instantly pushed back her chair and sprang to her feet. 'Sal, I don't know what I'm going to do about Noah. But what I *do* know is I'm going to show you right now that I meant everything I said about being a better sister.'

Marching up to Farhan, she held out her arms. 'Hand over the baby. And as for you, young Arin, you can take that look off your face right now. Auntie Del's on nappy duty today, so get used to it!'

29

Delilah pulled the front door shut behind her and headed for the outside bin, holding the small sack filled with Arin's soiled nappy at arm's length. After she reluctantly handed her phone to her nephew, the second nappy change had gone a lot more smoothly than the first and drooling over her mobile had kept him still long enough for her to strap on a clean nappy.

The morning and lunchtime with her family had passed quickly, and Delilah was feeling happier than she had in ages. Her relationship with Salome and Farhan was back on track and they had shared their plan with her to enrol Arin into a local nursery for a few days a week, allowing Salome to look for a part-time PR job. Delilah, for her part, had offered regular babysitting support to give the couple more quality time together.

As she lifted the lid of the grey refuse bin, Delilah caught a flash of movement in the corner of her eye and glanced up just in time to see Noah, head down, striding up the street in her direction. Without thinking, she dropped the lid and ducked down behind the bin, praying he hadn't seen her. *What the hell was he doing here in the middle of a working day!* Crouching into a tight ball with her back against the dividing fence, she pressed herself against the rough wood while her heart pounded furiously. She hadn't spoken to Noah since Zazie had admitted her plan to trick him into marriage, and Delilah was terrified of facing him when she knew he was being lied to. At some point, she knew she'd have to come clean with Noah, but she wasn't ready yet – and definitely not while she was clutching a bag with a soiled nappy.

When she heard the sound of a door slamming, Delilah counted to ten and then stood up cautiously, keeping a wary eye on the house next door while she opened the bin and tossed the nappy sack inside. She brushed down her coat and hurried along the path to the gate. With her eyes firmly fixed on the door to Noah's family home, it was too late to stop herself from crashing headlong into Noah's mother, who was approaching from the opposite direction.

'*Oh!* I – I'm so sorry,' Delilah gasped, her arms flailing as she tried to keep her balance. 'It's my fault! I should have been looking—'

'Yes, you *should*! You nearly knocked me over,' Mrs West cut in sharply, holding on to the gate to steady herself. Her caramel-brown eyes, so like Noah's, blazed with anger. 'But then being considerate of other people isn't your strong point, is it?' she added furiously.

Delilah flinched at the jibe, but this was the first time in years the woman had deigned to speak to her, and she seized the opportunity to plead her case.

'Mrs West, I know you're very upset with me, and I don't blame you,' she said humbly. 'What – what I did to Noah was unforgiveable and—'

'It was indeed unforgiveable.' Mrs West cut into Delilah's stumbling narrative once again. 'But I'm not the one you should be saying this to.'

It was hard not to feel intimidated by the woman's stony face and acid tone, but Delilah continued doggedly. 'I – I know. I've spoken to Noah and apologised...' She tailed off as Mrs West's eyes widened with incredulity.

'*You've* spoken to Noah? When was this?'

'Um... well, we've met a couple of times over the past few weeks.'

'That sounds very unlikely. He hasn't mentioned it to me.'

Bristling at the implication she was lying, Delilah fought the urge to point out Noah was an adult and under no obligation to tell his mother everything that happened in his life. But the news that Delilah was in touch with her son was clearly infuriating his mother.

'You really have a nerve, d'you know that? How dare you have the gall to even *breathe* near my son after the way you treated him?'

Her nostrils flared and her face tightened with anger, causing Delilah to take an involuntary step back. 'My Neville and I opened our home to you, but our trust was misplaced. I always suspected you didn't have staying power, but

I held my tongue for Noah's sake. I should have followed my instinct and persuaded Noah to finish with you before you hurt him so grievously.'

Although Mrs West would probably have considered herself too refined to raise her voice, Delilah would have infinitely preferred being shouted at to the quiet, cutting tone laced with contempt. By breaking Noah's heart, she had created an enemy in his mother – not that there had ever been much love to lose from that quarter. And yet, behind the verbal assault, Delilah could hear pain, and a tiny part of her understood the woman's deep visceral reaction to the girl who had so badly damaged her son.

'I hope Noah has made it clear he has a girlfriend now?' Mrs West continued, and Delilah winced at the triumph in her voice. But remembering her promise to Noah, she drew on the advice she had offered Zazie only days earlier and kept her tone even.

'Yes, he has. Look, Mrs West, about Noah and me. We – we're just friends.'

'*Friends!* And you seriously expect me to believe that's all *you* are prepared to settle for?'

'Noah's a grown man,' Delilah protested. 'He knows what he wants and – anyway, he's happy with Zazie.'

'Yes, he is. But, somehow, when it comes to you, my boy loses every bit of his common sense.' She took a step forward and her voice hardened. 'You are not to be trusted and I'm warning you, Delilah. *Keep away from him!*'

Seeing the contempt in the woman's face caused tears to spring into Delilah's eyes and spill down her cheeks. Overwhelmed by the venom in Mrs West's words and her own spiralling emotions, Delilah didn't immediately register the sound of the gate or see Noah until he was standing beside her.

'What's going on? I saw the two of you through the window.' He directed the question at his mother, who pressed her lips into a tight line and stared ahead with an expression set like concrete.

Delilah covered her mouth with a trembling hand, unable to hold back the tears cascading down her face. Noah glanced at her and his expression darkened. 'What did you say to her, Mum?'

'Nothing she didn't deserve to hear,' his mother said defiantly.

Noah looked from her to Delilah and then back again. 'Can't you see you've upset her?' he demanded.

'*I've* upset *her*? Have you forgotten so quickly how much she upset *you* –

and not just you but all of us with what she did! I don't know how you can even stand to look at her, much less...'

Noah's eyes narrowed. 'Much less what?'

'I may be getting on, son, but I am *not* naïve. I can see where this is going. First you start talking to her and the next thing I know, you'll be telling your father and me how everything that happened before was just a big misunderstanding and she's a lovely girl and not the nasty, self-centred madam she showed herself to be.'

Noah stared at her in outrage. '*Mum!*'

Mortified, Delilah fumbled in her pocket for the tissue she'd stuffed there earlier and swiped it across her damp cheeks.

'It's okay, Noah. Please don't fight with your mum because of me. She's got every right to be furious. I'm sorry. I'm so *so* sorry for what I did...' Her voice, husky with tears, broke as she looked pleadingly at Mrs West.

For a fleeting moment, the woman's expression seemed to soften, but then her mouth tightened, and it was as if a mask had come down. 'Are you sorry enough to leave my son alone now he's happy with someone else?'

'*Back off*, Mum!' Noah snapped. 'You've got no right to speak to her like that. Come on, Del!'

To Delilah's astonishment, Noah reached out a hand and she stared at him dumbly for a moment before slowly reaching out to take it, her skin tingling as his hand closed over hers. Her legs suddenly felt weak, and they seemed to move of their own volition when Noah gently tugged her towards him. She felt as if she'd been catapulted into a parallel universe as she found herself walking away with Noah while his mother stood open-mouthed on the pavement.

30

Thin rays of sunshine peeked through the heavy clouds overhead as Delilah walked down the tree-lined avenue, holding on to Noah's hand. She knew he was just being kind and she should let go, but she was reluctant to lose the comfort of his touch, and they continued on in silence. At the end of the road, Noah turned into the entrance leading into the park and Delilah went along without protest.

School was over, and in the small playground, a few adults watched on the sidelines as children wrapped in warm coats and jackets over their uniforms climbed the frames and jumped onto swings and seesaws.

As Noah still hadn't spoken, and Delilah had no idea of how to break the silence, they continued along the path running through the park, navigating children on scooters and parents pushing buggies, until they reached a stream flanked with tall trees overhanging its banks. They walked onto a narrow bridge over the stream and Noah stopped in the middle and released Delilah's hand. Leaning on the stone balustrade, he stared moodily into the murky grey water cascading over the mossy stones visible in the stream. Delilah glanced at him uncertainly, remembering how often in the past they had stood at this exact spot on the bridge, laughing and jostling each other as they competed to toss pebbles onto targets in the water below, and wondering why Noah had chosen to bring her here.

'I'm sorry about what happened. Mum had no right to speak to you like that,' he said, finally breaking the silence.

Shaken by the ugly scene with his mother, Delilah couldn't keep the tremble from her voice. 'She's still so furious with me for what happened. I don't think she'll ever forgive me.'

'It's just that she's – no!' He shook his head violently. 'No, I refuse to make excuses for her! She's my mother and I love her, but what she said was completely out of order.'

He sighed heavily. 'I don't know what it's going to take for her to understand that I need to live my own life, but I'll talk to her, Del. I promise.'

Lost for words in the face of Noah's unexpected defence, Delilah nodded and stared intently into the water. In the distance, she could hear the faint sound of children laughing, and she leaned on the wall, resting her elbow against his as they watched a couple of brown-feathered ducks waddle across the grassy bank and into the stream, their flapping wings sending fat drops of water into the air.

'Zazie said you went to see her at work,' Noah said eventually.

'Yes.' It was hard to tell from his voice how he felt about it, and she glanced sideways at him and then quickly looked away, following the progress of the ducks down the fast-flowing stream. She felt him turn towards her but didn't dare to meet his eyes for fear of spilling the beans about Zazie's shady tactics. Not that she was much better, Delilah thought sadly. She had kept so many things from Noah, and even now, he had no idea why she had really agreed to his stupid plan.

'I appreciate you doing that. I know you're busy,' Noah added after a while.

The ducks were now in the distance, and Delilah turned away from the stream to face him. This, at least, was her truth to tell. 'No, I'm not.'

'What?'

She thrust her hands into the pockets of her jeans and forced herself to meet his eyes. 'I'm not working. I've been suspended. Truth is, I'm not exactly the best trainee relationship counsellor and, well... let's just say that I've been told to sort out my own issues before I can get my job back. So, I've been trying to make amends to people I've hurt in the past and show my boss I'm self-aware enough to do my job properly.'

Delilah held her breath in the tense silence that followed, bracing herself as she waited for the bomb to drop.

'Is *that* why you showed up out of the blue asking for my forgiveness?'

Delilah nodded miserably. Now he knew she'd lied to him – or at the very least withheld the full truth – there was no chance on earth he'd forgive her. Everything she had gone through from dealing with Noah's hostility, trying to help Zazie, and facing his mother's vitriol, had basically been for nothing. She turned away as tears filled her eyes, and to her confusion, Noah gently turned her face back towards him, stroking away a tear that had spilled onto her cheek. Their eyes locked, and her breath quickened. She could see the rapid rise and fall of his chest and moments later, without breaking eye contact, he pulled her so close that she could feel his heart beating against hers. He lowered his head and the instant their lips touched, Noah groaned and pulled her closer, his fingers cradling her head. His lips, warm and sensuous, moved feverishly over her face and neck before returning to her lips, kissing her deeply until she couldn't think straight. She kissed him hungrily and stroked his face, relishing the taste of him and the feel of his stubble against her touch. She didn't care who might see them as she arched her body into his, burning with the need to hold him as close as possible.

Then, as suddenly as Noah had reached for her, he let her go, leaving Delilah gasping for breath and desperate to be back in his arms. He closed his eyes as if he was in pain and ran a trembling hand through his hair, his breathing as ragged as if he'd run a mile. Although a part of her wanted to curl up and die at the brusque rejection, a bigger part couldn't stop herself from moving up against him or reaching up to encircle his neck with her arms.

'*Noah...?*' she whispered with agonised urgency.

'Don't, Delilah.'

She flinched and stared at him in frustration. 'But—'

'—but *nothing*. I'm with Zazie now.' He wrenched her arms from around his neck and turned away, his shoulders heaving as he took in deep, uneven gulps of air.

His words were like a hot steel dagger piercing her heart and for a long moment, Delilah closed her eyes and wrapped her arms around herself, trying to absorb the pain. But she couldn't leave it.

'I know you're with Zazie,' she said quietly, 'but do you love her? *Really* love her?'

When he appeared to hesitate, she persisted. 'Because if you don't—'

'Of course I do!' he said harshly. 'Do you think I'd be putting myself through this mess with you if I didn't want Zazie and me to have a future together – if I *didn't* love her?'

It felt like she was drowning under a wave of pure anguish. 'So why did you kiss me?' she pleaded.

'I shouldn't have. It was a mistake. I was feeling sorry for you after what my mum said and... well...'

She could feel the heat start in her chest and work its way up to erupt into her face. If he had slapped her, it would have hurt less. If Noah's goal was to humiliate her, he was doing a great job, but she had nothing left to lose and deep in her soul, she knew Noah still had feelings for her. He *had* to!

'I've said I'm sorry for – for what happened between us a hundred times! Noah, what more can I do?' she begged.

'"For what happened"? You can't even say the words, can you? You *dumped* me twenty-four hours before we were supposed to take vows to spend the rest of our lives together. You broke up with me over the phone without a word of explanation and then disappeared. And then, after literally years of silence, you show up out of the blue because your job is at risk – to say what? *Sorry?* And I'm supposed to just let it all go and forgive you? What the fuck, Delilah! What don't you understand? You *broke* me!'

Delilah's hand flew to her mouth, stunned by the raw pain in his eyes. Her heart felt like it was cracking in her chest and any vestige of hope that the kiss had meant something disappeared, leaving her utterly defeated.

'Do you know how hard it's been to trust any woman again after what you did to me?' He looked away, and she could see the muscle at the side of his jaw working as he fought for control. After a few moments, he turned back, looking her straight in the eyes.

'Maybe I don't love Zazie in the same way I loved you, but she's a great girl. She's honest and transparent and I know she genuinely cares for me. But d'you know the biggest thing she's got going for her? She's *not* you!'

31

Delilah turned off the television and tossed the remote onto the side table before flopping back against the sofa. Her thoughts were jumping around too erratically to concentrate on the reality show featuring semi-naked contestants on an island trying to find love.

It was two days since Noah's brutal rejection in the park, and she had closeted herself in her flat, swinging between bouts of deep sadness and abject humiliation. She couldn't stop thinking about Noah and their kiss, and Zazie's constant texts with suggestions for worming her way into Mrs West's good graces brought further shame. Despite feeling guilty for kissing Zazie's boyfriend, Delilah was too outraged by the girl's brazen plan to trick Noah into proposing to speak to her, and she'd settled for responding to each text with a single thumbs-up emoji.

When Delilah had finally broken her self-imposed silence and had rung Salome, the call hadn't gone as she'd hoped. While her sister had listened patiently to Delilah's tearful recounting of the awful encounter with Mrs West and going to the park with Noah, when she reached the part about the kiss, her sister's shriek had been deafening.

'You did *what*?'

'*I* didn't do anything. Noah kissed *me*!'

'And you pushed him away, right?'

Delilah hesitated a fraction too long.

'Don't bother lying, I get the picture,' Salome said grimly. 'Delilah Braithwaite, what exactly are you playing at? You *know* the man's got a girlfriend! I warned you not to get mixed up in his relationship issues, didn't I? You had one job – apologise for what happened between the two of you and move on!'

This was no time for I-told-you-so's, Delilah thought despondently. Anyone with half a brain could have predicted that nothing good could come of helping an ex-boyfriend rescue his current relationship.

'Sal, no one planned for this to happen,' she said with a defeated sigh. 'I was upset, and Noah was trying to comfort me and... well, we – we just got carried away. But then he told me in no uncertain terms that it's Zazie he loves, so that's that!'

Salome was silent for a while, and then exhaled deeply, the sound coming clearly down the line. 'I'm sorry, hon. I know this can't be easy for you. I just don't want to see you get hurt. You've said yourself that Zazie's lovely and—'

'—and a lying bitch.'

'Wait... what?'

Immediately wishing she had kept her mouth shut, Delilah said hastily, 'Forget it. I'm just fed up with the whole thing, that's all.'

'Delilah! *Why*. Is. Zazie. A. Lying. Bitch?'

Salome was like a relentless terrier with a bone when she chose, and knowing from bitter experience that it was easier to give in rather than prolong the pain, Delilah reluctantly divulged Zazie's confession at the fashion shoot.

'What the *hell*?' Salome exploded. 'That girl isn't a lying bitch, she's pure evil! Who *does* that to someone they love? Del, this is awful! Noah absolutely *adores* kids – Maya's all over him whenever we bump into him, and you know she hates most people.'

'I know, I *know*!' Delilah muttered under her breath. She didn't need reminding her ex-boyfriend was a natural with children – especially when there was nothing she could do with the bombshell Zazie had dropped.

'You *are* going to tell him, aren't you?' Salome demanded. 'Noah can't get into something as serious as marriage with a woman who's lying to his face!'

'Zazie says they haven't really talked about having children, so I suppose technically she's not lying...' Delilah tailed off with a groan. 'Sal, it's none of my business. If I tell Noah, especially after what happened in the park, he's just going to think I'm the bitch who's trying to blow up his relationship.'

'Maybe so, but how can you live with yourself if you don't tell him, huh? No, Delilah! Noah's a good guy and he doesn't deserve this. You *have* to tell him!'

The testy exchange had left Delilah feeling more confused than ever, and she dragged herself off the couch, slipped on her trainers and reached for her hoodie. Too much thinking was giving her a headache, and two days moping in her flat and obsessing about her lost love was long enough. She needed to get out and clear her head.

She was almost at the door when her mobile buzzed. Praying it wasn't Zazie calling, Delilah glanced at her phone and her heart skipped a beat when she saw Noah's name flashing. She stared at the screen for a moment, wanting desperately to answer it and yet terrified of what he might say. She took a breath and then answered.

'Noah?' She felt her heart thudding painfully in her chest.

His voice sounded as crisp as if he was standing next to her. 'Can I come over?'

32

Delilah ripped off the jumper in frustration and tossed it onto her bed to join the discarded pile of clothes. It had been almost an hour since Noah's call and unless she planned to face her ex-boyfriend wearing nothing more than trousers and a bra, she didn't have much time left to find something decent to wear.

What was even more frustrating was that she still had no clue why he was coming over. *Get a move on, Del!* She faced the full-length mirror, turning to the side to check the fit of the black jeans hugging her small waist and curvy bottom. If she didn't want Noah turning up to find her half-naked... She hurriedly shut down her imagination before it went any further and opened her closet door to flip through the hangers again. Aiming for casual chic when your wardrobe was more like casual slob wasn't easy. She pounced on a silky black t-shirt with an asymmetric neckline she had missed earlier and pulled it off the hanger, slipping it on while her mind continued its feverish speculation.

'*Can I come over?*' The four words weren't much to go on, and Noah's tone had given nothing away. While his parting words before he'd left her standing on the bridge had been brutal, what if the kiss they'd shared had changed his mind about his feelings for Zazie?

Delilah ran her fingers through her twists and carefully brushed back her edges. Smoothing her eyebrows with her finger, she picked up a tube of mascara and then paused to stare at her face in the mirror. *You're doing exactly what his bloody mother said you would!* She bit her lip and tossed the tube, unused, back into her make-up bag.

'Noah is with Zazie! Noah is with Zazie! Noah is with Zazie!' She chanted the words aloud to block any rogue fantasies from slipping through and began to fold the clothes scattered across her bed. She was concentrating so hard on not thinking that it took a moment for the doorbell chime to register.

Adrenaline raced through her body, and she stood indecisively until the doorbell sounded again and jolted her into action. Dropping the jumper she'd been folding, she turned towards the door and promptly banged her toe against the corner of the bed. A stab of intense pain ran through her foot, and she hopped out of the room, cursing under her breath. By the time she reached her front door and pressed the Entryphone button to the building, the throbbing in her toe was agony.

She opened her door and heard Noah's footsteps bounding up the stairs, and within seconds, he was inside the flat. She waved him through, hobbling slowly behind him and biting her lip to stifle the moans threatening to emerge.

He walked into the living room and turned to watch her slow progress. 'What's wrong with your foot?'

'I just stubbed my toe on the bed,' she replied, sinking into the nearest armchair and rubbing her toe gingerly, trying not to whimper from the pain.

'Have you got any ice? Or frozen peas?'

'Huh?' Delilah looked at him blankly.

He sighed in exasperation and walked into the small kitchen at the end of the living room, pulling open the freezer and rummaging through its sparse contents.

'Do you ever buy food? This stuff looks like it's been here for years!'

She pulled a face and watched him take out a small bag of ice cubes. He shook half of it into the kitchen towel draped over the sink and twisted the towel into a tight ball. Coming back to kneel beside her, he gently lifted her foot, and her body immediately stiffened at his touch.

'Where does it hurt?'

She pointed silently to her small toe, and he carefully held the ice-filled towel against it. Despite her pain, she shivered at the sensation of Noah's warm fingers on her skin, and terrified he would see how his touch affected her, she snatched the cold compress away and flashed a nervous smile.

'Thanks, it's fine... I can do it myself.' She waved him towards the sofa. 'Sit down. Please.'

Noah eyed her for a second and then released her foot and stood up. He sat on the sofa facing her and nodded towards her foot.

'Does it feel better?'

Delilah nodded, pressing the makeshift ice pack against her numb toe. The stabbing pain was subsiding into a dull ache, but her bigger concern was why Noah was in her flat.

'So what brings you here? After what you said the other day, I didn't think you ever wanted to see me again.' She tried to keep her tone light, but it was hard to stop the hurt seeping into her voice.

Noah dropped his gaze and massaged the back of his neck. 'I know,' he said gruffly. 'What I said to you in the park... it was cruel and – and unnecessary. I wanted to check you're okay. I don't want any hard feelings between you and me.'

'Oh,' she said, her voice hollow with disappointment. She knew she could be the queen of wishful thinking, but despite the stern talking to she had given herself, she had still secretly hoped Noah was coming to confess he felt something for her.

'I suppose it's my turn to apologise.' With his hands clasped together and one leg jiggling furiously, Noah couldn't have looked more uncomfortable if he'd tried. 'I was well out of order kissing you in the park and then making things worse by attacking you instead of taking accountability for my actions.'

As if he couldn't bear to sit any longer, he stood up and wandered over to the window, peering through the blinds into the street before turning back to face her. He ran a hand over his face and then sighed heavily.

'I won't lie, Del. Sometimes it's hard to be around you after what went down with us before, and I—'

He broke off and walked over to crouch in front of her, looking deeply into her eyes. He was close enough for her to see the dark flecks in the brown of his eyes and smell the clean lemon notes of his cologne.

'You... what?' she asked breathlessly, a tiny spark of hope igniting despite herself.

He shook his head. 'I needed time to work through my feelings about the past. For a minute back there in the park, it felt like we still had unfinished business, but I've thought long and hard about this, and for your sake and mine, it's time to let go of my anger. I'm ready to try so we can both move on. Is that okay with you?'

'Absolutely!'

'So, we're good?'

'Of *course*!' Delilah nodded emphatically.

Noah drew himself up to his full height and grinned, and Delilah responded with a bright smile, wondering if he could hear the sound of her heart breaking. She could see the relief in his eyes, and she swallowed the bitterness she could taste in her mouth, determined not to show him how much she was hurting and invite his pity.

She changed the subject before she started to cry. 'I haven't spoken to Zazie, but she's been sending me texts with ideas about how she can connect better with your mum. How's that going?'

'Funny you should ask, cos that's the other thing I wanted to tell you.'

What fresh hell is this man about to announce? Delilah braced herself for more pain, praying for the day she could disentangle herself from Noah's life.

'There's been a breakthrough on that front, and the funny thing is Zazie didn't need to do anything. Mum called yesterday and invited us round to theirs for lunch next Sunday. She said she wanted to get to know Zazie better.'

'*Oh...!*' Delilah stared at him blankly.

'I know, right? The best part is Zazie's actually excited to go. She really seems to like you, and it looks like your advice has done the trick cos I swear before she met you, she'd have refused point blank or found some excuse. But when I told her, she seemed really excited and said if Mum's extending an olive branch, she's willing to meet her halfway.'

He smiled wryly. 'Look, Del, I know it's been weird for both of us, what with our history and everything, but you've really helped Zazie and me turn the corner on this situation with Mum, and I want to thank you.'

Delilah smiled through lips that felt as frozen as the ice cradling her injured toe. 'I didn't really do much, but I'm pleased for you, Noah. For both of you. I hope everything works out.'

Noah's expression sobered. 'Me too. I can't have the two most important women in my life at odds with each other. Mum and Zazie will probably never be best friends but if they can get along, I'm comfortable about taking things to the next level.'

Delilah nodded sympathetically even as her mind was furiously connecting the dots. The timing of his mother's invitation was no coincidence. Delilah's attempt to make peace with Mrs West had clearly backfired, especially after Noah's unexpected defence of his ex-fiancée. It seemed his mother was prepared to do anything to get rid of Delilah – including belatedly rolling out the welcome mat for Zazie. The irony that Zazie was planning to deprive Mrs West of the grandchildren she constantly harped on about was obvious, but she and Noah had agreed to put any acrimony behind them, and it wasn't her place to interfere. She could only hope Zazie would do the right thing and admit her feelings about having kids to Noah before it was too late.

Suddenly desperate for Noah to leave, Delilah dropped the sodden towel of melting ice on the side table and stood up. The emotional darts lobbed in her direction since Noah's arrival had overtaken the pain in her toe, and she could feel tears building up behind her eyes. Limping gingerly to the front door, she opened it, and Noah gave her a friendly hug that made her want to weep like a baby. She glanced at his arm, wondering again about the crown tattoo. What difference would it make even if it was still there, she thought wearily. Whatever was printed on his arm, Noah had left her in no doubt that he had moved on in his heart.

He stood in the doorway and held her gaze. 'It's time we both started a new chapter, Del. I want you to know I'm not holding a grudge any more. You came to me to ask for my forgiveness, and it's yours. I really hope you get your job back cos from everything I've seen, you'd make an awesome relationship counsellor.'

He cuffed her gently on the chin. 'Don't give up on your dream, you hear?'

Forcing a smile, Delilah nodded and watched him take the stairs two at a time before closing the door and leaning back against it. She let out the breath she had been holding, but that didn't stop the tears rolling down her face. Noah had forgiven her. She had finally got what she wanted, so why did she feel so empty inside? Walking back to sit on the couch that was still warm from Noah, she curled up into a ball and sobbed. Gone was the secret hope she had harboured for a reset in their relationship. Arne and Salome had been right, and even Armenique had warned her to keep her distance. Second chances only happened in romance novels, not in real life.

33

'*Please*, Polly! I've been working on myself like you wouldn't believe. For months, I've reflected on and assessed my past relationships like you said. I've explained to you how I've gone in search of my ex-boyfriends and taken accountability for my behaviour and made amends. I've seen Arne every single Monday except when he went on holiday, and I am so much clearer about myself. I totally get my biases and my triggers, and – and everything! I want – no, I *need* to come back to work. I promise things will be different.'

With little else to do except nurse her broken heart, Delilah had impulsively risked a final throw of the dice by calling Polly first thing on Monday morning. Polly had sounded pleased to hear from her and had listened carefully while Delilah explained her progress with therapy and detailed her reflections about the impact of her past relationships and her learning.

But, despite her manager's pleasant and sympathetic tone, it was clear to Delilah that her pleas to return to work were landing on stony ground, and Polly wasn't going to shift.

'I can tell you're making great progress and it's so encouraging that you've spent this time re-examining your past relationships, Del. It's clear you're working on yourself, and this will all help make you an amazing and compassionate counsellor. I'm delighted you're sticking with therapy. It's crucial and I knew you'd find the sessions helpful – and didn't I tell you Arne's the absolute best?'

'But Polly—'

'Delilah, listen to me,' Polly interrupted. 'Therapy isn't a magic switch. If you want to see real change, you need to do the work with Arne so you can sustain your progress for the long term.'

'But I don't need fixing!' Delilah burst out in frustration.

There was a short silence and then Polly said gently, 'This isn't about *fixing* you, Del. You are not broken. We all have unresolved issues; it's called being human. Going through therapy is so we can learn about ourselves and understand our conscious and unconscious patterns – what they are, where they started, what keeps them going, and how we improve ourselves so we can serve those in our care and not let our issues spill onto our clients. But counselling only works if we have explored and, most crucially, *changed* our behaviour. I want you to give this process a little more time, and you'll see the reward from the efforts you put in.'

When Delilah didn't answer, Polly went on. 'Keep up the good work and Arne will let me know when he thinks you're ready to come back, okay?'

No! Delilah screamed silently. *It isn't okay!*

On the brink of tears, she ended the call and flung her phone onto the sofa. She had embarked on the tortuous process of throwing herself on the mercy of irate former boyfriends, navigating painful memories in therapy and reviving her dormant feelings for Noah, only to have it thrown in her face. She had done all this to show Polly she had matured as a person and a counsellor... and it was all for nothing! For a moment, she felt like hurling herself on the floor and howling like a child, but even Maya had grown past throwing tantrums.

So, what now Del?

34

The gloomy weather lasted the rest of the week, mirroring Delilah's mood. The dark mornings and short days accompanied by non-stop rain lashing at her windows from morning until night merged into an endless blur of misery. After the call with Polly and for the first time since starting therapy, Delilah had cancelled her session with Arne. Noah's visit, compounded by the devastating realisation she was still in limbo with her job, had left her drained. She knew skipping therapy and avoiding the one person who could authorise her return to work was irrational and risky, but she was too emotionally spent to handle Arne's questions. Instead, she wandered between her bed and the bathroom, stopping occasionally in the kitchen to make a mug of tea or scrabble a makeshift snack from the dwindling supplies in the cupboard.

But staying away from Arne was doing nothing to take her mind off Noah. In completing Salome's challenge, Delilah had made some form of peace with each man on the list and moved on. Until Noah. The crippling pain now sapping every ounce of her energy wasn't embarrassment, shame, or a dented ego, but a breaking heart. She didn't know when it had happened, but somewhere between finding Noah and watching him race out of her flat into Zazie's arms, Delilah had fallen head over heels in love with her former fiancé all over again, and losing him once more had left her feeling worthless and utterly hopeless.

Noah loves Zazie. Noah loves Zazie. Noah loves Zazie. The three-word refrain ran on a constant loop in her mind interspersed with replays of the scene in her flat with Noah. As each day passed, Delilah grew increasingly listless and apathetic, and it was only her promise to babysit Maya and Arin while Salome took Farhan to dinner for his birthday on Saturday that finally forced her into the shower and out of her flat.

* * *

'Why are you crying, Auntie Del?' Maya demanded.

The child's anxious voice shook Delilah out of her daydream of Zazie walking arm in arm with Mrs West while a delighted Noah looked on. *Snap out of it, Del!* Quickly dashing away the tears she hadn't realised were there, Delilah opened her arms to cuddle her niece.

'I'm just feeling a little sad, Maya-moo,' she said shakily, squeezing her tightly. Glancing over Maya's shoulder, she could see Arin crawling stealthily towards the table holding Salome's precious blue pottery vase, and Delilah released Maya and scrambled off the sofa. Scooping the toddler from the floor before he could grab the table leg, she dumped him back onto the rug, laughing despite herself at the child's disgruntled expression.

Maya pursed her lips in disapproval. 'Arin's very naughty. Mummy's *told* him he's not allowed near that table.'

'I know, but he's still a baby and curious about everything,' Delilah explained. 'You know, you were exactly the same at his age.'

Maya dismissed the comparison and instead knitted her brows into a frown identical to Salome's. 'Why are you feeling sad, Auntie Del?'

Because the man I love happens to love someone else. Delilah bit back the words trembling on her lips and gave her head a virtual wobble. She was the grown-up, and it was her job to look after the children in her charge, not the other way round.

'I was just being silly, but I'm absolutely fine now,' she said with a bracing smile she hoped would reassure Maya. 'I have an idea, let's go upstairs and change Arin's nappy and then we can come down and play cops and robbers with your new walkie-talkies.'

Twenty minutes later, while a freshly diapered Arin surreptitiously gnawed Maya's teddy bear in his play pen, Delilah hid behind the sofa whispering into a walkie-talkie to Maya, who was stalking the corridor in search of an imaginary criminal. The sound of the doorbell startled Delilah, and she bumped her head on the sofa and hastily squashed the curse trembling on her lips. The walkie-talkie was still on, and Salome and Farhan wouldn't thank her for expanding Maya's vocabulary in that way.

She stood up and glanced over to where Arin was preoccupied with trying to pull off Bertie's re-stitched ear, and wrested the teddy bear from his hands. Pushing a pile of coloured plastic bricks in the corner of his play pen towards him, she went out into the hall.

'Who is it, Auntie Del?' Maya demanded, clearly irritated by the interruption.

'I don't know, darling. Mummy didn't say she was expecting anyone,' Delilah replied, pushing back her hair to peer through the spyhole. The bell rang again before she could make out who was there, and she wrenched open the door impatiently.

'*Oh!*' She gasped at the sight of Noah standing on the doorstep scowling with his finger poised to press the bell again.

'Can I come in?' he asked curtly.

Delilah nodded in bemusement and stood back to let him pass. This angry-looking man looked nothing like the jaunty, relaxed version that had left her flat less than a week ago.

'Come in—' She broke off as Maya dashed past her to hurl herself onto Noah.

'*Uncle Noah!*' She grabbed him by the knees, squealing loudly when he picked her up and swung her round in the air before setting her down gently. His irate expression transformed into a warm smile as he crouched to let Maya wrap her small arms around his neck and plant a wet kiss on his cheek.

Delilah smoothed her hair, suddenly conscious of the faded white crop top, torn jeans, and Disney cartoon socks she had thrown on before leaving home. When Noah released himself from Maya's arms and stood up, Delilah quickly pulled her niece towards her as if for protection and avoided his gaze by pretending to tidy Maya's thick curls.

'Salome's not at home,' she mumbled.

'I know. I spoke to her, and she said you were here looking after the kids.'

Delilah looked up, startled. '*Sal* told you I was babysitting. But why...? I mean, *how*...?'

'I need to talk to you,' he said abruptly. The smile he had reserved for

Maya disappeared, and he looked like a volcano about to erupt. Her stomach clenched and she scraped a nervous hand through her hair. She glanced down at Maya, who was watching them intently.

'Go into the kitchen, Noah. We can talk in there,' she said quickly. 'Give me a second and I'll put the telly on for Maya. The kids will be fine on their own for a few minutes.'

Hustling her inquisitive niece into the living room, Delilah switched on the television and flipped the channel to a children's show. 'Keep an eye on Arin for me, Maya-moo,' she said breathlessly. 'I'll just be in the kitchen talking to Uncle Noah for a few minutes, okay?'

Distracted by the TV, Maya nodded and sank cross-legged onto the rug, while Arin, who was concentrating on stacking a pile of toy bricks, didn't even glance their way. Ruffling his hair gently, Delilah stepped out of the room, leaving the door slightly ajar. Forcing herself to take a deep breath to calm her jitters, she smoothed her palms down the sides of her jeans. She and Noah had parted ways amicably, but he was clearly very unhappy and had apparently come in search of her.

She walked into the kitchen to find Noah standing by the window. Through the open blinds, the fairy lights Farhan had draped along the patio awning twinkled in the darkness. She cleared her throat, and Noah turned to face her with eyes blazing.

'Why didn't you tell me Zazie doesn't want kids?' he demanded without preamble.

Even without raising his voice, Delilah could tell Noah was livid, and caught unawares, she stood rooted to the spot. *How the hell did he find out?* Had Zazie confessed and admitted telling Delilah, or—? Her heart dropped, and she blanched as it dawned on her that she had confided in only one person. *Surely, Salome wouldn't have...?*

'How – how did you find out?'

'Salome told me,' he snapped, his voice thick with anger.

Delilah flinched at the savagery in his tone and closed her eyes, unable to bear the fury directed at her and wishing the ground would open up and swallow her whole. Salome was an absolute *snake* and the only secrets she was good at keeping were her own. For a split second she wondered if it was revenge for what she'd said to Farhan, but then dismissed the thought as quickly as it came. Sal wasn't petty, and they had both moved past that episode. What she did remember was how emphatic her sister had been that Noah deserved to know the truth.

'I'm so incredibly sorry,' Delilah said quietly, feeling completely wretched. 'Sal had no right to tell you.'

Her cheeks burned with shame at her own cowardice in staying silent, but her sister had nothing to lose in telling Noah, whereas she... She bowed her head and focused on the toes of her Bambi socks.

'*What the hell, Delilah!* Are you serious right now? *She* had no right?' Noah sounded incandescent, and Delilah looked up at him warily. 'At least Salome had the guts to tell me something I would have expected you, of all people, to warn me about.'

Noah's expression changed, and he looked at her with such hurt that she would have infinitely preferred his anger. 'You know how lonely I was growing up as an only child and how desperate I was for siblings, especially with Mum being so over-protective. You and I always talked about having kids one day – have you forgotten when we made that list of names we said would be off-limits for our babies?'

Noah looked so sad that Delilah wanted to cry, and she bit down hard on her lip to stop it wobbling.

'It wasn't my place to interfere in your relationship. You asked me to help you both, and it wouldn't have been ethical to take sides or break Zazie's confidence,' she said shakily.

Noah looked at her in disbelief. 'Del, you know better than anyone on this planet how much I want children. Why would you keep something like that from me? Was I so awful to you? Do you hate me that much?'

'Of course I don't hate you!' she burst out heatedly. 'If you really want to know, the main reason I couldn't tell you was because I didn't want *you* to hate *me*!'

Noah's eyes narrowed and he took a step towards her. 'Why would I hate you for telling me the truth about something so important?'

Delilah could feel her heart pounding, and she turned away before her face betrayed her feelings. It was hard enough listening to him accuse her of letting him down without further humiliating herself when he had made it abundantly clear he was over her. Zazie had lied to him, but that didn't change the fact she was the girl Noah had chosen, and Delilah couldn't bear his pity if he knew she still had feelings for him.

Noah closed the gap between them and turned her back to face him. 'Answer me, Delilah. Why would I hate you?'

'B-because you're h-happy and in love and I – I didn't want to be the one who ruined that for you,' she stammered. She tried avoiding Noah's eyes, but he cupped her face with warm fingers, making it impossible not to meet his gaze.

'I was scared—' She broke off, biting her lip hard to stop the words bursting to escape before she said too much.

'Scared of what?'

'That – that you might think I was trying to break you and Zazie up.'

He moved his hand away and looked at her curiously. 'Why? Because I got carried away and kissed you that time in the park?'

This was torture. Delilah stared at the floor and pressed her lips together so tightly her mouth ached. Then, it was as if a lightbulb suddenly lit up in her mind, and she sighed. It was pointless staying silent to protect herself when she was hurting anyway. She looked up and met Noah's gaze head on.

'Maybe *you* got carried away that day in the park, but I didn't. I wasn't confused or on some nostalgia trip. I *wanted* you to kiss me. To be honest, I just wanted you, full-stop.'

He didn't move as his eyes studied hers intently. 'What exactly are you saying, Del?'

'I just said it,' she muttered. 'I want you.'

'Want me as in...?'

She closed her eyes in sheer frustration. '*Please* don't make me say it!'

For a moment there was silence and then a tiny smile played on his lips. 'I'm really sorry, but I think I'm going to need you to say it,' he said softly.

'I still have feelings for you.' The words tumbled out before she could stop herself. 'I was scared if I told you Zazie was lying to you – well, you'd think I was being pathetic and jealous, and I couldn't bear the thought of you hating me.'

Noah shook his head. 'I could never hate you, Del.'

'Now, *that*'s hard to believe!' she scoffed. 'From the first day I arrived at your flat to ask your forgiveness, you've given a fantastic impression of someone who thinks I'm the worst person on the planet. You actually *forced* me to help you keep your girlfriend, remember? How did you think that was going to make me feel?'

Noah tugged on his earlobe with a wry smile. 'You make a good point, but I've already apologised for that. Listen, I know I shouldn't have pressured you to help me with Zazie and I'm sorry for putting you in that position. As for that first day at my flat... well, frankly, I was furious when you showed up asking for forgiveness without acknowledging how much you'd hurt me or even explaining why you did it.'

She nodded slowly, and then a thought struck her. 'Have you spoken to Zazie yet?'

'Yep. It was the first thing I did after Salome called me.'

Oh God! Delilah groaned silently. As far as she knew, she was the only one Zazie had told about not wanting children, and she was bound to blame Delilah.

'Did you tell her it was me who spilled the beans?'

'No, of course not. I went to see her and asked her point blank how she felt about us having kids if we were to get married. To her credit, she pretty much admitted right away that she didn't want them.'

'Sooo...?' Delilah held her breath.

'So, it's over between us. Obviously.'

'I'm sorry, Noah,' she said sincerely, a wave of compassion for him sweeping aside her own feelings. 'You love Zazie, and none of this must have been easy. I should have told you but—'

'—but I would have hated you. Yeah, you said.'

They looked at each other in silence, and then she said timidly, 'So now what? Can we be friends?'

Noah shook his head. 'Nah. I'm sorry, Del, but after everything that's happened, there's no way I can be friends with you.'

'Oh!' She stared at him, stricken. He had every right to be upset with her but after he'd made her admit her feelings for him, the words were like a brutal kick to the stomach.

'Don't look so sad, Del. I'm just being honest,' he said softly, then his lips broke into a teasing smile. 'Let's face it, there's no way you and I could ever just be friends.'

'Oh?' she said again.

Noah reached out and pulled her up to him, and when his mouth sought hers, she threw her arms around his neck and pressed her body against his. As his warm lips devoured hers, she tugged him closer, tracing the hard muscles in his back through the thin knit of his jumper. His fingers slipped under her top and cupped her breast and she groaned and kissed him harder. Somehow, through the haze of passion, she remembered where she was and pulled back, her heart pounding as she gasped for breath.

'I thought you wanted us to start a new chapter,' she murmured breathlessly.

Noah's breathing was as ragged as hers, and he pulled her back into his arms, holding her so tightly she could have sworn she felt his heart thumping. He nuzzled her neck and said huskily, 'I just realised we haven't finished the last one yet.'

Without warning, the kitchen door slammed open and Maya barged in.

'Arin wants to come out of the play pen,' she announced. Her eyes homed in on Delilah in Noah's arms, and she eyed them curiously.

'Auntie Del was feeling sad and crying before you came, Uncle Noah. Are you kissing her better?'

Noah linked his arms loosely around Delilah's waist and gazed into her eyes for a long moment. Then, he turned and nodded solemnly.

'I'm doing my very best, Maya.'

35

It felt like three months rather than three weeks since Delilah's last session with Arne, and even the reliably aloof Sigmund appeared to have missed her. Sidling up to where she sat, the cat allowed her a few strokes of his fur before shrugging her off and padding over to stretch out under the desk. While Arne made them coffee, Delilah scanned the room, her gaze falling upon a large sepia-toned photograph of a forest. Sunlight streamed through tall leafy trees with trunks that appeared enormous.

'Is that a new photo?' Delilah asked curiously.

Arne glanced up and followed the direction of her gaze. 'Ah, yes. I took the picture some time ago, but I had it framed only last week.'

He walked over with a brimming mug of milky coffee and set it down on the table next to Delilah. Instead of taking his seat, he went over to the picture and studied it while tugging gently on his beard. 'I like this photo very much. I lay on the ground to capture the trees at that angle. It speaks to me of perspective.'

'You mean the way the tree trunks seem so huge?'

'Indeed. It is a useful reminder how we can look at the same thing – or situation – in different ways. The position we choose will inform how we see things.'

'That's pretty deep. I only meant it's a nice picture,' Delilah teased. She grinned widely and Arne's eyes twinkled in response. He walked over and settled himself in the chair facing her.

'You look happy, Delilah.'

'*Very* happy!' It was impossible to hide her excitement, and she gave him a huge smile. 'I can't wait to fill you in on everything that's happened.'

'I was concerned when you cancelled not one, but two of our sessions, so I am pleased to see you back.'

'I know.' She scrunched her nose in apology. 'I'm really sorry about that. I know what a busy client schedule you have, and it won't happen again. Actually, I wanted to talk to you about signing me off. I've learned so much from our sessions, but I'm ready to go back to work. I tried telling Polly, but she won't hear of it until you give me the all-clear.'

Arne didn't appear surprised at her request, and he gestured as if inviting her to take the lead. 'Perhaps you can tell me what has brought you such elation.'

Delilah wriggled deeper into the armchair to make herself comfortable before relating the tumultuous events of the past three weeks. When she finished, she picked up her mug and swallowed the coffee thirstily before sitting back to gauge Arne's reaction. If her therapist was happy for her, his face clearly hadn't received the memo.

'It's all worked out well for me and Noah,' she added reassuringly, in case he was in any doubt. 'We've been together literally every day since then and it's like we've never been apart. We are so making up for lost time!'

Arne's expression didn't shift, and Delilah tried to rein in her mounting frustration. Things were back on track with Noah, and she was desperate to move on from therapy and get her job and her life back. But for that to happen, she needed Arne on her side.

'You do realise this is *good* news, Arne?' Delilah pointed out. 'Why don't you look happy about it?'

Arne tilted his head and studied Delilah thoughtfully. 'Tell me again why you broke up with Noah?'

Taken aback by the question, Delilah was immediately on the defensive. Why did he sound so negative? Surely he should be happy she had made enough of an emotional breakthrough to take a chance on love again.

'I told you. The same reason I broke up with the other guys. I was scared of commitment and—' She broke off with a sigh. She knew Arne well enough to know she couldn't fob him off with a superficial response.

'Getting emotionally close to someone has always felt scary and threatening,' she said, choosing her words carefully. 'But you and I have worked on that, and now I know I shouldn't connect love or intimacy to something fearful. I was able to open up and be vulnerable to Noah and express how I felt about him and I'm so thankful he feels the same. I'm confident we can make it work.'

'Why do you believe things will be different this time?' Arne's tone was mild, but somehow Delilah felt under attack.

'Like I said, I'm much more self-aware than the first time Noah and I were together. You've helped me understand my triggers, and that's something I never took account of before. Arne, I've messed it up once with Noah, and I know what I want this time,' she pleaded, desperate for his approval.

'You feel sure about your ability to commit to him this time?'

'Yes,' Delilah said firmly. 'It's still early days – after all, he's only just ended a relationship – and I'm not naïve enough to think it will all be plain sailing. He's assured me he's put the past behind him, but I know it's going to take time for him to really trust me again. It feels so good being back together and I'm really positive about us.'

Arne reached for a lined notebook on the side table and leafed through a few pages before peering at her over the top of his glasses. 'You feel ready to resume your work as a counsellor.'

She nodded, not quite sure if he was asking a question or making a statement. He glanced down again at the page in front of him. 'Delilah, do you understand why therapy is a mandated part of your training?'

Delilah willed herself not to scream with frustration. The man was just doing his job, and she wouldn't help her case by coming across as impatient or entitled. 'Yes, of course. Look, you know before I started working with you, I didn't think therapy was that necessary. But after our sessions, I do see why it's valuable. It's my job to support couples going through emotional challenges, which means I also need someone supportive and somewhere safe to offload my own baggage.'

'Not simply offload, but also unpack,' Arne corrected. 'To avoid repeating patterns or dynamics that are not working for you, you need to appreciate why they happen. When a counsellor hasn't taken the time to properly understand themselves, it becomes a problem for their clients. The more we understand, the better we are at stepping back so we can guide and facilitate healing in relationships rather than presuming and then weighing in or influencing the parties involved.'

Delilah winced, recognising only too well the description of how she had operated in the past. But that was then, and she was so much the wiser now. 'Arne, I do get that, but at the same time, therapy's not something anyone should do forever, is it?'

Arne shrugged lightly. 'Therapy is a process, Delilah, not an instant cure. It gives us the language, but you know very well how long it can take to repair a relationship with a partner. In therapy, we are working to repair our relationship with ourselves, and having insight alone doesn't change our behaviour. I understand your impatience, but while it appears as if you have made some big changes in a short period, it will take time and practice to truly shift your behaviour.'

Delilah's elation was slowly trickling away as she realised persuading Arne to sign her off was going to be tougher than she had anticipated.

'What were you hoping to achieve from our sessions together?' he asked, sounding curious.

'To get back to my job and finish my training,' she replied, trying not to sound as morose as she was now feeling.

'There was a reason you were suspended. Let me ask, Delilah, do you believe you know yourself well enough to recognise your own biases?'

When she nodded, he continued. 'What do you think you must do to persuade Polly that you can support your clients more objectively going forward?'

'I don't know. I suppose, prove to her that I'm not dominated by my past relationships – which was the whole point of the apology exercise…' She tailed off uncertainly. What did he want her to say?

'I believe there is still a great deal you and I need to explore. For instance, examining your family dynamics can be crucial to knowing yourself better. What we learn as children reveals clues to our beliefs and behaviour as adults. Will you permit me to share this observation?' Arne paused and when she didn't react, he continued.

'You appear to shy away from discussing your family history, and if I'm to be frank with you, this suggests to me there is some form of trauma you do not wish to revisit. While it may be painful to do so, I urge you not to ignore the past because without understanding and processing what happened, you will continue with patterns of behaviour which prevent you from healing and from accepting the love you deserve.'

Stunned by the therapist's clinical dissection, Delilah stared at him wordlessly, the blood draining from her face. Without any warning, it felt like the safe, comfortable cocoon that had represented her sessions with Arne had been smashed open, leaving her raw and exposed.

'Delilah?' Arne's voice was deep with concern, but she couldn't find the words to reassure him, and it wasn't until he pressed a glass of water into her palm that she came back to herself. Draining the glass, she wiped a hand across her mouth, conscious of Arne crouched in front of her, his face only inches away.

'Do you feel better?' His brilliant blue eyes were unblinking in their focus and Delilah nodded slowly.

'I apologise if what I said has upset you—'

'It's fine,' she mumbled, horribly embarrassed by her extreme response and desperate to move on.

'But if I am to do my job as your therapist, then there are times I must challenge you. I am your ally in this journey and, as such, I am obliged to hold up the mirror for you to see things that perhaps you do not wish to see. This is the work we must do to help you find healing, and your strong reaction to what I said just now reveals something important to our understanding.'

Apparently satisfied that she was fine, Arne straightened up and returned to his chair while Delilah fiddled awkwardly with the empty glass. She glanced at the clock; there was still another twenty minutes left of the session, but she wasn't sure she could stand much more.

'My observations have made you deeply uncomfortable,' Arne remarked, as if he could read the thoughts chasing round her mind. 'None of us welcomes discomfort, but sometimes we must find the courage to sit in it and reflect on what drives that discomfort.'

Delilah closed her eyes. 'I... I just don't like talking about the past. Maybe it's because Mum died when I was so young. Also, if I'm honest, I don't remember large chunks of life before and after it happened, and it makes me anxious and upset when I can't retrieve my memories.'

'But Delilah, this is precisely why you should not continue with a blank past and hide from it, but rather explore further where this anxiety comes from,' Arne said earnestly. 'This loss of memory and the anxiety you talk about is often linked to people who have experienced unstable or threatening environments in their childhood.'

Delilah flinched, but when she said nothing, Arne persisted. 'When we feel anxiety, it is our body responding to a perceived sense of danger. But while we can't avoid anxiety or make it disappear, we *can* try to understand what drives the anxiety, so it doesn't overwhelm us or disrupt our relationships.'

Unable to maintain her silence, Delilah burst out, 'But I'm happy *now*. I feel fine and positive, so why can't you just accept that?'

Arne studied her for a moment and then he leaned forward. 'What is it you fear about therapy, Delilah? Do you imagine it will swallow you up and leave you helpless? I can understand your concern, but I assure you that will not be the case. On the contrary, when we open up to explore our past, we are giving ourselves the chance to tell – or, in your case, to remember – the story of what happened to us, however bad or shameful we might think it is. Bringing what is in the dark out into the light is not for you to relive that trauma, but so we can see what it is and make sense of it. That way, you are no longer stuck in it. My goal is for you to look forward and flourish in your chosen vocation.'

Delilah released a despondent sigh. Somehow, Arne had managed to extinguish the joy she had wafted in with as effectively as an unexpected deluge of rain on a picnic lunch.

'So how long do I have to keep doing this?'

'I don't want you to see our sessions as some form of punishment, Delilah,' Arne said mildly. 'In the same way it takes time to build habits, it takes time to change behaviour. But this gets easier over time, and as we work together, you will create new habits that serve you and your clients better.'

The therapist's reassurances fell on stony ground and Delilah set her jaw stubbornly, smouldering in silence. She had spent so much time on this whole process and listening to Arne, it sounded like she'd never be good enough to do her job. To make things worse, he was obsessed with her past, and she was fed up with the constant probing. Her future with Noah looked bright, and that was what she wanted to focus on. For the first time, Delilah wondered if her job was worth all this aggravation. Did she love it enough to risk Arne forcing her back to places she had no desire to revisit?

Sigmund slunk out from under the desk and padded over to her, staring up at Delilah with clear green eyes. For a wild moment she had an eerie feeling the cat knew exactly what she was thinking. Shaking off the disturbing idea, she gave it one last try.

'Arne...' Delilah started, and then she slumped back in the armchair with a dispirited sigh. 'Please listen to me. I've spent weeks hunting down my ex-boyfriends and I have learned so much more from that than I think you're giving me credit for. I can't change what's happened in the past, but I've done everything possible to take accountability and make amends to everyone – including my sister and her husband! I've learned my lessons and I'm not afraid of committing to a relationship any more. Bottom line is, I'm an adult and I *know* I can make things work with Noah.'

'Adults are not immune to unhealthy relationships, Delilah. That is precisely what your job is about, no? You know the data from your training – a significant percentage of adults who struggle to build healthy relationships were exposed to toxic relationships in their childhood or had their trust broken, and they will often replicate this behaviour.'

Arne persisted, his tone deliberate. 'The data also tells us that children who feared being hurt or abandoned can grow into adults who try to protect themselves from potential pain. Sometimes by keeping emotional distance in their relationships, and sometimes... by abandoning relationships altogether.'

Arne's intent gaze and soft voice were a powerful and hypnotic combination, and in that very moment, it felt to Delilah that he had looked deep inside her and mined her secrets without her consent, as if he had reached inside her body and ripped out and exposed what she had kept hidden. But she couldn't let him know that, and so she remained frozen in her seat.

Arne observed her in silence and then said, 'I think that's enough for today. I know you wish to return to work, Delilah, but I don't think you are ready.'

He sat back in his chair and the action jolted Delilah out of her state of paralysis. Suddenly it was all too much, and she was incandescent with rage. Like a bomb exploding on the bed of a placid lake and turning it into a churning river, a wave of corrosive anger rose from the pit of her stomach and surged up into her throat with such force, she had to press her lips together to stop the bile from spilling out. With a fury she could scarcely contain, Delilah leapt to her feet, drawing a startled meow from a passing Sigmund.

How *dare* Arne violate her privacy and judge her? What did this virtual stranger with his wild hair, baggy brown corduroys, and stuffy Argyle vest presume to know about her or her life? Rigid with anger, Delilah's lips worked soundlessly as she tried to speak, but unable to utter a coherent word, she grabbed her bag and jacket and stormed out of Arne's office, slamming the door behind her.

She raced down the steps as if pursued by demons and wrenched open the heavy front door. Pushing her way through the throng of people on the busy high street, Delilah ran until she was out of breath and her chest hurt so badly that she was forced to stop. Bent over with her head down and her trembling hands gripping her thighs, she heaved in great gulps of air, shuddering as her mind flashed back to the bewildered expression on Arne's face before she had fled his office.

Her breath emerged in ragged bursts as she staggered down the road, desperate to put as much distance as possible between herself and her therapist's office. Every doubt and reservation she had quashed about therapy as she grew more comfortable with Arne came flooding back with a vengeance. Polly was absolutely right: Arne was good at his job. No, not just good, she corrected herself grimly, the man was bloody brilliant! He had so skilfully lulled her into a sense of security that she had almost forgotten herself. He had fooled her for a while but, in the end, he had been out to trick her – just like Verity, the po-faced therapist.

She knew she was risking her career by running out on Arne, but Delilah no longer cared. *I don't need Arne, I don't need Polly, and most of all, I don't need therapy!* She would change jobs if she had to, but the one thing she knew for sure was that she was never *ever* going back!

36

Turning over in bed, Delilah looked across to where Noah lay on his back, deep in sleep. She plumped up her pillow and rested her head on the crook of her arm, watching the silent rise and fall of his naked chest, partly exposed by the sheet that had fallen away. It always amazed her how Noah breathed so softly and scarcely moved during the night while she tossed and turned trying to quieten her mind.

It was hard to believe three weeks had passed since the night he'd gate-crashed her babysitting duties. Since then, he'd spent almost all his free time with her or at her flat, and it was starting to feel like the three years apart had never happened.

But if things with Noah were back on track, Delilah thought soberly, everything else in her life remained an unresolved mess. She had ignored Arne's calls and messages, and so far there had been no word from Polly, which suggested Arne hadn't yet snitched on her. Her manager had made it clear the sessions with Arne were mandatory, and if she learned Delilah had walked out of therapy, it would be inviting an inevitable firing. Even if she looked for another counselling job, it would be problematic trying to explain why she hadn't finished her training. In any case, working as a counsellor would mean returning to therapy and— She shook her head and purposefully shut down any thoughts of Arne. She was done with him.

Punching the pillow as if it was responsible for her situation, Delilah flopped back onto it and mulled over her situation. Her half-hearted attempts to search online jobs boards had resulted in a ton of random jobs, but nothing of any interest and—

'Good morning, beautiful!'

Startled, Delilah turned to find Noah watching her with a sleepy smile. She shuffled over to close the gap between them, snuggling under the warmth of his arm and breathing in his unique Noah scent.

'You looked like you were a million miles away,' he growled, his voice rough with sleep. 'What's going through that pretty head of yours?'

She didn't feel particularly pretty lying there without a scrap of make-up and her hair tucked into a black satin bonnet, but she wasn't about to argue. She kissed him lightly and rested her head against his chest.

'Just thinking I need to kickstart my job search. I can't hang around forever waiting for Polly to take me back. I'm already weeks behind Armenique and the others on my training programme, and all this sitting around is doing my head in. It's probably best if I look for another job.'

Noah's deep voice rumbled through his chest. 'Are you sure about that? I thought you loved your job. Can't you talk to Polly and work something out?'

Delilah snuggled deeper into his arms, wondering how much detail to get into. Noah knew she had been seeing a therapist, but she had never explained it was a precondition of her job, and now she'd ditched Arne, there was no point bringing it up.

'It's not just Polly...' She tailed off with a sigh. 'I've tried my best but maybe relationship counselling isn't the right direction for me. Anyway, enough about that. Let's talk about you – what's on *your* mind?'

'Right now? Nothing much. Just enjoying lying in bed with the most incredible girl in the world in my arms.'

'I am rather incredible, aren't I?' she teased, and he promptly tickled her ribs, leaving her giggling helplessly. She buried her face in the crook of his neck and mumbled, 'I'm so glad you've taken the day off work. Now, you can project manage me all day instead of your sweaty construction crew.'

'When you put it like that, how can I say no?' He squeezed her tightly against him. 'I'm so crazy about you,' he said, his voice muffled by her shoulder.

She couldn't stop the shiver that ran through her at his words, and she wrapped her arms around him and tried to push away the unwelcome prickle of unease. Moments later, when Noah rolled on top of her and kissed her deeply, she stopped thinking about anything at all.

37

After spending most of the morning in bed, Delilah and Noah finally left her flat for a stroll into town. Walking hand in hand through the neighbourhood park, they stopped to sit on a bench, watching people walk their dogs and the occasional jogger run past them on the pathway that circled the park. Overhead, the blue sky was darkening as clouds clustered into a grey blanket, slowly blotting out the late morning sunshine. The temperature had been unseasonably warm when they'd left the house but was quickly dropping, and Delilah was beginning to regret not bringing a jacket. A sharp gust of wind cut through her light sweater, and she rubbed the sudden goosebumps on her arm.

Noah reached for her hand and squeezed it gently. 'Looks like we missed the best weather while we were in bed.'

Delilah smiled coyly. 'I know, but it was so worth it. Best way to start the day.'

'Couldn't agree more.' He released her hand and wrapped his arm around her, and she snuggled against him. It was so good to see the tactile and affectionate Noah she had known in the past, with none of the moodiness and coldness he had displayed towards Zazie. She stifled a pang of jealousy at the thought of Noah's ex-girlfriend. It was hard to forget that only a few weeks earlier, he had been so involved with another girl, he had been contemplating proposing to her. But then, Delilah reminded herself, Noah had stood up to his mother in front of her in a way he had never done for Zazie, which had to mean something.

'Has Zazie been in touch with you since – well, you know?' she asked tentatively.

'No,' Noah said tersely. 'Just as well cos I've got nothing to say to her.'

'Don't you think maybe you two need to have a proper chat and get closure?' Delilah persisted, even as the voice in her head was screaming at her to shut up. *Are you trying to drive him back into her arms, you idiot!*

'You really can't stop yourself going into counselling mode, can you?' Noah drawled, his voice tinged with humour.

'Well, when people react strongly to someone, it means there's still feelings there,' she pointed out. 'I just want to make sure I'm not the rebound girl.'

'Del, if anyone was on the rebound, it was me with Zazie.' He shifted on the bench to face her squarely. 'I won't pretend I didn't care about her because that isn't true. When I met Zazie, I was struggling to get over you, and she was fun and easy to be with. I was desperate to move on from you and me and to be happy again. Maybe I was forcing things with her a bit, but Zazie really cared about me – or at least, I thought she did,' he finished grimly.

'I *know* she cared about you! Look, I'm not saying what Zazie did was right, but no one's perfect and it isn't always easy to be upfront about things if you're afraid you're going to hurt someone, or even lose them.'

'Yeah, well being honest is super important to me. *You're* not holding anything back from me, are you?' He studied her earnest expression quizzically.

'No, of course not,' Delilah said quickly. She reached up and stroked his face gently. 'I'm glad you're over Zazie. I won't lie – it was torture watching you loved up with someone else.'

Noah turned his head to kiss the palm of her hand before tracing a path down her arm with his lips. His hand slipped under her top, and she shivered at his touch and pressed herself against him. He kissed her hard, and his warm fingers stroking her left her aching for more. A cyclist whizzed past, and Delilah pulled away from Noah, laughing.

'You need to behave or we're going to get arrested,' she breathed, her voice catching at the naked desire in his eyes.

'I don't care who's watching,' he murmured, but she resisted the temptation and sat back, slipping a hand through the crook of his arm to lovingly trace the small crown tattoo on his forearm.

'I'm shocked you still have this,' she marvelled. 'I would have sworn you'd removed it or covered it over with – with something else.'

'Didn't occur to me,' Noah said with a shrug. 'You're always gonna be my queen.'

'That's *so* sweet! Who knew you were such a romantic?' She beamed up at him and squeezed his arm, a fuzzy ball of happiness lodging itself inside her. She and Noah would be fine, she vowed silently. Zazie was his past, and there was nothing to fear about the future.

'Okay, so now it's your turn to demonstrate a bit of romance,' he said with a grin. 'I distinctly remember you promising to get a tattoo when I did this one, and we both know that never happened. We could go to Stan's parlour now if you're up for it?'

His eyes dared her to accept the challenge, and Delilah pulled a face and shuddered. 'Ugh! Sorry, but I can't handle the idea of that needle drilling into me.'

'And here's me thinking I'm worth any amount of pain. Just so you know, Zazie was planning to get one done with my name on it,' he said plaintively, and then burst out laughing when Delilah rolled her eyes.

Struck by a thought, Delilah hesitated and then asked quietly, 'Is your mum still not talking to you?'

The news that he was back with Delilah had sparked a furious row between Noah and his mother. Even learning about Zazie's scheme to deprive her of grandchildren had done nothing to lessen Mrs West's fury at her son for ignoring her warning about the dangers of trusting Delilah. Since then, she had refused to speak to him until, as she put it, 'he came to his senses'. While Noah had been at pains to assure Delilah she wasn't to blame, it was hard not to feel guilty for causing a rift between mother and son.

'It was bound to happen at some point. Mum's never been happy with anyone I've brought home and it's time I put down some boundaries. Don't worry about it – I'm not. Trust me, she'll come round,' Noah said easily.

Delilah scrutinised him covertly, but he really didn't appear bothered, which was a total switch from when Zazie had been the one in the firing line. When Delilah cautiously voiced the thought, Noah simply shrugged and hugged her to his side.

'It's different with you and me. Granted, things between us didn't end well the first time around, but that's in the past. Give her time – even Mum can't stay upset forever. At the end of the day, she knows I've been obsessed with you from the first time we met.'

Delilah winced at his choice of words and tried to ignore the flutter of trepidation they caused in her gut. She knew Noah wanted their relationship back to how it was before she'd run out on him, but there were times when the pace of change felt somewhat overwhelming. As they spent more time together, it was becoming trickier for Delilah to balance her instinctive need to take things slowly with showing Noah she was enthused about their future and committed to making things work. While she was happy to be back with Noah, it probably didn't help that they spent all their free time glued to each other's side. It had been weeks since she had gone out with Armenique or spent time with her other friends, and while Noah wouldn't have minded, after everything they'd gone through, Delilah felt guilty about even suggesting time apart.

Salome had found a part-time job with her old firm who were delighted to have her back and was juggling the demands of her new job with making time for Farhan and the kids, which made finding time for the heart-to-heart chat Delilah sorely needed almost impossible. Besides, Salome was so firmly Team Noah that she'd have been horrified to hear Delilah voice any concerns about navigating the relationship.

But Delilah didn't need any reminders that the last time she had felt under emotional pressure from Noah, she had panicked, and their relationship had ended in disaster. After her sessions with Arne, she had learned enough about herself to recognise that emotional stress was a trigger, but she had no idea how to explain this to Noah without opening a Pandora's box which would be impossible to close.

They sat quietly on the bench watching a family of ducks waddle past and head towards the stream while Delilah mulled over Noah's words. After a while, she broke the silence.

'Babe, you know I'm so happy we're together, right? But you've just come out of a relationship with Zazie, and you should really take some time to process that. It's still early days for us, and – well, we're still getting to know each other again.'

She kept her tone light, placing a hand on his chest as if to stop him running too far ahead. He took her hand and held it tight.

'Don't bring Zazie into this. That was a completely different situation, and my feelings for her are nothing like we have. Del, this isn't exactly our first rodeo – we were literally *hours* away from getting married! How much more is there for us to know about each other?'

'All I'm saying is, let's take it slow and not let things get too heavy too quickly,' she pleaded. 'We've got all the time in the world, and I just want to make sure we don't get ahead of ourselves.'

Noah frowned, and she stifled a sigh. It was hard to blame him for looking confused or suspecting she might be trying to backtrack, and she wanted desperately to reassure him. A loud rumble of thunder broke the tense silence, and she looked up at clouds that had grown ominously dark. She shivered and turned back to Noah, kissing him hard and holding on to him until she felt the tension ease from his body.

'That's more like it,' he muttered, stroking back her hair and caressing her cheek gently. His eyes lit up with a hint of mischief. 'This might be a good time to tell you about my brilliant surprise.'

'You look like the cat who got the cream. What are you planning?' she asked warily.

'No need to look so suspicious, my queen,' he laughed, kissing her nose. 'You'll love it, I promise!'

Still feeling unaccountably twitchy, Delilah felt her scalp prickle with anxiety, and she forced a laugh. 'You know I hate surprises.'

'Relax, girl! You'll love it.' Noah glanced up at the darkening sky and stood up, pulling Delilah to her feet and grabbing his jacket from the bench. 'It's going to rain. Let's get out of here.'

38

As Delilah hurried out of the park with Noah, there was no trace of the earlier sunshine. The rain clouds were rapidly thickening, and the sharp breeze had picked up strength, whipping dead leaves and abandoned litter on the high street up into the air. Minutes later, a flash of lightning ripped across the sky followed by a loud clap of thunder, and suddenly the heavens opened to torrential rain.

Delilah shrieked and grabbed Noah's hand, and they raced across the road to the greengrocers to stand under a flimsy canopy overhanging a display of fruit and vegetables while the rain thundered down. Spotting a café nearby, they dashed along the pavement, almost tripping in their haste to get through the door.

Inside, the only sign of life was a bored-looking blonde woman leaning on the cash register and listening to the radio. The dim lighting didn't disguise the dated décor and basic furnishings, but with the thunderstorm raging outside as their only alternative, Delilah quickly slid into a booth by the window while Noah squeezed his tall frame into the seat opposite.

Plucking a handful of tissues from the dispenser on the table, she dabbed her wet arms while Noah tried to brush off the raindrops clinging to his close-cropped hair.

'Bloody hell! That was wild!' Leaning forward, he reached across the table and gently wiped a few droplets from Delilah's face with his thumb.

'What can I get you both?' The woman at the counter strolled over, making a show of tightening the straps on a tiny apron that barely covered the top half of her skintight jeans. Tucking a long strand of blonde hair behind her ears, she fixed her gaze onto Noah, or rather onto the damp black T-shirt clinging to his broad shoulders and muscular torso.

'Del, what do you fancy – tea?' Noah asked, tossing his rain-spattered jacket onto the dark green faux-leather banquette. When Delilah nodded, he glanced at the waitress.

'Two teas, please.'

'Fancy anything else?' The woman nodded towards a small selection of sandwiches and pastries under a glass counter by the cash register, but her raised eyebrow and a slight inflection in her tone made it clear that food wasn't the only thing on offer.

Delilah immediately bristled, but Noah shook his head in warning before she could speak. 'Nah, we're good, thanks,' he said evenly. 'Just the tea.'

The waitress went off and Noah, his lips twitching, reached across the table for a quietly seething Delilah's hand.

'The cheeky cow!' Delilah fumed. '*Imagine!* She seriously thinks it's okay to flirt with you while I'm literally right here! And who the hell would risk their life eating one of those dusty cakes that look like they've been sat there for days!'

Noah burst out laughing and Delilah glared at him for a moment, and then reluctantly smiled. 'Sorry, but it's so annoying when someone thinks they can just come on to your man like that.'

'Hey, don't apologise to me. It's actually quite nice to see you get a bit jealous. At least it shows you care.'

'Of *course* I care,' she protested. He raised an eyebrow, looking unconvinced, and Delilah added quickly, 'I just don't want us to rush things. That's all I was trying to say before.'

The waitress brought their tea and while Noah emptied three sachets of sugar into his mug and stirred the contents vigorously, Delilah gnawed her lip anxiously. Her communication skills toolkit wasn't doing much to help her find the words that would keep Noah happy and give their relationship space to deepen at a pace she could handle. It wasn't unreasonable for Noah to doubt her commitment, given their history, but with so many things in her life out of kilter, she couldn't help feeling pressured by the weight of his expectations.

Delilah stifled a yawn while trying to focus on Noah's story about an incident at work. Being in love hadn't improved her poor sleep patterns which, if anything, had worsened over the past few weeks. Broken nights filled with vivid, tearful dreams she couldn't recall when she woke up were leaving her drained and unsettled, a state of mind not helped by the uncertainty of her job situation. Knowing she had to speak to Polly was one thing, and doing it was another. In the meantime, with no definitive answer about the status of her stalled career, Delilah felt stuck.

But it wasn't the frustration of treading on verbal eggshells with Noah or even the uncertainty surrounding her job that was really throwing Delilah off balance. As much as she tried to deny it, the situation with Arne was weighing heavily on her. While she hated his intrusiveness and feared his tactics, she also knew he was right that their sessions had only scratched the surface. She still couldn't explain the fury Arne had provoked in her that day in his office, and she was troubled by the way things had ended. If she was honest, she was also badly missing having someone objective she could talk to about the conflicting emotions building up inside and the nagging fear that they would overwhelm her.

Delilah's positive mood of the morning was changing along with the rain that had now turned into hailstones noisily battering the café windows. She knew she should talk to Noah about the worries pressing on her, but she dreaded the idea he might think she was blaming him or their rekindled relationship. Listening to him with half an ear and injecting the occasional murmur of agreement, she stared into her half-empty cup, rehearsing different scenarios for communicating with Noah.

'Hey, Earth calling!'

Startled, Delilah looked up. 'Sorry,' she apologised. 'I was listening, I swear. My mind just wandered for a second.'

Noah leaned in, his eyes bright with excitement. 'Well, stay focused cos there's something I want to tell you. Remember that surprise I mentioned?'

'Remember I hate surprises?' she countered, smiling to take the edge off her words.

'Well, you're definitely not going to hate this one! Drumroll, please... Okay, never mind. Guess what? I've booked us a trip – five whole days in Morocco!

We can finally have that honeymoon we cancelled. I've got the time off work, and we go next week. I know you've been feeling down about not working so I thought a few days off with just the two of us would cheer you up. Now, imagine you and me walking through the souks of Marrakesh, then chilling on a beautiful beach.' He grinned and bowed. 'Go on, here's where you tell me what an amazing boyfriend I am.'

Delilah dropped her cup onto the saucer with a clatter and stared blankly at his jubilant expression. With so much uncertainty in her life, the last thing she felt like doing was going abroad on holiday. It was clear Noah expected her to be elated by his news when all she felt was dismay, and the excuses came immediately.

'Noah, that sounds expensive. I can't afford—'

'You don't have to. It's my treat!' He looked so pleased with himself that she felt awful for not jumping with joy at the prospect of a few days together in the sun. She looked through the window where the hailstones had turned back into sheeting rain, struggling to find the right words.

'I don't – I don't think this is the right time...' she started hesitantly, turning back to face him. 'I need to speak to Polly, remember, and, um... well, you never know. She might still want me to come back to work, and I'll need to be available. Besides, I've put in some job applications, and I should stick around in case I get called for an interview...' She tailed off with a helpless shrug.

'You'll have your phone on you, and we'll only be away for a few days,' Noah said patiently. 'Nothing you've said can't wait until we get back.'

When she still looked troubled, his expression shifted. 'I thought this would make you happy, so why are you looking like I've just offered you two weeks of hard labour?'

She dredged up a weak laugh at his attempt to lighten the mood but couldn't find the words to reassure him.

'What's going on, Del?' Noah's face had lost its humour.

Delilah suddenly felt exhausted. She rubbed her temples, feeling guilty for seeming unappreciative, and wishing she could be anywhere but here. Noah was trying to be supportive, but she had so much on her plate already without the added stress of managing his emotions.

'I thought we'd agreed to take things slow,' she said finally.

He looked pained. 'No, *you* said that, not me. I don't get it – why are you being so negative? I've been practically living at your place, so how does going on holiday for a few days suddenly become a problem? Jesus, Del, it's not like I'm asking you to *marry* me!'

Delilah flinched as if he had struck her and turned away, staring at the rain-soaked pavements outside through a blur of tears.

'Can I get you some more tea?' The waitress appeared at their table and Delilah shook her head without turning.

'We're fine, thanks,' Noah said heavily.

Delilah blinked back the tears and turned back, and after staring at her curiously, the waitress shrugged lightly and walked away.

'Sorry,' Noah muttered. He rubbed the back of his neck and exhaled loudly. 'I'm just frustrated. What's going on in your mind, Del? Please talk to me.'

She peeked up through her lashes at him, consumed with guilt for ruining what had been, until now, a perfect day. 'I... I... It just feels like...'

'Like what?'

She could tell he was trying not to sound exasperated, but when she tried to explain, her chest tightened, and her throat felt clogged. Noah had every right to be furious with her and she knew she owed him the truth, but as much as she could feel them hurtling towards disaster, she had no idea how to pull them back.

'Okay, now you're really scaring me. Delilah, what's wrong?' Noah leaned in closer, and his voice took on an urgency mirrored on his face. '*What* is going on with you? Is it something I've said or done or...?'

The persistent barrage of questions instantly pushed Delilah onto the defensive and her words spilled out before she could filter them. 'You're *pressuring* me, Noah! It – it... all of it. It just feels like a lot right now, and...'

She floundered, lost for words, and swallowed hard. Everything had been going so well. *Why did he have to push things all the time?*

Noah couldn't have looked more shocked if she'd slapped him. For one long, agonising moment he simply stared at her, and then he slumped back in his seat. Any trace of his earlier brightness had drained away as he brushed a weary hand across his face. Staring down at the table, he slowly shook his head.

'Are we really here again?' he asked quietly.

'What – what do you mean?' Delilah stammered, her stomach churning.

Noah looked up at her, and she could have wept at the blend of disbelief and despair in his eyes. 'I mean, are you getting cold feet about us again? Are we really back where we were three years ago... after... after *everything*?'

She swallowed the sob tearing at her chest and leaned forward, clutching his arm as if it was a life rope. 'Noah! It isn't you. I *promise*! There's a lot going on in my head that I'm trying to process and you – us... sometimes it can feel like—'

'Like *what*?' His eyes looked bruised with pain as he harshly interrupted her halting attempts to explain herself. 'I thought you were happy we're back together. I didn't realise being with me was so damned stressful!'

The tears spilled unchecked down Delilah's cheeks while her trembling fingers clung onto Noah's arm. She felt rather than saw the waitress looking curiously in their direction, but she didn't care. All she wanted was to wipe the sadness from Noah's face.

'*Please*,' she whispered tearfully, feeling utterly wretched. 'It's not you – it's me. It's *me*! I'm the one with issues. You've been nothing but lovely. After everything I've done, you still want to take me on holiday and instead of sounding grateful, I'm being an insensitive cow! Noah, please... just give me time.'

'Time for *what*? How much time?'

'I don't know!' She shook her head, knowing she sounded irrational even as she silently pleaded with him to understand what she couldn't explain.

Noah's gaze travelled over Delilah's distraught, tear-stained face for what felt like forever. 'It's not just you – I'm part of this. If you've got issues then they affect me too, so *talk* to me! I love you, Delilah, and I'm 100 per cent in this. What do I need to do to prove it?'

Despite the words, his voice sounded hollow, as if he had already given up on them.

'I'm... sorry, Noah...' Delilah's chest was so tight that she could scarcely get the words out.

He stared at her, bemused. 'What's happening here, Del?' he said forcefully. 'Please don't do this to us. I love you... Dammit, *I adore you*.'

In an instant, everything merged into a blinding kaleidoscope. The words, the rain beating against the windows, feeling trapped inside the booth, Noah's hurt, angry face demanding her love, demanding answers she couldn't give.

Terrified, Delilah looked around frantically, desperate to escape.

'*Delilah!*'

Noah's urgent plea was like an injection of adrenaline, like a bolt of lightning shooting through her and pumping up her heart rate so fast, she thought she would pass out. She stared at him with wild eyes, her mind, her body, *everything* screaming at her to run.

'I'm sorry!' she gasped, wringing her hands helplessly. 'I – I can't—'

Overwhelmed and panicked, she couldn't think straight. She dragged herself out from behind the table and stood up, trembling. As she stared down into Noah's stricken face, the words she so desperately wanted to speak remained stuck in her throat.

Anguished, she turned and stumbled past the empty tables to get to the door. Through a haze of tears she saw the waitress openly staring, but Delilah didn't stop. Wrenching open the café door, she ran out into the rain.

39

Delilah ran down the street until she was out of breath, her eyes streaming with tears that were washed away by the heavy rain as soon as they fell. The raw pain in her chest felt like someone had reached inside to rip the plaster off a deep wound that had never healed. She stopped under a doorway to catch her breath, her entire body shivering uncontrollably. The moment there was a slight lull in the intensity of the water cascading over her precarious shelter, Delilah stepped out into the rain and fled towards the only person who could save her.

Please, please be there! The words played on a loop as she waded through flooded pavements and dodged oncoming traffic to cross the waterlogged main road into the town centre. By the time she reached the door to Arne's building, she was drenched. She wiped the relentless rain from her face with the back of her hand and pressed hard on the bell, pounding her fists on the door and sobbing hysterically. He *had* to be there, he *had* to be there...

Hearing the click of the lock being released, Delilah pushed open the door and stumbled inside. Her drenched clothes dripped water onto the stairs and her saturated trainers squeaked loudly as she dragged herself up to the first floor. When she reached the landing, Arne was standing inside the door to his office, and he stood aside to let her in. Although she knew she looked like a drowned rat, other than an initial exclamation in his language, Arne made no comment. Instead, he went into the adjoining bathroom and returned with a thick towel, silently handing it to her before turning up the electric heater and pulling it further into the room.

'I wish I had some dry clothing to offer you,' he said finally, his voice sounding apologetic as he watched Delilah wipe her dripping arms and rub the towel over her wet hair.

She shook her head and swallowed a sob, feeling calmer now she was safely inside the warm, tranquil office. She pressed the damp towel against her eyes, trying to staunch the flow of tears and sat in the familiar armchair, vaguely aware that the therapist had taken a seat across from her. The irony of being back in the chair in which she had so confidently insisted she was fine and had every faith in her relationship with Noah hit her like a body blow. Remembering her fury at Arne and her stubborn conviction that the past was done with set off a flood of fresh tears. Against all odds, she had found Noah again, but her past was destroying any chance of happiness. She had sworn to never return to Arne, but she needed him, and he was the only one she could trust to help her.

'He'll never forgive me!' she mumbled brokenly. 'Arne, I... I ran again. After everything we've been through. Noah left Zazie and came back for me. I thought I could do it, but I've let him down again. I'm a broken, awful, *awful* person and I don't deserve anyone's love!'

All she could see was Noah's face filled with pain which, once again, she was responsible for, and it hurt so badly, she couldn't bear it. Crushed with guilt, she buried her face in the towel as violent sobs racked her body. Why, why, *why* had she let Noah fall back in love with her when she wasn't capable of making a relationship work? *It's all your fault, Del! You should have known better!* She was so distraught and intent on berating herself that it took a moment to realise Arne was speaking.

'Delilah, look at me.'

Trembling, she raised her head and stared at him through a veil of tears.

'Where are you, Delilah?'

'What... what do you mean?' She gulped back a sob and gripped the towel in her fist so tightly, her knuckles ached.

'Where are you?' Arne repeated. 'Right at this moment?'

'In your office,' she croaked, her expression mirroring her confusion.

'Exactly.' He sounded so satisfied that she stopped crying and stared at him, dumbfounded.

Arne held her gaze without wavering. 'You didn't run *away*, Delilah. Not this time.'

She started to protest, but he raised a hand and shook his head. 'This time, you ran *towards* help. This time, when you felt scared, you made a different choice. If you didn't want a different outcome this time, you wouldn't be here.'

She absorbed his words in silence. *Was Arne right?* The last time she ran away from making a commitment to Noah, she had sought refuge in a cemetery, trying to justify her actions to a woman who had been dead for fifteen years and couldn't force her to face the truth. This time, she had come to a man who wouldn't tell her what she wanted to hear. A man who would make her confront the reason she had run – and had been running for so long.

Arne was studying her silently and, once again, it was as if he could read her thoughts. 'In our first session together, I promised I would never push you to share anything with me, but that anything you chose to share would go no further than us. Delilah, do you remember when I told you that if we don't acknowledge and deal with the unresolved issues from our past, we are setting ourselves up to repeat them?'

Delilah threaded shaking hands through her wet hair and twisted the towel in agitation. A part of her wanted so badly to say the words out loud, to tell Arne everything. But the other part – the part that had protected her for so long – was screaming at her. *You can't tell anyone, Del!*

'You are safe, Delilah. You can trust me. Talk to me. Tell me what happened to you.'

Arne's warm, reassuring voice combined with the heat from the fire was slowly relaxing Delilah's damp, chilled body. She drew in a long, deep breath and willed herself to speak. She had come here for a reason. Exhausted from the constant battle with herself, it was time to lay down the burden.

40

'It was me who found her.' Delilah's voice emerged as a whisper.

'Found who?' Arne asked softly.

'Mum. She was in the kitchen, on the floor. I'd just got home after my final college class before the Christmas break.' As Delilah released herself to the memories, her voice dropped into a monotone.

'It's pouring with rain outside, and my coat is soaked, but I'm hungry and want to make a sandwich before I go up to my room. I drop my jacket onto the staircase and go into the kitchen. I don't see her at first. I take some ham and cheese out of the fridge and put them on the counter and when I close the fridge door, I see red fabric on the floor behind the kitchen island. It's Mum's skirt. I walk around the island thinking she must have dropped it when she was doing the laundry – and then I see her lying there. For just a moment, I think she's asleep and then... and then I see her head...'

The muted ticking of the clock was the only sound in the room.

'Delilah, where are you?' Arne's voice sounded deeper than usual.

Her breath was emerging in shallow bursts, and she felt her heartbeat pounding painfully fast in her chest. She clasped her knees tightly. 'I – I'm here.'

'Where is that?'

'In your office.'

'Good. We're in this together. I'm here with you, and you are safe. Take a couple of deep breaths and then tell me what you saw.'

Delilah closed her eyes and took in a gulp of air to calm her speeding heart rate. 'It was gone. The – the back of her head was gone. It was like someone had just chopped it off. There was blood everywhere.'

'What did you do?'

'I used to watch horror movies on TV, and I would always scream. But this time—' She shook her head as she tried to remember the events she had blocked from her mind, and which returned only in her dreams. 'This time, when it was real life, I couldn't scream. I couldn't get a single sound out of my mouth. I just stood there staring at Mum lying on the kitchen floor wearing her red skirt and her favourite white lace blouse. I knew she was dead, and I knew *he* had done it.'

She let go of the towel and watched it fall to the floor. Then she looked up at Arne, her expression a blend of anger and defiance. 'I knew *he* had finally done it. After years and years of telling her, of telling *us* how much he loved her – no, how much he *adored* her – and couldn't live without her, he'd actually killed her.'

Arne leaned forward, his arms resting on his thighs as he gazed intently at her. 'Who's "he", Delilah?'

Her body was still, the only movement coming from her fingers twisting around each other as if playing a complicated game of cat's cradle. She released a pent-up breath and closed her eyes, her throat closing in on itself as she tried to get the words out.

'Her husband. My father,' she muttered hoarsely.

She opened her eyes but if Arne was shocked, his expression didn't show it. Sigmund had been stretched out in his favourite spot under Arne's desk, and as if sensing her distress, he padded over to Delilah. For the first time since Delilah had started therapy, Sigmund leapt up onto her chair and settled himself on her lap. Feeling herself anchored by the warm weight of the cat, Delilah stroked his fur, and the rhythmic movements slowly eased the constriction in her throat and helped steady her breathing.

'What happened next?' Arne asked gently.

'I stood there for ages and then it hit me that maybe *he* was still in the house. And then just the idea that *he* was still alive while Mum was dead was too much for me. I couldn't bear it, and I – I grabbed a knife from the block on the counter and raced up the stairs. I honestly don't know if I could have done it – killed him, I mean – and I suppose I should be grateful I didn't get the chance to find out, but at the time I wasn't thinking. I just felt angrier than I'd ever felt in my life. That's when my voice came back. I started screaming, and then I ran into their bedroom holding the knife, but there was no one there. It was only when I was leaving the room that I noticed the bathroom door was partly open and his leg...'

Delilah's hand stilled as her voice trailed away. The memories she had buried for so long were pushing up against the walls she had erected, knocking out each brick one by one and revealing flashes of images like disjointed pieces of a crossword puzzle. Slowly, slowly, as the pieces locked together, the big picture came into view.

Pushing open the bathroom door with one hand, the knife gripped in the other. The sight of the handgun on the floor by his body. The dark red blood splattered onto the white floor tiles that Mum always kept spotlessly clean...

Sigmund stirred in Delilah's lap, bringing her back into the present. She resumed stroking the cat while she described to Arne the confused and chaotic aftermath of the gruesome discovery of her parents' bodies. Calling the emergency services, and then calling Salome.

'Sal was in her final year at uni and was planning to come home a couple of days before Christmas,' Delilah said dully. 'She stayed on the phone with me until the ambulance and the police arrived, and then she rushed out to catch the next train. Farhan picked her up from the station and brought her home.'

Arne stood up and went over to the fridge, coming back moments later with a small bottle of water and a glass. He filled the glass and placed it on the table next to her and went back to his seat, watching as Delilah picked it up and drained its contents.

'I can only imagine how difficult it has been for you to trust me with the truth,' Arne said heavily. 'What happened to you is a terrible burden for anyone to carry, still less for a girl of seventeen.'

Delilah sighed in agreement. 'It was beyond awful. To be honest, a lot of what happened after that is a blur. Apparently, it – the *incident*, as the police called it – was all over the news for days, which I suppose wasn't surprising. *His* family were all in the Caribbean and not a single one of them came over. Mum was an only child, and her parents had died years before, but she had an auntie and a couple of cousins she was close to who used to come over regularly with their children for cookouts. After it happened, they would come round, bring food and sit with us, but after Mum's funeral, they didn't visit as much. I'm sure they felt uncomfortable around me and Sal, and we saw less and less of them. After a while, they just stopped coming.'

'How did other people react to you?' Arne asked.

'Because I was a minor at the time, the papers didn't report my name, so it never comes up when people do a search on me. That's why I was able to carry on with my life without anyone knowing. Salome changed her name as soon as she married Farhan. After Mum and *he* were buried, I went back to college, but I never told anyone – I mean, let's face it, who would want to be friends with a girl whose psycho father murdered their mum?' she said bitterly.

'Delilah, what happened was horrific, but it wasn't your fault.'

She brushed off Arne's assurance. 'Maybe, but that doesn't stop people from thinking it might be something that's in your blood. That's what Farhan's parents thought, but he wouldn't abandon Salome. They got married as soon as she graduated, and for ages his parents refused to have anything to do with him. It wasn't until Maya was born that they all finally made up, and now you'd never know there'd been a problem.'

'How did you cope?'

Delilah shrugged. 'I had Salome and Farhan, and that was all that mattered. When Sal graduated and found a job, we sold the house. I wonder if Mum always knew how it would end, because it turned out she'd bought a hefty life insurance policy years earlier. Between the payout from that and the money from the house sale, we were financially secure. Salome and Farhan got a place together and I moved in with them. After a while, when I felt ready to live alone, I bought my flat.'

She drew in a deep breath and looked at Arne, her eyes moistening when she saw no judgement in his face. 'I'm sorry I've kept it from you all this time, but I was so ashamed. And I was terrified that if I told you the truth, you wouldn't think I was fit to be a counsellor. Who needs someone with my background advising troubled clients?'

Arne shook his head emphatically. 'It takes great strength and resilience to come through everything you have described to me, Delilah. Your experience has helped you understand the depth of our human frailties in a way few people are exposed to. This understanding brings empathy, which is an invaluable attribute for any counsellor.'

'But doesn't that make me a hypocrite? I'm asking people to forgive their partners when I can't forgive—' She broke off with a groan and squeezed her hands into fists. 'God, I can't even say his name! I swore that day that I'd never call him Dad again. He doesn't deserve it! What kind of father deprives his kids of their mother?'

The silence stretched out for several minutes, and then Arne cleared his throat and looked at her quizzically. 'You said he would often profess love for your mother. What he did must have come as a great shock and yet, you said earlier that you knew immediately he was the one who had taken her life. Why was that?'

'He was completely unpredictable. He'd go through bouts of depression and stop speaking to us for days at a time. It was like he didn't even notice we existed. If we got upset about it, Mum would beg us not to bother him and just give him space. At other times, he turned into this cheeky-chappy, happy-go-lucky man who didn't have a care in the world, hugging and kissing Mum every chance he got, and constantly telling me and Sal how lucky we were to have her in our lives. Even when she was cooking, he'd come into the kitchen and turn on the radio and start dancing with her until they'd both collapse laughing. "*Your mum is so beautiful. I adore her!*" He said it so often, it was like a mantra...'

She shook her head in wonder. 'It's funny how you don't question things when you're a kid. Your dad goes through mood swings and can ignore you for a week, but you tell yourself that's just the way he is. Because Mum was a lawyer and earned well, he'd stop working whenever he couldn't deal with being around people. I don't know if it was his illness that made him so possessive and obsessive, but mostly Mum acted like she was okay with it. She never seemed resentful that he refused to get help. If anything, it seemed like knowing he needed her made her love him even more. For years she would tell me and Sal that you can love a person back to wellness. But, in the end, even for her, it got too much. A few weeks before it happened, Mum told me and Sal that she felt trapped and was thinking of leaving him... but then she never did. Who knows? Maybe she told him that day and that's why he did it. Anyway, that's how I knew straight away that it wasn't some random burglar. That it was *him*.'

41

As late afternoon turned to dusk, the room grew darker, illuminated only by the glow from the electric fire. During a lull in their conversation, Arne stood up to close the blinds and turn on his floor and table lamps, bathing the room in a soft light. Without asking, he brewed a fresh pot of coffee and brought a full mug over to where Delilah sat. The warmth from the fire had long since dried her wet clothes, and with the comforting weight of Sigmund curled up on her lap, she lounged comfortably in the spacious armchair.

Arne sat down and took a sip of his coffee, and then peered at her solemnly over the rim of his glasses.

'You have been through a great deal, Delilah. I am very glad you were able to share this with me.'

Reaching for her coffee, Delilah held it away from the dozing cat while she took a couple of sips. It had been draining to go back in time and revisit the most traumatic day of her life, although, oddly, it hadn't been as scary as she had feared. Knowing Arne was there had made her feel safe, and she knew she'd done the right thing by finally confiding in him.

Arne put his mug down on the side. 'How are you feeling?' he asked.

Delilah considered the question while she mentally checked in with her body. Other than a slight cramp in her legs from trying not to disturb Sigmund, she felt at ease – and light, as if a weight had shifted.

He nodded when she told him and stared down at his folded hands in contemplation. 'I imagine surviving this experience together has cemented the close bond you have with your sister. I am struck by your differing responses to the events of your childhood and the divergence in the directions your lives have taken.'

'For ages, Salome acted like it never happened,' Delilah said with a tinge of bitterness. 'Even later, talking about it with me was taboo because I refused to see a therapist and she couldn't handle me freaking out on her. She says going to therapy has helped her come to terms with everything, but then she still acts like if she can make everything around her perfect, it will stop bad things happening.' She shrugged. 'I don't know... maybe because she has a family to take care of, it's easier for her to focus on Farhan and the kids.'

'Trauma is very much an individual experience, Delilah,' Arne pointed out. 'We all see and process things differently and sometimes the gap between experiences is not easy to bridge. Some people can move through trauma, while others get stuck and need something different to heal from the same trauma.'

Sigmund stirred and stretched, jumping off her lap as unexpectedly as he had arrived. As she stretched her cramped legs out in front of her, Delilah's gaze fell onto the black and white photo Arne had taken of the trees in his native forest.

'It's a bit like that photo up there, isn't it? The same trees look very different, depending on the direction you're looking from.'

'I would say so. You mentioned your sister had left home for university, whereas you, as the younger child, were at home witnessing the deterioration in your parents' relationship firsthand.' He paused as if contemplating his next words. 'It must have been frustrating to see your mother seemingly accept your father's behaviour.'

'I hated the way she let him get away with it!' Delilah said, a deep flush creeping up from her neck and into her cheeks. It felt disloyal to say it, but she knew Arne wouldn't judge her.

'Mum let herself be bullied and manipulated. She could have insisted he get medical attention, but instead she'd just make excuses for him. She wasn't scared of him, exactly, but maybe she was scared of what he might do to himself if he got stressed. All we ever heard was "*Girls, keep the noise down, your dad is tired and needs to rest*" or "*Girls, give Dad some space. He doesn't feel up to talking.*" Somehow, how Sal and I felt when our father stayed in bed for days without speaking or walked past us in our own home as if we didn't exist didn't seem as important.'

'Do you think you can try to forgive—?'

'*Him?*' Delilah cut in with a bitter laugh. 'No! Never.'

'I meant to say, do you think you can try to forgive your mother?' Arne asked gently.

'*Oh…!*' Delilah said blankly. She was so used to placing the blame for her mother's death where it rightfully belonged that she hadn't acknowledged the anger she had deflected away from her and how much it hurt that she and Salome hadn't been worth protecting. Her mother had risked her children's lives as well as her own, but how could you be angry with someone who loved you and had died? And yet…

'Why did she make us mistrust our own instincts about *him*? He was so unpredictable that Sal and I never felt safe, but it's like Mum conditioned us to doubt or ignore our feelings. When someone's being treated poorly and yet they're also telling you it's okay, you learn to numb your feelings, so it doesn't seem so bad. But the honest truth was that it felt terrible when *he* got like that. I knew it wasn't right, but Mum insisted everything was under control. My God, if you can't trust your own mother, who *can* you trust?'

'Unfortunately, when those we rely on to care for us as vulnerable children become the ones who cause us pain, it breaks the trust we have for our parents,' Arne observed. 'Once that sacred trust is breached, it's understandable how any subsequent relationships can appear risky.'

'I'm starting to see why I'm always overthinking and second-guessing myself. For years, I couldn't trust myself to pick the right job, never mind the right man,' she said bleakly.

'I imagine it was tough for your mother to balance the demands of a mentally ill spouse with the needs of her children.'

'*He* was a grown man, and we were children. She should have put *us* first!' Delilah burst out, immediately feeling ashamed for blaming the victim. But then, she wondered sadly, weren't they all victims? Yes, Mum was the one who died, but she and Sal – and even Farhan and his parents – had all been forced to live with the consequences of one man's actions.

Arne tilted his head as he weighed the merits of her words. 'Your feelings are valid, Delilah. You and your sister were also victims,' he said softly, his words echoing Delilah's thoughts. 'You were not complicit in what your father did, and yet his actions left you humiliated and too traumatised to fully live your life. You are not responsible for what happened, and you shouldn't feel ashamed about a past you had no choice in. The person you loved breached your trust, which has caused you anxiety when it comes to closeness and intimacy. Our stored memories can create fear, and our bodies will respond to this. However irrational, such fear can provoke an overwhelming physical urge to flee – such as the crisis you experienced today with Noah.'

He unfolded his hands and sat forward in his chair. 'When we are reluctant to trust, we build walls to keep any potential hurt at bay – you know this, Delilah, because you've challenged yourself to look at the patterns in your previous relationships. Unfortunately, walls don't only keep people out, they also trap us inside as we find reasons to avoid getting close to others, and thus isolate ourselves from the relationships we need to pursue a full life.'

Even if Delilah hadn't been too exhausted to push back, her disastrous track record with men made it impossible to argue. Polly had been right all along, she acknowledged gravely. The years of seeing her mother emotionally manipulated by a man who claimed to worship her had fed so many unconscious biases Delilah had about relationships. Her assumption that, when given the chance, men would control, manipulate and coerce women had coloured her interactions with clients. Instead of facilitating honest communication between the couples in her care, she had weighed in, projecting her own prejudices and making things worse.

But it wasn't only her clients who had suffered the backlash of Delilah's childhood trauma. She thought wretchedly of the hurt in Desmond's eyes, of Kwame's fury that she had been able to bury the memory of how she'd abandoned him, and Carl, still too crushed to ever want to see her again. And then there was poor, sweet Remi who, despite everything, had actually hoped for a second chance. As her mind drifted back over the years since her mother's death, she could see the pattern. A past littered with the debris of men with whom she had jumped into relationships and given them every reason to love her, only to escape just as quickly when they got too close or showed even a trace of the obsessive love she had witnessed as a child. And yet, not all men were like the one she had grown up with. One, in particular, would never be the kind of man her father had become.

Delilah's reflections steered her back to the reason she had run to Arne in the middle of a raging thunderstorm, and she stood up and paced across the room. The image imprinted on her mind of Noah's devastated expression before she turned and ran out on him a second time made her stomach churn. After everything it had taken for them to find each other and for him to trust her again – even jeopardising his relationship with his mother in the process – the idea of letting him down again was gut wrenching. She had apologised for her first betrayal, but this time simply saying sorry would not be enough.

She turned to Arne in despair. 'So, what do I do about Noah?'

'That's not for me to say.'

'You're supposed to be the expert,' she muttered in frustration. Just this once, couldn't Arne stop dissecting everything and simply *tell* her what to do?

'Come now, Delilah. It's tempting to want a black and white response, but you know it isn't my role to give you an answer you can find yourself.'

He gestured towards the chair and Delilah returned to sit down, looking at him with apprehension.

'The first time you ran from Noah, you said it was because you were afraid, yes?'

When she nodded, he continued. 'Fear leads us to catastrophise and look for the worst version of a situation, so try to remember that your fears are just that. Fears. They are not the truth. Here's what I want you to do.'

She leaned forward, holding her breath in anticipation. At this point, she was so desperate to make things right with Noah that she would have done anything Arne suggested.

'I want you to recognise that what you are doing is panicking and imagining your worst fears. Do not run ahead of yourself. Instead, focus on where you are right now and not what the future might bring. It is possible you and Noah will find happiness together, but, if not, what's the worst-case scenario?'

'He'll hate me and never want to see me again,' she said miserably.

'And what will that do to you?'

'It would break my heart...' Her voice tailed off as she imagined life without Noah's infectious energy and teasing smile. Without his generosity, his thoughtfulness, and his readiness to defend her against anyone, including his own mother. Life without the feel of Noah's arms around her and the way he made her giggle by nuzzling her neck whenever he kissed her.

'Yes, it would, but you would survive.' Arne's words broke into her thoughts.

'Surviving isn't enough,' she burst out. 'I don't *want* to be without Noah!'

'I know, but we were exploring your worst fears. So let's also consider the best-case scenario. What would that look like?'

Delilah took a deep breath and closed her eyes. She pictured them in the park, standing on the bridge watching the ducks paddle downstream. She saw clear blue skies and felt the warmth of the sun. She saw Noah smiling at her, reaching for her, the crown tattoo clearly visible on his arm. She opened her eyes, even more dejected by the realisation of what she had lost.

'It would look exactly like it does now,' she whispered. 'Or, at least, like it did before I destroyed him again. Oh Arne, I just want to be free to love without feeling like I'm in danger!'

'Can I make an observation?' Arne said mildly.

'Go on,' she said with a deep sigh, wondering why he bothered to ask. They both knew he would speak his mind, whatever she said.

'How we behaved in the past doesn't define the rest of our lives – or even our future relationships. We can unlearn poor behaviours and replace them with new and better ways to manage ourselves and our emotions. When you were a child, you didn't feel safe to voice your feelings about what was happening around you, and so your emotional language was suppressed. But now you are an adult, you can relearn that language. So, tell me, Delilah, what is it you want?'

'I want to be with Noah. I really, *really* do! I ran away from him the first time – and today – because he said he adored me. I've heard those words before, and it didn't end well. I want to move out of my past and focus on my future, but I also don't want to replicate my mother's behaviour. I don't want to be with someone who's so dependent on me for their happiness that I feel suffocated. So, how can I love Noah – or let him love me when – when I *know* the damage love can bring?'

'It takes work, Delilah. When your default response is to run away, it takes work to sit in those feelings of anxiety and dread until they pass, and then stay and face your fears. You've seen it's impossible to bury pain, put on a mask and hide secrets in the hope that things will somehow resolve themselves. It takes courage but acknowledging what you feel – and expressing what you need – are the first steps towards taking personal responsibility.'

Arne studied her gravely. 'You have a strong support system with your sister and her husband who model a healthy love. You have described to me how Salome and Farhan dealt with their challenges as a couple; they communicated honestly and openly to address the crisis in their marriage. You also have my support, Delilah. If you are willing, we can work together to address the trauma you experienced and help rebuild your confidence to sustain a healthy relationship with Noah.'

Everything Arne said made sense, but his offer would only work *if* she had a relationship to sustain in the first place, Delilah thought in mounting frustration.

'Arne, I beg of you,' she pleaded. She clasped the palms of her hands together, prepared to throw herself onto her knees, if necessary. 'Tell. Me. What. To. Do. To. Get. Noah. Back!'

Arne scratched his beard thoughtfully and a faint smile played at the corner of his lips. 'You ask me for answers, Delilah, and yet you are a trained relationship counsellor. You know very well that true intimacy cannot happen without honest communication and a willingness to be vulnerable. We can avoid conflict if our partner is aware of the wounds from our past. When we share information, we are giving them understanding about why we react, or overreact, in certain circumstances. Does this man who loves you not deserve to know about such a consequential event in your past – especially if the real threat to your relationship is not what happened, but the fact of you keeping it from him? What would *you* advise your client if she was withholding a secret of such magnitude that it prevented her bringing herself fully to her partner?'

When he put it like that, there was only one answer. 'I would encourage her to talk to him and tell him everything, of course!'

Arne's broad smile confirmed she'd got it right, but her momentary elation was quickly replaced by panic. There was no saying how Noah would react to the truth she had hidden from him all these years.

'But what if—'

'Delilah, whatever happens this time, you can handle it,' Arne broke in. 'If Noah is the right man for you, then you must trust that he loves you and will understand.'

When she had arrived at Arne's office earlier that afternoon, Delilah had felt desperate, lost, and utterly defeated. Now, standing up to leave the sanctuary he had so generously offered, it was as if she had shed a burden she'd grown so used to carrying that she'd almost forgotten it was there.

'Take your own advice, Delilah.' Arne's smile of reassurance was the injection of courage she needed. 'Go and talk to Noah. He deserves the truth.'

42

'What do you want?'

Noah's eyes were like chips of brown ice, and Delilah flinched at the coldness in his voice. The loving, good-humoured boyfriend of the past three weeks had vanished, leaving in his place a man who glared at her with unconcealed hostility.

Delilah had spent a sleepless night tossing and turning while trying to prepare what to say to Noah, but she still didn't have a clue how to tell him. Taking a tiny crumb of comfort from the fact he hadn't shut the door on her, she took a cautious step up the stone steps leading to his front door in the hope of reducing the gap between them.

His eyes flashed a warning, and she stopped, uncertain whether to stand her ground or retreat, but the stakes were too high to back down, and she continued defiantly to the top of the steps. She was close enough to see his jaw tighten and for a split second she thought he was about to slam the door in her face.

'I know I'm the last person you want to see, but I need to talk to you – no, actually, I need to show you something.'

His eyes narrowed, but he stood back and held the door open. Pulling her jacket tightly around her, Delilah stepped over the threshold and ran up the flight of stairs leading to his flat. His front door was ajar, and she walked in and made her way towards the lounge before turning to face him. He stared at her stonily, and it took everything not to give up and flee.

'Thanks for giving me a chance to explain,' she started breathlessly. 'I—'

'What do you want to show me?' he interrupted impatiently, his curt tone sending the clear message she was wasting his time.

She wrapped her arms around herself protectively. She had known this wouldn't be easy, but it was agony to see Noah looking at her with such coldness when all she wanted was to be in his arms.

'It – it's not here. I need you to come with me.'

He looked sceptical, and she reached out and grasped his arm, feeling a stab of pain when he recoiled from her touch.

'Please, Noah,' she said urgently. 'I promise I'll explain everything and answer any questions you have – but not here. Please come with me...' Her voice tailed off at his unyielding expression.

'Give me one good reason why I should put myself through another round of you blowing hot and cold. I don't know what you're playing at, but honestly, I've had enough – *Jesus*, Delilah, why do you always make things so *hard*?'

'I don't blame you. I know I've been a proper nightmare, but even if you decide you can't forgive me, I want you to understand why. *Please*, Noah. Just hear me out.'

He studied her face, and his mouth twisted into a humourless smile. 'I really don't have a clue how your mind works,' he said finally. But his voice had lost its edge, and she waited, hardly daring to breathe.

Just when she thought her lungs would burst if he didn't speak, Noah nodded. 'I probably need my head examined for agreeing to this but give me a minute to put some shoes on.'

43

The cemetery was quiet for a Saturday morning, with only a few people to be seen tending to graves. Delilah tramped through the grass, still wet from the previous day's downpour, conscious of Noah beside her, his long legs easily keeping up with her pace. This was the first time she had brought him here, and after explaining where they were heading, he had lapsed into silence. He was clearly still furious with her, and on the short bus ride over, he had carefully positioned himself on the seat to ensure their bodies didn't touch.

They walked down the path skirting the chapel, and as they approached the roped-off section of old graves, Delilah glanced at Noah with sudden apprehension. Noah wasn't Arne; it wasn't his job to listen without prejudice and understand the complexity of trauma and emotional dysfunction, and there was every chance he would reject her when he learned the truth about her family. But they were here now, and there was no turning back. If she wanted to keep Noah in her life – assuming he was even still interested – she had no choice but to come clean.

Leading the way, Delilah picked a path around the muddy ground between the graves and past the statue of the cherub, coming to a stop in front of her mother's grave. The brass vase had tipped over, spilling a bedraggled, storm-battered posy of flowers onto the white marble, and she crouched to set the vase straight. She thought back to the painful conversation with Arne and felt the prick of tears behind her eyes. As children, she and Salome had sought comfort and protection from the person they had loved and trusted the most and, hard as it was to admit, she had let them down.

'We needed you, Mum. You should have put us first,' she whispered under her breath.

Perhaps it was only the rustle of leaves from the breeze sweeping through the branches of the oak tree overhead, but as she contemplated the gilt inscription on the marble headstone, she heard her mother's voice. *Forgive me, Del.* Delilah closed her eyes for a long moment, absorbing the healing words she had so needed to hear. *Help me make him understand, Mum,* she pleaded silently.

Straightening, she walked back to Noah and looked up at him, trying to muster the courage for what was needed. His earlier grim demeanour was now one of wariness, as if uncertain about what was coming.

When she opened her mouth, however, the lines she had rehearsed on the bus ride to the cemetery disappeared, and she stared at Noah blankly. Then, Arne's words pushed through her mental haze. '*We can avoid conflict if our partner is aware of the wounds from our past. When we share information, we are giving them understanding about why we react, or overreact, in certain circumstances.*' Arne had urged her to be open and vulnerable and now, under the shade of the giant oak tree, for the first time, Delilah let down her guard with Noah.

* * *

When Delilah finally stopped speaking, there was silence. Noah had listened without interruption and now he knew everything. She didn't dare look at Noah, but when the silence stretched out, she forced herself to look up, and for a long moment, they gazed silently into each other's eyes. *What if, for once, Arne was wrong*?

'Noah?' she started tentatively, her throat tight with fear.

Without saying a word, Noah reached for her and wrapped his arms around her. At first, she stood rigidly, unsure of what it meant, but then she relaxed into his hold.

'I'm sorry,' she choked, her voice muffled against his shoulder.

'You have nothing to be sorry about, Del. It wasn't your fault.'

His words echoed what Arne had said in his office, and she clung to him, trying desperately to believe them.

'I wish I'd known about this, Del. I would have understood so much that didn't make sense to me.'

She sniffed back tears. 'I wish I'd told you sooner, but when we first met, I'd lived my life in two parts – before and after *he* killed my mum. After seeing how Farhan's family reacted – how even Mum's family reacted – there was no way I could admit what had happened to anyone I cared about. It was much easier just to say my father died when I was a child.'

He raised his head and pulled back to look at her. 'I'm so sorry this happened to you. You acted so weird with me one time when I asked how your mum died that I thought she'd gone through some awful illness you couldn't talk about. You and Salome were so tight and didn't seem to need anyone else, so I never really questioned what happened to your parents.'

'With Mum gone, it was just the two of us,' Delilah murmured, resting her head against Noah's chest. 'He didn't just kill Mum. He took away the life my sister and I had and then left us with the stigma of his crime. Luckily, Sal had Farhan, and even more luckily, I had Sal.'

Noah dropped a soft kiss on the top of her head, and Delilah sighed. 'I told you before that I've been going through therapy. Polly – my manager – insisted on it if I wanted my job back. I thought I'd blanked out the "before" part, but Arne helped me see how it was driving so much of what I've been doing in the "after", and how pretending things were fine didn't stop the past infecting my life. Since I've started seeing Arne, I'm working on blending the before and after. It's been agonising because I've grown so used to being guarded, but he's helping me face my demons and sort my head out when my emotions get overwhelming. He's amazing – really patient and understanding and kind – and he really *listens*. I feel safe with him because he's not the slightest bit judgy, but he's also not afraid to challenge me when I'm deflecting instead of expressing my feelings. You know, I hated the idea of therapy at first. I was so scared I'd lose my job if anyone found out about my past and thought I was unfit to be a counsellor, and I did everything to stop him finding out the truth – until yesterday. Arne says we learn certain behaviours as children to survive our family situations, but they don't serve us in our adult relationships. After I ran from you in the café, I knew I didn't want to be stuck in this pattern of sabotaging my life any more and that if I didn't get help, I would lose you for good – and I couldn't *bear* that!'

Noah looked into her eyes and sighed. 'I'm sorry, Del. Truly sorry. I was so fixated on trying to protect my own emotions, I didn't stop to ask the right questions. I assumed you were playing with my feelings again and that you didn't care about me.'

For a long time, they stood holding each other as Delilah talked to Noah about her sessions with Arne. When she haltingly explained how Noah's words during their phone call had triggered her into bolting the day before their wedding, he simply hugged her tighter.

'You weren't to know,' she admitted sadly. 'Even I didn't connect the significance of that word to my reactions until I opened up to Arne. While I can't say for sure if I'll ever be fully healed, he's confident I will get to a place where I can properly manage my emotions and make better choices.'

She looked up and searched Noah's eyes anxiously. 'But at least now I can stand here and talk to you and be open without feeling like hiding.'

Noah kissed her gently and stroked her hair away from her face. 'Thank you for being honest with me, babe. Whatever you need from me, it's yours. I want us to work more than I've wanted anything in my life.'

She smiled at him tremulously, deeply moved by the sincerity in his voice. 'I'm so sorry about yesterday – and before. What I did to you was beyond awful. I let you fall in love with me and then abandoned you.' She swallowed hard. 'You loved me so much, but I felt overwhelmed and helpless and – and terrified I'd be consumed by my feelings for you and lose control like *he* did or, even worse, that I'd let *you* become consumed by me like Mum did. It's taken time to figure all this out, but I promise I'll do better by us.'

'Well, it's way too late for me to stop loving you, but next time you feel like running, tell me and I'll run with you.'

His eyes twinkled, and Delilah giggled and punched him lightly on the shoulder. Okay, so Arne *was* right, she thought happily, but having Noah back was worth conceding her therapist had won the argument.

Noah stroked her cheek and then his expression sobered. 'You haven't said where he is.'

Delilah stiffened, and her eyes darted involuntarily towards the far side of the cemetery. 'I don't want to go there!'

'I understand, babe. Honestly, I do,' Noah said, his voice soothing. 'But he can't keep dominating your life. Look how much it's taking out of you to keep hating him. Why not let go of the hurt and bitterness so you can put that energy into something positive?'

'It's easy to say, but how do you forgive the unforgiveable?' Delilah retorted bitterly. 'Besides, if I forgave him, I'd be letting Mum down.'

'Forgiving your dad doesn't mean you're abandoning your mum, Del. What happened is unimaginable, and he was your father so you're going to feel conflicted, no matter what. But what he did is on him. *He* was the one who took away your sense of security and ripped your life apart. All I'm saying is, you don't have to forgive your father, but you need to make peace with what he did. I know letting go of trauma isn't like turning off a switch, but I need you to understand you will not fight this battle alone.'

She looked away, and he held her gently by the shoulders until she turned back to meet his eyes. 'Listen to me, Del. *You're* the one I care about, not him. I want you to be happy and I don't want the past to stop you living fully in the present.'

'But *is* it okay to be happy?' Delilah said dejectedly, her voice sounding more like a sigh. 'For years after Mum died, I felt guilty if I so much as laughed at a joke.'

Noah gave her shoulders a reassuring squeeze. 'I'm right here, sweetheart, and we'll face it – *him* – together. Let's do this, okay?'

44

Delilah hadn't set foot in that part of the cemetery since the day they had buried her father, and as they approached the spot, she felt her heart pounding and the hairs rise up on her arms. She shivered and would have pulled back if Noah hadn't urged her forward, his grip on her hand warm and reassuring.

Moments later, she stopped. There it was. Her breath caught in her throat as she stared at the faded lettering engraved on the worn brass plaque. *Justin Braithwaite.*

They stood in silence, the birds chirping in the morning sunshine and the chilly February breeze rustling the leaves of the surrounding trees. Slowly, Delilah felt her heart rate calm and the tightness in her chest ease. She let go of Noah's hand and took a step closer to the unadorned grave.

This patch of damp grass with its rusty plaque was all that remained of the man whose actions had devastated her past and threatened to destroy her future. She would never know what had driven him or understand how he could take the life of someone he claimed to love, but it wasn't her mystery to solve or her burden to carry.

Something positive has to come from such an evil action, she thought soberly. Noah was right. She didn't have to forgive her father, but she did have to let her anger go – not for his sake, but because it was corroding her inside and pushing her towards destructive choices. She could hear Arne's voice: '*Find compassion for the hurt child you were then and give it to the woman you are now.'* She thought of the bewildered, frightened child caught up in the complex emotional dance of the adults around her. None of it was her fault, and she deserved to love and be loved. It was time to heal the hurt child and be at peace with herself. It was time to accept that it was over; that she was safe, and he was gone.

Noah stepped forward to stand beside her, and when Delilah's hand crept into his, he held onto it tightly, as if he would never let go. She closed her eyes and inhaled deeply, breathing in the scent of damp grass, freshly dug soil and the faint lemon tang of his cologne.

Then, with Noah by her side and his hand firmly holding hers, Delilah exhaled.

45

Arne gently shooed Sigmund off his lap and leaned forward in his chair. 'Why do you want to go back to work, Delilah?'

Delilah stared at the floor, mulling over her options. She could offer a glib response and say what she thought Arne wanted to hear, or she could use the lessons she'd learned and tell the truth.

She took a breath and then looked up to meet his gaze. 'Because it's the only job I've ever had where I truly felt like I fitted. I wasn't great at it, because I was blind to so much about myself, but that didn't mean I wasn't being real. Helping people who are struggling with unhealthy relationships means everything to me. I understand that I don't know half of what I think I know, but I'm not scared or embarrassed any more to ask for help. I know from our sessions how important it is to have people I can bounce ideas off and share my doubts and insecurities with, and I'm ready to do it right this time.'

Arne leaned back, and a slow smile worked its way across his face. 'Bravo, Delilah. I think you're ready, too.'

She had been so focused on expressing her feelings that it took a few moments for Arne's words to register.

'*Really?*' she whispered, her voice cracking with incredulity.

'Really.' Arne nodded. His brilliant blue eyes suddenly looked suspiciously moist, and he cleared his throat loudly. 'I will send a message to Polly this afternoon. She has missed having you on her team and this will be very welcome news to her.'

Delilah's smile was so wide that her face hurt, and it took all her willpower – and the real fear of Sigmund hissing at her – not to whoop out loud. She hadn't realised until this moment just how badly she wanted her job back. This time, however, it wasn't to prove anything to Polly, Farhan or Salome – or even to herself. It was to help people find a way through the conflict in their relationships without harming each other.

Then, just as suddenly, the doubts flooded in. 'What if it turns out I'm still being biased?' she asked hesitantly.

There was silence, but she had learned that when Arne paused, it wasn't judgement. He had heard her, and he was reflecting.

'Delilah, the insights you have gained during our time together won't change your behaviour overnight. That will take practice and being patient with yourself,' Arne said gently. 'Any setbacks will be part of the process of learning, but I'm confident you have enough awareness of your sensitivities to recognise when you are in danger of breaching boundaries with your clients. Don't forget that you also have your colleagues and your supervision group to advise you when you face such challenges and, as we have agreed, you will continue your sessions with me.'

'But what if—?'

'Therapy is also about recognising your strengths, Delilah,' Arne cut in before she could continue. 'Remind yourself how far you've come over these past months.'

He stood up and walked towards the door, leaving her with no choice but to pick up her bag and jacket and do the same.

Arne opened the door and stood back, and when she hesitated, he gave her an encouraging smile. 'You will be fine, Delilah. You have the tools to reframe false and negative beliefs into what is real and possible – so use them.'

Once again, her Viking giant of a therapist was right. Delilah nodded, only just restraining herself from hugging him fiercely. Instead she gave him a huge smile and took off down the corridor, running past Sadie's office and down the stairs with her heart bursting from joy. She knew what getting help had done for her, and she couldn't wait to do the same for others.

EPILOGUE

Delilah glanced up at the clock on the wall. With only fifteen minutes of the session left, her clients were still at loggerheads. This was the second of three Saturday morning sessions which Sandy, a heavily made-up blonde in her late thirties, had booked for herself and her husband Graham. With no breakthrough yet in their communications, Graham's laboured attempt to mirror the statement his wife had just made as proof that he could listen had not landed well.

'For God's sake, Gray, that is *so* not what I said!' Sandy exclaimed. 'It's so bloody typical of you. Do you see now, Delilah? He never listens to me!'

Graham flushed angrily, and Delilah raised a hand. When she had their attention, she said calmly, 'Now, Sandy, remember our goal is to focus on solutions, which means being clear about the problem. It's not helpful to use blanket statements like "never" because when you say Graham never listens to you, that's not true. Let's try this. I think what would be more useful to Graham is if you can be specific about a time you felt unheard and then tell him what you observed.'

Sandy pursed her lips and said grudgingly, 'Right. On Sunday, I asked him to move my dressing table nearer the window to give me more natural light when I'm doing my face.'

'And what did Graham say?'

'Absolutely bloody nothing! He blanked me – waved me away like I was an annoying fly that had got into the room.' She glared accusingly at her husband who was squirming in his chair with a face like thunder.

'What did Graham's response tell you, Sandy?' Delilah asked.

'That he doesn't love me and couldn't give a toss about what matters to me!' Sandy said tearfully, fumbling in her handbag for a tissue. She sniffed loudly and dabbed under her eyes, and Delilah gave her a sympathetic smile.

'The reason we've spent so much of our session today talking about communication is because, as we've just seen, something as trivial as asking for help to move furniture can quickly blow up into a crisis. Now, instead of both of you trying to prove you're right and the other one is wrong, let's try and understand the truth of what was really going on. Sandy, what do you think you could have said to Graham, either at the time or afterwards, to help him understand how his response made you feel?'

Sandy huffed. 'Well, it was obvious I was upset cos I had a go at him, didn't I?'

'Yes, but what could you have said to help him understand *why* you were upset, and what you needed from him?'

Sandy looked across at Graham, who had slumped back in his chair looking miserable, and her expression softened. 'I suppose I could have told him what I've just said to you,' she admitted.

'And Graham, when Sandy asked you to help her – what did you hear?'

Graham held up his hands, suddenly looking sheepish. 'Look, it was in the middle of the football and if I'm honest, all I heard was noise. We were in extra time and the boys had just scored from two-one down. I wouldn't have heard a bloody earthquake at that point.'

'So Sandy's timing was the problem, not that you didn't want to help?'

Graham nodded with an anxious glance at his wife. Sandy refused to meet his eyes, and Delilah studied them both for a moment.

'Graham, what would you have said if Sandy had explained – after the game was over – that it makes her feel unloved and devalued when you ignore her?'

Graham reddened, and then said gruffly, 'I'd have told her she was being a silly cow! She's my world, and I'd do anything to make her happy – just not... you know, not when the team's about to take penalties.'

'Oh, *Gray*!' Sandy's lips trembled. 'I've never heard you say anything so sweet before.'

Delilah checked the clock and let out a satisfied sigh. 'Okay, folks, our time's up for today. I'm really pleased to see you building better connections with each other. Before our final session next week, I'd like you both to practise what we've discussed today. Go through the steps rather than jumping to conclusions about what the person said. Ask yourself what you heard and then what you're making up in your head about it. Express how that makes you feel, and what you need to feel better. And remember your tone of voice – you don't want your body language to sabotage your message.'

She stood and walked to the door, holding it open while the couple gathered their belongings.

'You okay, Graham?' she asked, biting back a smile at his grumpy expression.

He shrugged on his jacket and scratched his thinning hair. 'All seems a bit long-winded, if you ask me,' he grumbled.

'I know changing our habits can feel uncomfortable, but these exercises will work for both of you, if you do them properly. It'll get easier with practice, I promise,' Delilah said cheerfully.

'I'll give it a try, love. Anything to make sure I'm not back here again after next week.'

He reached for Sandy's hand and his gloomy expression changed into an indulgent smile. 'Come on, you silly sausage. We don't want to be late for kick-off. The boys are playing at home this afternoon.'

As soon as she'd ushered Graham and Sandy out, Delilah closed her laptop and grabbed her jacket. She shut her office door and popped her head around the half-open door to Armenique's office.

'You still here?'

'Yup,' Armenique answered distractedly, typing swiftly on her laptop. 'Just finishing my notes and then I'm done for the day.' She looked up from her computer with a smile. 'Doing anything special this weekend?'

Delilah grinned. 'I'm off to meet Noah at his place, and then we're going over to his parents' for lunch.'

Armenique folded her hands in prayer. 'I wish you luck, my friend. May the forces of good protect you,' she intoned solemnly before breaking into her trademark cackle. 'Nah, have fun, girl. How are things going with the Wicked Witch these days?'

Delilah laughed. 'Let's just say we'll never be besties, but at least she's civil.

Noah's made it clear she's got to be nice to me and she's definitely making the effort. Thankfully, his dad loves me, which more than makes up for her.'

'Well, say hi to Noah and have a nice lunch,' Armenique said with an airy wave. 'See you at supervision on Monday?'

'Definitely!'

Leaving the building, Delilah walked to the end of the lane and turned into the high street. The bus stop was just past the tattoo parlour on the other side of the road and as she approached the pedestrian crossing, she was struck by a sudden thought.

Almost an hour later, Delilah emerged from the shop in time to see her bus approaching. Racing the few metres to the stop, she got there just as the bus pulled in and climbed on board, taking the nearest seat while she caught her breath. Her left wrist stung from Stan's handiwork, but when she peeked under the small plaster to admire the two entwined initials, she couldn't stop herself breaking into a huge grin.

A glance at her watch confirmed she and Noah were going to be late for lunch, which would not please Mrs West. But somehow Delilah had a strong feeling that when Noah saw her new tattoo, he wouldn't mind at all.

* * *

MORE FROM FRANCES MENSAH WILLIAMS

Another beautifully warmhearted, romantic read from Frances Mensah Williams is available to order now here:

https://mybook.to/FrancesMWNewBackAd

ACKNOWLEDGEMENTS

I have always been deeply curious about what motivates people and drives their actions, which many might say is a useful trait for a writer! In preparing to tell Delilah's story, I delved into a ton of literature about therapy, counselling, and psychology, and learned so much about human behaviour and the impact of trauma on our personal and romantic relationships.

I would like to thank the therapists and relationship counsellors who shared their insights with me, particularly Alison Brown, who immediately 'got' who Delilah was, and gave me valuable pointers on the impact of childhood trauma. Alison, I hope you don't mind me naming a (nice) character after you! I really appreciate your time and generosity, and any errors in interpretation are entirely mine.

Sadly, real life tragedies unfolded for me while writing *Tell Me About It*, and I sometimes wondered if I'd ever finish the story. My heartfelt thanks go to my amazing agent Gyamfia Osei for her deep compassion, unflagging enthusiasm, and constant encouragement. A huge thank you also goes to Emma Beswetherick, my editorial director at Boldwood, for loving this novel from the get-go, and for being such a kind and incredible champion.

My special thanks go to the women who hold me up and who embrace, cheer, and support me every day in this journey called life. To my tribe of sister-friends – you know who you are – I love and appreciate you beyond words.

Fx

ABOUT THE AUTHOR

Frances Mensah Williams CBE is the author of acclaimed contemporary fiction novels, including *Imperfect Arrangements*, set in contemporary Ghana, and *Strictly Friends*, set in the Caribbean. She is an entrepreneur, consultant, executive coach, and TEDx speaker, and was awarded a CBE in 2020 for services to Africans in the UK and in Africa.

Sign up to Frances Mensah Williams' mailing list for news, competitions and updates on future books.

Visit Frances' website: www.francesmensahwilliams.com

Follow Frances on social media here:

instagram.com/francesmensahw
facebook.com/FrancesMensahWilliams
x.com/FrancesMensahW
bookbub.com/authors/frances-mensah-williams

www.ingramcontent.com/pod-product-compliance
Lightning Source LLC
Chambersburg PA
CBHW011800010726
47497CB00012B/3220